The Shifter Romances The Writer

Nocturne Falls, Book Six

Kristen Painter

THE SHIFTER ROMANCES THE WRITER:
Nocturne Falls, Book Six

Copyright © 2016 Kristen Painter

ISBN: 978-1-941695-19-7

Published in the United States of America.

Welcome to Nocturne Falls, the town that celebrates Halloween 365 days a year. The tourists think it's all a show: the vampires, the werewolves, the witches, the occasional gargoyle flying through the sky. But the supernaturals populating the town know better.

Living in Nocturne Falls means being yourself. Fangs, fur, and all.

For romance writer Roxy St. James, living in Nocturne Falls means a fresh start. And as soon as her unbearable ex signs the divorce papers, that new beginning will be a reality. Unfortunately, her ex doesn't seem ready to let her go and the subtle threats he's been making leave her no choice but to confide in her oh-so-handsome neighbor, who just happens to be a deputy with the sheriff's department.

But Officer Alex Cruz isn't just the law. He's also a panther shifter, a secret he's sworn to keep (along with the truth about Nocturne Falls) from the very foxy Roxy. Humans aren't supposed to know the town is filled with supernaturals. Then she starts seeing things she shouldn't and thinks she's losing her mind. His attraction—and concern—for her wars with the promise he's made.

Will his truth be more than she can handle? Or will it cause her to write him out of her life?

This book is for Emily,
my favorite teenage superfan.
Now go do your laundry.

APRIL

Buying a home on her own was the most wonderful, frightening thing Roxy St. James had ever done. Even publishing her first book hadn't been this exhilarating. Or scary.

Although it might have been just as difficult. Not as difficult as the divorce she was going through, but for today, she wanted to forget about that and focus on this next step in her life.

As she parked behind her realtor's car outside of the third house of the day, Roxy questioned if she'd ever find the right place. Realtor Pandora Williams got out and headed to the door, but Roxy sat for a moment, looking at the house. There was a charm about this house that the others hadn't had. She hoped that carried through to the inside and that she could finally imagine herself living here.

Because, more than anything, she wanted to be here in this town where she had a friend and a chance to start over.

She nodded. This house absolutely could be the one. She got out of the car and inhaled. The air was different in Georgia than it was in New Jersey. Fresher, maybe. Or just new. And perhaps that's all she was feeling. Just a sense of being somewhere different.

So maybe it was the way the light filtered through the branches of the mature trees in the neighborhood or the way the breeze picked up as Roxy lifted her face to the sun, but this house, in this neighborhood, felt right.

And Roxy needed things to feel right. The divorce had put a dark haze on things for too long. This town of Nocturne Falls—and the home she'd eventually make here—was going to be her fresh start. Her new beginning.

Sure, Nocturne Falls was miles away from New Jersey and her life there, but a clean break was the only way she could come up with to shake off her past. Most importantly, her ex.

Her awful, controlling, soul-crushing ex.

Besides, New Jersey was his home state, not hers. She was a New York girl. And the Jersey neighborhood was filled with his family and friends. People he'd since poisoned against her. People she'd never liked that much anyway.

At least here in Nocturne Falls, she had a real friend. Delaney James—no, it was Ellingham now. Her old college friend had married an amazing man and was a few months away from having a baby. Good for her. Love ought to work for someone.

Roxy snorted at that thought. How ironic that she, Roxy St. James, a woman who made her living writing romance novels, could have gotten love so wrong. She sighed out a breath. Whatever. That was behind her now. Her fictional heroes were enough to keep her warm. And she didn't need to believe in forever and soul mates and love without conditions in order to write books about those things.

Fiction was fiction for a reason.

Nope, no man for her. She would be happily single. Maybe she'd get a dog. Or a cat. But cats and romance writers were just such a cliché. Either way, she would definitely be getting an aquarium. Fish were peaceful. And she needed peaceful.

Pandora opened the home's front door then turned to look at Roxy. "What do you think? Cute, right?"

Roxy left her mental wanderings behind and smiled as she headed up the walk. "Very cute. I really have a good feeling about this one. And this neighborhood is great."

"I told you I saved the best for last." Pandora preened. "And I'm not just saying that because I live a few blocks away. Wait until you see the inside."

Roxy stepped through the front door and let out a happy sigh. "Oh, yeah, this is gorgeous."

Pandora smiled like a proud mama. "They redid the house last year. New floors, new cabinets, new countertops, the whole thing. Of course, I don't think they counted on getting transferred, but their loss is your gain."

The house looked magazine-worthy, all shades of gray and white and brushed chrome but still warm and welcoming. It was far more sophisticated than anything Roxy had imagined she'd find in this little Georgia town. Frankly, it was far more sophisticated than anything she'd pictured herself living in.

"C'mon," Pandora said. "Let me show you the rest."

Roxy followed her through the house, oohing and aahing at the kitchen (tons nicer than the kitchen she'd had in New Jersey, which was a real plus since cooking was a great way to procrastinate instead of writing), and the master bedroom and bathroom were so perfect they were like a spa retreat.

She turned slowly, taking it all in. "I could live here. Like, really live here. That big walk-in shower? I might never get out of that thing."

"Pretty impressive, huh?" Pandora took her into one of the smaller bedrooms. "Any one of these other bedrooms would make a great office, but this one is the closest to the master."

"It's a good size and just what I need." Roxy bit her lip. "I could finally have that big saltwater fish tank I've always wanted."

"Hey, if you want a fish tank, we have a company in town that I can hook you up with. No pun intended." Pandora grinned. "They set them up and maintain them."

"Really? That would be awesome."

"I'll get you Undrea's card. She's a total expert on all things fishy. She custom-builds tanks in her shop, so she can do anything you can dream up." Pandora put her hand on the door. "Let's go look at the other two bedrooms and the second bath."

They turned out to be just as perfect as the rest of the house. Roxy stood in the living room with Pandora. "Okay, I love it. But I'm almost afraid to ask how much."

"It's at the top end of your budget, but it *is* four bedrooms, completely remodeled, has a two-car garage, and I haven't even shown you the bonus part yet."

"There's a bonus?" Roxy couldn't imagine what else there could be. "Wait. Is there a pool? A hot tub? A koi pond?"

Pandora just crooked her finger. "Follow me."

Roxy did. Right out the rear sliding doors onto a big bricked patio, which definitely had enough space for a hot tub if she ever decided to pull the trigger on that purchase. The entire backyard was fenced in, like a lot of the yards in the neighborhood, and was a large, lovely green space.

But she saw immediately what Pandora had been talking about. A two-story outbuilding sat at the rear corner of the property. It had cedar shingles, round windows, gingerbread trim and an exaggerated peaked door to match its roof. Roxy tipped her head. "Okay, that's interesting. And cute. But what is it exactly?"

Pandora looked up at the structure. "The owners had two girls who desperately wanted a tree house, but as you can see the two trees in this yard wouldn't support that sort of building. So their dad had this designed for them as a playhouse, but it's really so much more. It has electric and its own heat and air unit. I thought it might be something you could use as a writer's retreat. Or even a guest room if you had some of your writing friends visit like you said you might."

"Can I go in?"

"Absolutely." Pandora handed her a key. "Take a look. See what you think."

Roxy walked back to the building on the flagstone path, unlocked the door and stepped inside. Her first thought was fairy house. Sunlight spilled through the portal windows and a large skylight overhead. There was plenty of space for a pull-out sofa, an easy chair, a small fridge and coffee maker—all the comforts a writer might need.

A spiral staircase led to the second floor. She went up and had a look. Long transom windows on either side opened to let in light and air. She could stand up at the peak of the roof with about a foot of space overhead. It wouldn't be too hard to get one of those memory foam mattresses up here and turn this loft into a sleeping area. That would be pretty cool.

She could totally see herself writing in this magical little place when the confines of her office got to be too monotonous. And possibly napping in this loft.

And it could definitely serve as another place to house a guest when she invited her writer friends in for a retreat, something she'd been desperate to do but her ex had never allowed. She could hang some light strings, stock the fridge with wine and snacks. It would be perfect.

Pandora had knocked it out of the park with this house.

Roxy came down from the loft and walked back to Pandora on the patio, smiling the whole way. "I love it."

"I thought you would. There's still the garage to look at. Not that exciting, but you should have a look at the whole place before you make an offer. Sound good?"

"Yes." But Roxy didn't need to see any more to know she'd finally found home.

"Mom. Mom. *Mom.*" Alex Cruz sighed and flattened his hand over his forehead. His mother continued on in a mix of English and Spanish, but he didn't need to hear every word to know what she was talking about. Because it was the same conversation they'd been having for the last five years.

"I'm not getting any younger, Alex. I want grandbabies while I can enjoy them. I want to know that my only son has found a good woman to take care of him when I die."

He rolled his eyes. "Mom. I'm not your only son. Remember my brother, Diego? Your other son?" Granted, Diego as a father was a sobering thought, but if either of them was going to give Carmen Cruz grandchildren, it was probably Diego. And sadly, those grandchildren would probably not be planned.

Sort of shocking that Diego hadn't ended up with a few kids already.

"Eh, Diego will never settle down."

"He *is* living with a girl."

"At least he's doing that much." Carmen Cruz made an exhausted noise. "But the only time he hasn't lived with a girl is when he was in the Marines. That means nothing."

"True." Diego went through women like a frat boy went through shots. "Also, you're fifty-nine. Death is a long way off."

"You don't know that."

Deputy Blythe walked past Alex and crinkled up her face as she mouthed the question, "Mom?"

He nodded at his fellow officer, and she shook her head in sympathy. Everyone he worked with at the station knew what this conversation was about.

"I do know that, Mom. We're shifters. We live a long time."

"Then what if something happens to you? Your job is very dangerous."

"Besides the fact that we heal faster than humans and are much harder to kill, Nocturne Falls is about the least dangerous place a cop can work. Nothing is going to happen to me in this town. I give a few tickets, I arrest the occasional drunk and disorderly. Sometimes I divert parade traffic. Nothing remotely dangerous."

"You could be shot."

He closed his eyes for a moment. "Yes, I could be. I could also be swept up in a tornado or get food poisoning. My chances of any of those are all about the same." Which was unfortunate, because either one would be preferable to this conversation.

"Now you're just mocking me. Why are you such a bad son? Why do you want me to be unhappy? Wolfgang Blackborne would never treat his mother this way. If he had a mother. Which he doesn't because she was burned at the stake for being a witch."

Alex squeezed his eyes shut harder. Ever since his mother's favorite telenovela had been canceled, she'd gotten hooked on romance novels. She talked about the characters like they were real. He was glad she'd found something to be passionate about, but he couldn't keep up. "Pretty sure that guy is fictional, Mom."

In the background, Alex heard his father yell, "Carmen, leave that boy alone."

That would never happen. He took a breath. "Mom, I love you, but I have to go. I'm on duty. I'll talk to you soon. Give my love to Dad. Bye."

He hung up as she was still talking, but there was only so much he could take. Why couldn't his mother understand that, to him, a wife wasn't just a role to be filled? He wanted to love the woman he married so deeply, he couldn't imagine life without her. He wanted her to be his best friend.

And he wanted her to be the *one*. His true love. His soul mate. Sadly, that wasn't something he was sure existed, considering the women he'd dated. Yes, they were all nice and kind and attractive. But none of that mattered, because none of them had flipped that switch inside him that let him know they were meant to be.

Until that happened, he was content being alone.

Maybe not *content*, but he'd accepted being alone was better than spending time with the wrong person. Diego was proof of how awful that could be.

Alex leaned back in his chair as Deputy Blythe walked past again, paperwork in hand. She stopped at his desk. "You okay?"

He looked up. "Yeah, fine. Just…thinking."

"Sounds dangerous." She grinned. "You want to get a couple beers after shift at Howler's?"

He shook his head. "Not tonight. I need to study."

"Dude, you've got two months before that sergeant's exam."

"And I don't want to waste them."

She shrugged. "There's going to be a lot of disappointed female tourists. You know how they love a uniform. And who am I going to hang out with?"

He laughed. "The female tourists have enough men in this town to drool over." And he wasn't interested in a human or a tourist, so what was the point? "If you need someone to hang out with, call some of the guys from the firehouse. Or just wait for them to show up. They're always at Howler's anyway."

She nodded, smiling. "True. And those uniforms *are* awfully cute." She snorted. "See you later."

"Later."

He finished his shift and headed home. The evening was perfect. He'd go for a run before dinner, then grill himself a steak. But when he got to the house, there was a car in his drive he hadn't seen in a long time. He parked alongside it, got out and started toward the figure on his front porch.

The figure came out from the shadows, a hand raised in greeting.

Alex nodded. "Hey, Diego. What's up?"

His brother shrugged. "You know, just thought I'd see how you were doing. Hang out for a bit."

"Nice to see you." Then Alex narrowed his eyes. "You just here for the weekend?"

Diego hesitated. "More like until I find somewhere else to stay. I hope that's cool."

Alex managed not to sigh, but this was pretty typical Diego. He never showed up just because. "Does that mean you and Nina are done?"

"I'm with Penny now. Or I was." Diego shrugged and leaned against the porch railing. "Penny and I are sort of taking a break."

And there it was. "You mean she threw you out?"

"Harsh."

"But true, right?"

12

Diego frowned. "I just need a place to stay for a couple nights, tops."

Alex loved his little brother, but the man was thirty. By now, he ought to have his business together. "Of course, you can stay. But more than a week and you have to start looking for a job because that's when rent kicks in. Six hundred a month, plus utilities, your share of the chores and you buy your own food."

Diego's frown didn't move. "What kind of job am I supposed to get?"

"The same kind you've had before. Bartending or mechanic. You're good at both of those." Diego had bartended on and off, but his real skills were with engines. That's what he'd done in the Marines, and Alex was pretty sure there wasn't an engine in existence his little brother couldn't fix. The Camaro taking up the other space in his driveway was proof of that.

But Diego sighed and shook his head. "I don't know, man."

Alex held firm. "You can always move back to Mom and Dad's."

"Like that's really an option."

Alex shrugged and said nothing.

"Yeah, all right." Diego's grumpy expression finally turned into a sly smile. "Is it true you can be yourself in this town? Like, full-on shifter?" His eyes gleamed feline gold.

"In a sense. Don't go shifting in front of tourists or running through the streets in your panther form, but generally Nocturne Falls is wide open when it comes to supernaturals like us. Or any kind, really."

Diego nodded. "Cool."

"It is." Alex rested his hand on his utility belt and tried to put a teasing tone in his voice. "Just don't make me remind you I'm the law in this town. Or I'll return you to Mom and Dad myself."

"Yeah, yeah. I'll behave. I'm a former Marine, you know."

"I know." He should have stayed in. "But in all seriousness, this is my town, Diego. I don't want you causing trouble."

"I won't. I swear."

"Good." But Alex's gut wasn't so sure about that.

MAY

Roxy loved her house. *Loved*. Maybe more than she'd ever loved her ex-husband. And if she was going to be married to anything, it might as well be something this awesome.

Actually, it wasn't just the house. It was her new life here in this new town. The freedom of being on her own was life-changing. Invigorating. Joyous. The move and the process of getting settled in her new house had pretty much derailed her writing productivity, but she was also rediscovering who she was, and taking some time off was good for the soul.

So was life without Thomas hovering over her, trying to control her every action and constantly telling her what she was doing wrong. He'd emailed her again this morning with some nonsense about how she was ruining both their lives with this divorce. She hit delete almost instantly. And with great satisfaction.

Living without that kind of negative weight was a revelation. Maybe this was how prisoners felt after being released. But just thinking about him amped up the stress of the divorce to a new level.

If only he would sign those papers and let her get on with her fresh start.

And today, the last piece in the puzzle of that new life had arrived. Her late father's '69 Corvette convertible. She'd inherited the cherry-red machine years ago when he'd passed and had kept it in storage ever since. For a multitude of reasons, she'd hidden the car from Thomas. It had been tough to pull off, but she'd done it.

At one time, she feared she'd have to sell the car and use the money to escape her marriage, but then her paranormal romance series had taken off and she'd been able to save up the necessary funds to get a good attorney.

Now she could finally drive the car and enjoy it. She knew that's what her dad would have wanted, although he would have understood, and approved, if she'd sold it to be rid of Thomas. This was the better outcome, though. By far.

Her dad had taken on the role of both parents after her mother's hospitalization and subsequent death, so having this car felt like having him with her again. Today was a good day.

She paid the long-haul driver and turned to look at the car. There was no question it needed to be serviced, but all those times she'd snuck away to the storage unit to start the car and occasionally take it for a short drive had paid off by keeping it in running order.

At long last the day had come for her to take it for a real drive. Blow the carbon out, as her dad used to say. Seemed fitting that it was happening as part of her new life. And on Monday, when she went to the DMV to get her new Georgia license, she'd get new plates for the car too. Maybe vintage plates, if they did those.

She went inside, tied a scarf over her dark curls, popped on her biggest shades and grabbed her purse. Then she went back outside, put the top down and climbed in. The engine purred to life with a deep rumble that vibrated right through her.

There was no way not to smile. The day was gorgeous, thanks to the perfect weather and the car was a thing of beauty. A sleek machine that scared her just a little but mostly filled her with exhilaration and joyful memories of her father and the times they'd gone for rides together. She patted the dash. "This is for you, Daddy."

And just what she needed to relieve the stress of

this divorce. Thomas was about to be the furthest thing from her mind. At least for a little while.

She was shifting into reverse when a male voice called out to her.

"Sweet ride."

She glanced over. A handsome man, her neighbor, stood in the side yard. He looked to be about her age, well built and obviously very proud of that fact based on the tight T-shirt he wore. She'd seen him a couple times, but they'd never spoken. Something about him, maybe his cocky smile, maybe his overly confident posture, said loud and clear that he was not her type. But she could imagine him very easily on the cover of one of her books. And he was probably a very nice guy despite her first impression of him. And since he was her neighbor there was no point getting off on the wrong foot. She smiled. "Thanks."

"'69?"

"Yep." The wind blew past her, and he seemed to…sniff it. If he'd been one of her paranormal romance heroes, that wouldn't have been weird at all. But he wasn't. So it was.

His grin took on a feral edge. "My favorite year."

Or maybe not so nice a guy. Her smile faded.

He jerked his thumb toward the house behind him. "That's my '69 Camaro. Rebuilt it myself."

She shot a quick glance at the black muscle car sitting in the driveway and nodded tentatively.

"How nice." But she was done talking cars. All she wanted to do was drive. "Have a good day."

She looked behind her, backed out and took off down the street. If that was her neighbor, they were not going to be getting together for BBQ's. Guys like that found out what she did for a living and instantly thought she was an easy target. Like she was looking to do some up close and personal research.

Uh, no.

And unless he was a vampire or a werewolf, he really had nothing to offer her. She laughed at that thought. If vampires and werewolves actually existed, that would be something. They'd probably be nothing like the heroes in her books. In fact, they'd probably have all the same issues real men had, like working full time, paying bills and doing yardwork. That would kill the fantasy pretty fast. Except for the yardwork part if they were half naked and sweaty and ripped…

She glanced in the rearview mirror. Whatever that guy thought, she wasn't about to start getting chummy with her neighbor. That was a fast way to make things awkward. No, thank you. All she wanted was to be left alone, live her life and write the books that made her readers happy and her new single life possible.

Maybe she'd think about dating in a year or two.

Or never.

She could probably live with never. Especially if she got a dog. Or a houseful of cats.

The air whipped past. Sad, really. She considered herself a great catch, but she wasn't about to let another man into her world and risk ruining all this happiness. And why was she even thinking about this? Her divorce was still who knew how long away from being final.

Enough. She cranked up the radio, found some good tunes and settled in to enjoy the ride. The back roads of Nocturne Falls took her past some beautiful scenery and some amazing houses. No clue who lived in the big mansion near the winery, but the place was epic. Delaney had mentioned that her husband's grandmother had a house that was beyond all else. Could that have been it?

She sped on, loving the winding roads and unexpected turns. This town was not only the perfect place to live (Halloween every day was a paranormal romance author's dream), but it was proving to be the perfect place to own a car like this.

The Corvette would never be her daily driver. Her trusty hybrid was much more suited for that. But for weekends? And outings? And just plain fun? The Vette and these roads were a match made in Car & Driver heaven.

She owed Delaney lunch and a major thank-you for getting her to come to Nocturne Falls.

Something told her this place was going to be life-changing.

Her foot got a little heavier on the gas, and she zipped through another right-left-right turn combination. She whooped out loud, the grin on her face causing her cheeks to ache. She could practically feel her dad smiling down on her.

Then the wail of a siren interrupted her perfect day.

The Corvette sped past Alex's patrol car as he was sitting at a stop sign, about to turn back toward town on his normal route. He doubted the driver had even seen him since she'd made no attempt to slow down.

He flipped on the siren and went after her, catching up in a quarter mile. Then she slowed and pulled onto the shoulder.

Nice car. New Jersey plates. That was a long way to drive a classic car on vacation, but then, stranger things happened.

He stepped out and approached the vehicle. "Ma'am, are you aware you were doing seventy in a fifty-five mile per hour zone?"

She glanced at him, a pair of big sunglasses hiding her eyes. "Yes."

Not the response he'd expected. Usually, a

traffic stop brought on tears, arguing, excuses—you name it, he was used to it. But admittance of guilt? That was a rare one. He blinked behind his aviators. "Any particular reason you were going that fast?"

She seemed to be fighting a smile. "Because I can?"

He wondered if he should administer a field sobriety test, but his sensitive nose didn't detect even a hint of alcohol. Still, there were other substances that might be making her this bold. All he was picking up on was something sweet and floral. Not a bad smell at all. Not the slightest hint of anything supernatural, though. She was a hundred percent human. Like most tourists. "It's illegal and unsafe to exceed the speed limit, ma'am."

"I know. But sometimes you just need to let loose, you know?"

"License and registration, please, ma'am."

She sighed loudly as she dug in her purse. "Could you cool it with the ma'am business? We're probably the same age."

She handed over her information and he checked. She was twenty-nine. Five years younger than he was. Roxanne Sykes from New Jersey. And not bad-looking, now that he could see her without sunglasses and a scarf over her head. "I'll be right back."

"No hope for a warning, huh?" She smiled optimistically.

"No, ma'am." He walked back to his car while she frowned after him. Warnings were for locals, not tourists. He plugged her info into the system. Nothing outstanding. He wrote up the ticket and walked back.

He held out his clipboard. "Sign here please."

She signed.

He returned her ID and registration, along with a copy of the ticket and instructions about how to pay it. She stuffed it all in her purse, obviously not happy with him. Which was to be expected. "Have a nice day, ma'am."

"I was. Until you showed up."

"Just doing my job."

She looked at him, brows raised and just peeking over the rims of her sunglasses. "Are we done?"

He nodded. "Yes, ma' —"

She yanked the shifter out of park and drove off.

Women. He shook his head as he walked back to the patrol car. At least she hadn't resorted to tears. That always made him feel like such a heel.

A call came in on the radio. A noise disturbance at one of the local hotels. He responded and drove away, the ticket he'd just written all part of his day.

By the time that day was over, he was happy to go home. He didn't feel much like studying, but the test for sergeant was coming, and he wanted to be prepared. He changed out of his uniform and into shorts and a T-shirt, then grabbed a beer from the fridge.

Diego was lounging in the hot tub on the back deck, a beer at the ready. And probably not his first.

Alex stared at his brother through the kitchen window. Diego had the radio turned up and his eyes closed like he didn't have a care in the world. Pretty amazing that someone who still didn't have a job after three weeks could feel that way. Irritation curled in Alex's belly, but some of that was aimed inward. After all, he'd allowed Diego to move in.

But what were his options? He sighed. He knew what they were. He should have said no. Made his little brother face reality. Like every other adult had to do. Alex took a long pull off the bottle, the cold liquid diminishing some of the heat building in his gut. He loved his brother, but this conversation needed to happen.

He pushed the slider open and walked onto the deck.

Diego opened his eyes. "Hey, bro, jump in. The water is perfect."

Alex stayed put. "How did the job hunt go today?"

Diego shrugged. "You know how it is."

"No, I don't. That's why I asked."

Diego drank his beer before answering. "It's tough out there."

"Where did you apply?"

Diego frowned. "I didn't make it out today. I found a couple places in the paper, though. I'm going to call them in the morning."

"You didn't even make phone calls today? Diego, come on. This is the third week you've been here. You should have had a job two weeks ago."

"I got busy with other things."

"What other things could you possibly have to do? You're unemployed. Living in my house. And there are dishes in the sink, so clearly those other things don't include cleaning up after yourself." Alex looked away for a moment, feeling the beast within him rise. He knew his eyes must be gold.

Another breath and he found enough calm to speak again. "You have one more week. Get a job or you need to find other living arrangements."

"You're going to throw your baby brother out? Pretty heartless, bro."

"I am your brother, Diego, not your parent. You want to live like a child, unencumbered by work or bills? Move home with Mom and Dad." Alex strode back inside and shut the slider. He leaned on the kitchen counter and heaved out a breath.

He hated feeling like his brother was taking advantage of him, but that's what it had come to.

He'd known that would happen, but he hadn't listened to his instincts. That was his mistake. As an officer of the law, he knew better than to ignore his gut. Now he was paying the price.

The mail was on the counter, so apparently Diego had managed one chore. Alex flipped through it. Bills and junk mail. Except for one envelope. Looked like a card of some kind. And it wasn't for him.

The name on the envelope was Roxy St. James, and the address was next door. He'd been so busy he hadn't met the new neighbor, but he knew he had one. The Tamakas had been good neighbors. He hoped Roxy was too.

No time like the present to make an introduction, he supposed. Besides, he needed a break from Diego. He stuck his beer back in the fridge, grabbed the envelope and walked next door.

He knocked on her door and waited. Maybe she wasn't home. There was a car in the drive, one of those eco-friendly types, but she could be out for a walk or in the backyard.

He was about to knock again when the door opened and a petite brunette in yoga pants and a cropped T-shirt appeared. She had a mass of curly hair and big brown eyes that were as strong and warm as the Cuban coffee he loved.

The three inches of soft, tanned stomach on

display were equally as mouth-watering. He looked toward his house so he wouldn't be caught staring. That was no way to make a first impression. "I'm Alex, your neighbor from next door." He made eye contact again as he held the envelope up. "I got your mail by mistake."

She squinted at him for a hard second, then snatched the envelope out of his hand. "Are you kidding me?"

He stared at her. Why did she look familiar? "No, I really did get it by accident—"

She crossed her arms, tucking the envelope under them. "Just my luck. The cop who pulls me over lives next door."

He inhaled. And recognized her perfume. But without the scarf and the sunglasses—"Why does it say Roxy St. James on that address?"

"Not that it's any of your business, but St. James is my maiden name. And it'll be my legal last name again as soon as my divorce is final."

He shoved a hand through his hair. "Sorry about the ticket. I would have given you a warning if I'd known you were local. I thought you were a tourist."

Her glare didn't lessen. "Oh, so you're *that* kind of cop."

He really wasn't. "I'm not saying I'd do favors for you based on the fact that you live next door, but I could have given you a warning. But tourists are sort of how the town makes money in general." He sighed. Her expression wasn't changing. He didn't want to have this kind of tension with the woman who lived next to him. "I can make the ticket go away."

She went silent for a few seconds, then huffed out a breath. "Too late. I already put the check in the mail."

"That was fast."

"I don't like having that kind of stuff hanging over my head."

He respected that. "I'm sorry."

She frowned, and her expression finally softened as she exhaled a long sigh. She was remarkably pretty when she wasn't scowling at him. "Don't be. You were just doing your job. And I *was* speeding. Still, it kind of put a damper on my day."

He tried a smile. "How about I let you off the next one?"

Her brows knit together, then she laughed. "You're that convinced I'm going to be speeding again?"

He broadened his smile, glad he'd gotten a happy response out of her. "I saw the car. I'd be speeding again. Unless that wasn't your car?"

"No, it's mine. It's in the garage."

"Good place for a machine like that." He stuck his hand out. "I'm Alex, by the way." And then immediately remembered he'd already told her his name. She *was* a little discombobulating. "Sorry we met the way we did, but maybe we can move past that."

She hesitated. "Only if you never call me ma'am again."

He nodded. "Done."

She shook his hand. "Then I think we can move forward. I'd rather be friends with the cop next door than enemies. You know, in case I throw any wild parties."

Her hand was soft and delicate, but her grip was firm. "As long as I'm invited."

She smirked as they ended the handshake. "I'll keep that in mind, but honestly, it's not likely to happen. I'm pretty boring. I work from home and generally leave the house as little as possible. Although Nocturne Falls might change that. Seems like a really fun place."

"It is. Or it can be. I don't go out much myself either." At least not since he started studying for the sergeant's exam.

She squinted at him. "I actually thought I met you earlier. I mean you my neighbor, not *you* you. Anyway. There was a guy standing on your property when I left to take my drive this morning. Sort of looked like a younger version of you."

"That was a younger version of me. My brother, Diego." Alex sighed. "He's staying with me while

29

he gets back on his feet." Or until Alex evicted him.

Roxy smiled. "That's nice of you. Hey, you want a beer?"

He hesitated. It wasn't every day an attractive woman asked him in for a beer, but she was human. He didn't want to lead her on if she was thinking they were going to be more than neighbors.

"I'm not a mass murderer or anything, I swear. I only kill fictional people."

He frowned. "What?"

She laughed. "I'm a writer."

"Oh." A beer with his new, hot neighbor? Or back to his own house and the Diego invasion? "A beer would be great." He'd just make sure she knew he wasn't looking to get involved, that he wanted to keep things strictly on a friend level.

Especially because he couldn't exactly explain that he only dated other supernaturals.

"You sure I'm not interrupting anything?"

Roxy shook her head at Officer Hotness aka Alex, the man candy who lived next door. "You're not. I'm on a break." By which she meant she was procrastinating on writing the book she should have been halfway through by now, but whatever. Getting to know her handsome neighbor was definitely more important. And maybe the only way she'd avoid tickets in the future. "C'mon in." She pulled the door open wide and stepped back.

"I just thought maybe I was interrupting your workout."

She made a face, then glanced down at what she was wearing. Cropped T-shirt and yoga pants. They could definitely be interpreted as workout gear. "Because of my outfit? These are my work clothes. I go for comfort."

"I see that." He stepped inside. "Not that you

don't look good. You do. I mean, you look fine in comfortable clothes."

He shifted uncomfortably, and she laughed. "Relax, Officer Cruz." She headed for the kitchen, tossing the card he'd brought over onto the counter. He was really cute when he was flustered. And not writing her a ticket. "Light beer okay? That's all I have."

"Sure. And call me Alex, please."

She pulled two out of the fridge and handed him one.

He took it, twisted the top off with his bare hand, then gave it back and gestured for the other one.

She gave him the other bottle while she stared at the one he'd already opened. "Um, these aren't twist-offs."

The sound of the second bottle cap hitting the kitchen counter filled the brief silence. He smiled oddly. "Are you sure? They came off pretty easy."

She just nodded. He didn't seem like he was showing off, but that little act was sort of impressive. Just like his biceps. The man looked *very* fit.

He lifted his bottle toward hers. "Here's to new neighbors. And friends."

"To new neighbors. And fewer tickets written by friends." She winked as she took a sip of her beer.

He nodded and laughed before drinking his. "So you're a writer? What do you write?"

And there it was. His reaction to her answer would be very telling. Because she wasn't going to sugarcoat it or dance around the truth. That life was over. This one was all about truth and not being afraid. She leaned against the kitchen counter and lifted her chin. "I write romance novels."

"Seriously?" He took a seat on a bar stool at the counter.

She wasn't sure how to interpret that, but the question still put her on the defensive. "Yes."

He grinned. "My mother is addicted to romance novels. I think she reads one a day. She's hooked on this series right now…the Black Moon Brothers, or something like that. The hero is a werewolf *and* a vampire."

Roxy bit back a laugh. "You mean the Blood Moon Brotherhood?"

"Yeah, I think that's it. You know it?"

She nodded, doing her best to look nonchalant. "A little. Been writing it for three years."

He blinked at her. "For real?"

She nodded. "Yep. That's how I bought this house."

"Wow." He mumbled something in Spanish she didn't understand.

"What was that?"

"Just that my mother will kill me if she finds out

I gave her favorite author a ticket." A sudden look of panic came over his face. "I can't tell her I met you. Or that you live next door. She'll be here tomorrow. She'll try to move in with me. Or you. There's no telling, really. She's crazy like that."

Roxy laughed. "I'll sign a book for her if you want."

He shook his head. "Maybe we could save that for her birthday. It would raise too many questions if I sent her something like that out of the blue. Really nice of you, though."

"Her birthday, then."

He smiled and toasted her with his bottle. "Congrats on your success. My mother says you're her book club's favorite author. She's all worked up about the next book in the series. I take it it's a big one?"

"It's the final book before I start a spin off series and *Blood Moon Rising* is the one I've been teasing since I started the series. It wraps up Wolfgang's story. He's the pack leader."

"The werewolf and the vampire."

"Werevamp, but yes." She took a drink. "I'm behind on it a little. Er, a lot, actually, but moving kind of took up most of my writing time. Unpacking takes forever."

He glanced around. "Still working on it?"

"Yes and no. I didn't have a ton of stuff." Her house was a little sparse, but she'd covered the basics. Everything else would come with time. And after the book was done. The boxes in the garage weren't going anywhere. She shrugged. "Divorce has a way of exhausting you, mind, body and soul."

"You moved from New Jersey."

"Yep. And I plan to be at the DMV on Monday getting my new plates and license. Getting pulled over reminded me it's time to do that already. But it means one more day I won't be writing. Not much anyway."

His mouth bent in an utterly sexy half smile. "My mother can wait. She rereads the other books all the time."

Roxy sighed. "I'm happy to hear that, but I hate to disappoint my readers by prolonging a book too much, so I need to get cracking."

His lids lowered a bit. "Then you probably shouldn't be wasting time talking to me."

She shook her head slowly. "This isn't wasting time. It's being neighborly." She tipped her bottle toward his house. "So, your brother…he likes to think he has a way with women, am I right?"

Alex grunted. "Please tell me he did not come on to you."

"Yeah, no. Maybe a little." She laughed. "I handled it."

"I'll talk to him. And I'm sorry. Diego thinks he's God's gift to women, but if his last girlfriend hadn't kicked him out, he wouldn't be living with me. I don't know what to do with him. But he's family. My kid brother. What am I supposed to do?" He let out a soft sigh. "I didn't mean to dump all that out."

"It's okay." It was kind of sweet that he was willing to share so much right after they'd met. Maybe he was still trying to make up for the ticket. But she got that kind of sharing a lot. She'd always chalked it up to being an author. People liked to tell their stories to writers. "Family comes first, right?"

"Right. You have any brothers or sisters?"

"Nope. Just me."

"How'd you end up in Nocturne Falls from Jersey?"

"Delaney James. Ugh, Ellingham. I keep calling her by the wrong name. We were good friends in college, although I'm a year older than her due to getting a later start on school. We kind of bonded over almost having the same last name. Anyway, yes, I lived in New Jersey with my husband. Most of my so-called friends have sided with him in the divorce, but they were his friends first so no surprise there. I stupidly let my own friendships lapse. Too much work, not enough play."

"I know all about that."

"Well, that led me to reach out to some old friends from school on social media, and Delaney was one of the first to respond. One thing led to another, and here I am. Fresh start and all that."

She laughed nervously. "I'm talking too much. I do that."

"No, you're not talking too much, and whoever made you feel that way was wrong."

A warm spot blossomed inside her. She'd never had a man say something like that to her. The opposite, yes. Many times. And all from Thomas. "Thanks," she said softly. "Old habits die hard, I guess."

"This is a good town to make a fresh start in. And a great place for you to live considering what you do. Halloween three hundred and sixty-five and all that."

She nodded. "That's a big part of how Delaney sold me on moving here. You can't get much more inspirational for a paranormal romance writer than a town that celebrates Halloween every day."

"That's for sure."

"Hey, can I bug you if I ever need cop stuff? Procedural advice, that sort of thing? I can research it online, but it's always better from a real-life source." And it would give her an excuse to talk to Officer Hotness again. Without speeding. Because while she definitely wasn't interested in being involved with anyone, being friends with a guy who could model for one of her book covers was never going to be a bad thing.

He smiled. "Sure, anytime. I'll give you my number."

"Great." That had worked out better than imagined. Maybe she'd be able to make some friends in this town after all. Especially if everyone who lived here was as nice as Alex and Delaney. She glanced around the kitchen. "You know, I don't have anything to write on in here. Kind of sad that I'm a writer with no tools, huh? Let me grab a pen and notebook from my office. Be right back."

She left him drinking his beer and went to get paper, returning a few moments later. "Here you go. And here's my business card with my number on it in case you need me. Not that you're likely to have any romance-writing emergencies."

He jotted his number down. "You never know. There's always my mother."

"Right. You sure you don't want a signed book for her? I'm happy to give you one now *and* on her birthday."

He slid the notebook back toward her. He had nice handwriting, firm angled strokes that exuded confidence. Sexy handwriting. Which was totally a thing. "Okay. Maybe it'll distract her from her usual conversations with me about when I'm going to get married and settle down. Thanks again. You have no idea how much this is going to do for my favorite-son status."

She laughed. "You really feel bad about that ticket now, don't you?"

He groaned. "You're not going to let me forget that, are you?"

"Nope. Let me just go grab a book and—"

"On second thought, if I bring that book home, Diego's going to ask me all kinds of questions about it. And if he finds out who you are, he will definitely tell our mother." He frowned. "I have to figure out a time to get the book from you when he's not home. Which is always."

"Is the station anywhere near the post office? I have to check my P.O. box tomorrow. I could swing by and drop it off. If you're working on Saturday, that is."

"I am working. That's really nice of you. Tell you what, you bring me the book tomorrow, and I'll buy you lunch at one of the best places in town. I won't feel so bad about the ticket then."

That sounded an awful lot like a date. A thought that must have shown on her face because he put his hands up. "Just lunch as friends. To make up for the ticket. Nothing more than that, I swear."

She nodded. "I really should get back to writing after my errands, but I also want to get to know the town, and I'm having a saltwater fish tank installed in my office in the morning, so the day will probably be a bust writing-wise anyway. Lunch as friends would be great. And I'll bring you the book."

"Excellent. Meet me at one at the station, and we'll walk from there. Cool?"

"Cool."

"Thanks for the beer." He stood. "I should get back or Diego will be ordering pizza with my credit card."

"Okay. See you tomorrow. It was nice getting to know you." She walked him to the door, then watched him through the sidelight a few seconds longer. The man had a powerful, graceful stride that could only be described as feline. And there was something about him that was instantly compelling. Something she couldn't quite name. Maybe it was knowing what he did for a living.

Maybe it was how nice he'd been to her. And how he hadn't mocked what she did for a living.

Whatever it was, Alex Cruz was hero-worthy. And based on how lunch went tomorrow, he just might find himself in a book.

When Alex walked in, Diego was standing in front of the fridge with the door open. The puddle around his feet was growing as more hot tub water trickled off him and onto the kitchen floor.

He turned when he heard Alex. "There's nothing to eat in this house."

The muscles in Alex's jaw tightened. Muscles that had just been very relaxed over at Roxy's. He tried to stay calm. "Hey, you're getting water on the hardwood. Throw a towel down, will you? And there's plenty to eat. There's a tray of Mom's arroz con pollo in there. I took it out of the freezer this morning. It just needs to go in the oven for forty-five minutes."

"I'll starve to death by then."

Alex brushed past his brother to get the casserole out of the fridge. "You can always go out to eat."

"You mean buy my own food?" Diego rolled his eyes. "You didn't buy that. Mom stocks your freezer every time she visits."

Alex set the oven temp, put the casserole in, and headed back to his bedroom to get his iPod. "I'm going for a run."

"Cool. You want me to go with you?"

"No."

"Hey, where were you?"

"Returning the neighbor's mail." He left it at that, hoping Diego would too.

"Was that the chick with the Vette? Dude, she's hot for an older woman."

Alex stopped dead in his tracks. "Older? She's a year younger than you."

Diego snorted. "Yeah, but women age differently. You know."

Alex turned to stare his brother down. "No, I don't know, and if you honestly believe that, you have more growing up to do than I realized."

Diego's brows shot up, and he grinned. "Someone likes the new neighbor."

"As a friend. That's it."

Diego shrugged. "In that case, maybe I'll go next door and ask her out."

"No, you won't. Leave her alone."

"Why? You're not interested. You just said so."

"And if I was interested?"

Diego scratched himself. "Then I'd be hands off. You know that, bro. That's always been our code."

"In that case, I have a lunch date with her tomorrow."

Diego's eyes widened. "For real?"

"Yes."

"You know she's human, right?"

"I'm aware."

Alex went into his bedroom as Diego yelled out, "Nice work, bro."

Alex sighed and stared at the ceiling. He'd have to tell Roxy what he'd said in case Diego said something first. Which would be exactly like Diego. Alex grabbed his iPod and headed back to his pretty new neighbor's house to tell her the news.

Roxy was about to head to her office with the intention of making some headway on the new book when she remembered the card Alex had brought over. She went into the kitchen and picked it up off the counter. No return address, but there was some stickiness in the corner like the label had peeled off.

The cancellation on the stamp was too smudged to read.

She got a steak knife and ran it under the edge, then pulled the card out. She stared at it, unable to comprehend what she was looking at for a moment.

Enjoying your new house?

The words were scrawled in black marker on a lined notecard, the kind people used to write recipes on. Or plot points. The handwriting wasn't familiar. But it felt threatening. And deliberate.

She dropped the card on the counter and backed away. She watched it for a few seconds, like it might do something. Then she put her hands on her hips and got a little frustrated with herself. "This is silly. It means nothing."

But that wasn't true. It meant something. Otherwise, what had been the point of sending it? No doubt it had come from Thomas. Like their marriage hadn't been punishment enough. The man just couldn't let her be.

A knock on the door made her jump, and she shrieked before she could stop herself. She snarled out a groan, angry at herself for reacting that way. She strode to the door and pulled it open. "Yes? Oh, hey, Alex. I didn't expect to see you again so soon."

His brows bent together. "Did I just hear you scream? Everything okay?"

She waved her hand. "It was nothing. A spider. You know." She wasn't about to tell him about that silly piece of mail. "What's up?"

He glanced toward his house, a very long-suffering look on his face. "If you happen to run into my brother, our lunch tomorrow is a date. Like, an actual date. I told him that to keep him from asking you out. As you surmised, he's kind of a player, but if he thinks I'm interested in you, he'll leave you alone. It's the bro code. Or something like that. Anyway, I thought you should know so you don't get blindsided. Or think I'm trying to pull something."

She tried to suppress a smile. "Got it. Our lunch date is a date, but only if Diego asks."

"Right. Sorry to bother you."

"No problem. And no bother. Hey, one question."

"Sure."

Not that the weird note had made her jumpy about having strangers in her house, but… "Do you know Undrea Seely? She installs and maintains fish tanks? She's cool, right? I mean, she seems that way and she came highly recommended, but—you know what, never mind. I'm just being weird."

But he answered anyway. "I don't know her personally, but yeah, I hear she's nice." His brows lifted. "Is that who's installing the tank for you?"

Roxy nodded, liking that Alex had actually listened to what she'd said. Maybe that was just the cop in him, but it made her feel nice. "Yep. So it would be okay for her to be in my house alone? I just might not be here the whole time, and I was wondering."

"You don't have anything to worry about."

"Okay, thanks. That's what I was thinking, but never hurts to ask. See you tomorrow. For our non-date date."

He smirked. "Yeah." Then he gave a wave and jogged down her path to the sidewalk.

Her gaze lingered a little longer than was neighborly, but Officer Cruz was in very good shape. His running shorts showed off muscular legs that were hard not to admire. She finally pulled herself away from the door as he disappeared down the street. Time to get back to her office.

And back to the main man in her life, Wolfgang Blackborne.

She settled into her chair, tapped the touchpad to bring the screen to life and logged in. Her manuscript sat there, formatted and waiting, the blank white pages of the Word document mocking her with their emptiness. She stared at the screen for a moment, then put her fingers to the keyboard and started typing.

Wolfgang Blackborne stared out across the jagged castle ruins. Wind scoured the Scottish moors, buffeting his face and tugging at his long, leather coat. His childhood home had once been a majestic place. But that had been three hundred years ago. Before he'd been turned into the beast he now was.

He'd thought his life was about to be perfect again. That he'd be able to rebuild here, create a legacy for the family he and Marabella would conceive. But he'd lost his beloved Marabella. And his brother had betrayed him.

Now he cared only for one thing. Vengeance. And with the help of his pack, he was finally going to get it.

Roxy nodded. That was good. That was a start. Only eighty thousand more words to go. She sighed and started tapping away, losing herself in the world of the Blood Moon Brotherhood until her stomach started to growl.

She looked at the time. She'd been at the keyboard for almost two hours. That was enough for the day, considering it was getting late. She got up, went into the kitchen to fix something to eat and saw the note again.

She picked it up and was about to pitch it in the trash when a small voice in her head said not to. She really didn't want it in her house, but maybe she'd hang on to it for another day or two.

Just in case.

She gingerly stuck the card back into the envelope and set it on top of the fridge, which required some stretching, but also meant out of sight, out of mind. She brushed her hands off and decided another beer, or two, was in order while her low-fat, all-veggie frozen pizza for one heated up.

She got the pizza in the oven, then turned on the TV and sat on the couch while it baked. Feet up on the coffee table, she scrolled through the channels, not paying so much attention to what was on as to what was happening tomorrow.

Lunch with Alex. The non-date date. She grinned. Whatever it was, it would be fun. He was a nice guy, and she needed to get out and see the town some more anyway. Maybe afterward, she'd stop by and see Delaney. Get the real scoop on her neighbor.

Hmm. Maybe she should get a picture of the two of them together and post it to her social media. Her fans would go nuts over Officer Cruz in his uniform. She shook her head. She wouldn't do it, no matter how many likes it might get her. Some things weren't meant for public consumption, like her private life.

Roxy nodded, pleased with her plan for the next day. Who knows? She might be so inspired after lunch with Alex that she'd get some writing done in the afternoon.

The next day started bright and early with the arrival of Undrea Seely, owner of Tanks A Lot. Undrea was stunning, in an unintentional sort of way. Her rose-gold hair was pulled back in a long braid and she wore denim overalls with a simple cotton tank top. Her amber eyes were bright and happy. "Morning! Ready to get fishy?"

Roxy laughed. "Yes. I have been looking forward to a tank like this ever since I was a little girl. I can't wait."

"I know you've probably moved some stuff in since I was here to measure so do you mind if I have a look at the space once more before I bring everything in?"

"Not at all." Roxy walked her back to the office.

All she'd really added was a desk, a chair and a bookshelf. "I hope there's enough room for you to do what you need to do."

Undrea nodded. "Yep. We're in good shape. I'll start the setup."

Roxy hadn't seen anyone in the van with her. "You have help, right?"

"Absolutely. I've got Aaron in the truck."

"Just two of you? Isn't the tank kind of heavy?"

"Um…" Undrea shrugged. "Not really. Not until it's filled with water. These acrylic tanks aren't nearly the weight of the glass ones."

"Oh, yeah, I remember you telling me that. And clearer, too, right?" Still seemed like a lot of tank for two people, but Undrea was the expert.

"That's correct. You'll see. You're going to love this when it's all set up."

"I can't wait." Roxy was buzzing with excitement. She'd wanted a tank like this ever since she and her dad had kept goldfish. She knew now that getting the fish had been her father's way of distracting her from the loss of her mother, but as a kid, she hadn't understood that. She'd loved the time they'd spent together, staring into the tank and talking about the fish. Listening to the soft bubbling of the filter. It had done the job he'd intended, to a certain point. Spending time with him had taken care of the rest.

She smiled and wished he could see this when it

was all done. To be able to sit and work near something like this would take all her stress away. "Okay, well, I'm going to grab my laptop and get out of your way. I'll have my cell phone, so call me if you need me. I'll just be in the backyard, but that way you won't have to go searching for me."

"You got it." Undrea headed to her truck.

Roxy picked up her laptop, stuck her phone under her bra strap, since her yoga pants didn't have pockets, and went outside. She hadn't written in the fairy house yet, which was what she'd named the playhouse, but today was as good as any to give it a try.

She unlocked the door and climbed the spiral stairs to the loft. She'd had a memory foam mattress put up here last week and she'd loaded it with pillows, turning it into a great napping and writing nest. She positioned herself at the head of the mattress, back against the wall, and fired up her laptop.

Her phone vibrated with an incoming message. Maybe Undrea had run into a snag. Roxy checked it, cringing immediately as soon as she saw Thomas's name pop up on the screen. Unbelievable. He just couldn't leave her in peace.

She tapped delete and went back to her laptop, ready to focus on some words and not her bothersome ex. If he needed to talk to her, he already knew he could send messages through her attorney. Huh. Maybe that's why he'd sent that note about the house. It was his way of showing her he could still get to her.

Jerk.

Twenty minutes and several pages later, she realized that she either needed the AC on or some fresh air. The loft was a little warm. And since it was May, fresh air won out. She set her laptop aside and crawled over to one of the transoms.

The height of the fairy house and her position on the mattress meant she could look right down into Alex's backyard. The morning sun cast streaks of light and shadow over his property, making it a little tricky to figure out what she was looking at initially.

Well, now. *He* had a hot tub. That much she could see.

She grinned as thoughts of peeping on him while he was in that hot tub drifted through her mind. That would be wrong. Right? Probably. Ooo, but fun. She closed her eyes for a second and tried to imagine him without his shirt. As a writer, she had a vivid imagination. Her mental picture of him only made the loft hotter.

She laughed softly and opened her eyes. Time to get the window open and—she stared into his backyard.

There was no way she was seeing what she was seeing. A panther. A big, black, *freaking* panther.

She rolled away to lie flat on her back on the mattress and stare up at the pitched roof. Where on earth could that have come from? Then it occurred to her that the panther might not be real. This was Georgia. Not…wherever panthers lived.

She'd seen a shadow, that was all. And the stress of moving and being behind on her book and *Thomas* was making her see things. She took a breath. That's all it was. Just a weird shadow. Or a very large housecat. One of those things. Totally explainable.

She rolled back to the window.

There was no panther in the backyard. Just Diego. Shirtless and stretching. She frowned. He was hot. Too bad he was also so full of himself.

Okay, so she *was* seeing things. It happened. Never to her, but stress made all sorts of weird things happen to the body. That had to be the reason. Stress. Because she didn't want to think that her mother's history was repeating itself in her. No, it was this divorce. It was giving her the kind of stress that made her want to drown in chocolate.

Which reminded her, she really needed to go by Delaney's shop. She added that to her list of errands for the day, then blew out a long sigh and went back to writing.

Two hours later, her phone rang.

"Hello?"

"Hey," Undrea said. "Your tank is in."

Roxy sat up a little straighter. "Water and everything?"

"Yep. We bring the salt water with us. It still has to condition for a few days, then I'll be back with fish. But come take a look. You can get a pretty good idea of how amazing it's going to be."

"I'm on my way." Roxy hung up, closed her laptop, stuck her phone back under her bra strap and headed into the house. She left the phone and her laptop on the kitchen counter before going into the office.

She found Undrea in there, standing in front of the new tank and smiling like she was unveiling a masterpiece.

"Oh, wow." The tank spanned the length of the rear wall and had been designed to look like a built-in. The water was cloudy with unsettled sand, but it was still beautiful. The coral inserts were bright and colorful, and Roxy could definitely imagine how gorgeous it would be with fish. "I love it. So much."

Smiling, Undrea lifted the remote in her hand and clicked a button. The lights shining into the tank changed to blue. "That's the moonlight setting."

Roxy squeezed her hands together. "I should have more words to say, but it's kind of left me speechless. I'm so happy right now, you can't imagine."

"I'm glad to hear that." Undrea switched the

lights back to daytime and set the remote on Roxy's desk. "The timer's set to cycle the lights as needed. I use live sand and rock that's cured ahead of time at my shop, so everything's basically ready to go, but I like to run the tanks empty for at least twenty-four hours, then check the salinity and adjust as needed."

"Do I need to do anything?"

"Nope. I'll be back tomorrow morning to test the water and possibly add some wrasses." Undrea picked up her clipboard. "Just sign and date this first invoice and I'll be out of your hair."

"All right." Roxy leaned in to scribble her name. Undrea's perfume smelled like fresh salt air. Roxy smiled. Pretty appropriate for someone in her line of work. She glanced up.

And saw gills behind Undrea's ear.

Roxy blinked and focused on the paper in front of her. She added the date. Not gills. A scar. She tried to look again, but Undrea had moved away.

The woman tore off a copy for Roxy and put it on her desk. "We're good to go."

Roxy nodded, her mind swirling. "Okay. Thank you so much."

"See you tomorrow."

Roxy walked Undrea to the door, then went back into her office and sat in her desk chair. It was almost funny that life with Thomas had been so awful that the grueling process of divorcing him was now giving her hallucinations. She closed her eyes, then remembered the tank.

She swiveled her chair around and stared into it, imagining fish gliding around in their quiet, perfect little world. She exhaled and already her stress levels felt lower.

She sat there for a while, just thinking. Had she actually imagined she'd seen a panther in Alex's yard? And gills on Undrea? She snorted. She needed this tank more than she'd realized. Thinking about Alex and his yard made her check the time.

"Holy cow!" It was five after twelve. If she was going to meet him at one, she had to get going.

First, she grabbed the book she'd promised to bring and stuck it in her handbag so she wouldn't forget it, then she raced through her routine, showering and doing her makeup with as much speed and care as possible. Her hair got wound into a quick twist because she was definitely driving the Vette. It was sort of a necessity if she was dining with Alex.

It was May and this was Georgia, so she went with white denim capris, a cute top and wedge flip-flops that gave her an extra three inches. That might put her at eye level with Alex's chin.

She was out the door and on the street in forty minutes, which didn't give her long to find the sheriff's station, but thankfully the GPS on her phone knew how to get her there. Checking her P.O. box would have to wait until after lunch.

Finding a parking spot took a little longer, but somehow she managed to walk into the Nocturne Falls Sheriff Department at twelve fifty-seven.

She stopped at the front desk, where a perky older woman greeted her with a big, "Hi there! What can I help you with?"

"Hi. I'm Roxy. I'm here to meet Officer Cruz."

The woman's eyes lit up. "Oh, is that so? Officer Cruz, huh? He's a handsome one, isn't he? And such a good cook. Did you know that about him? He's really—"

"Birdie, I already have a mother trying to marry me off." Alex walked up to the counter. "I don't need you doing it too." He smiled at Roxy. "Hi."

She smiled back. "Hi."

Birdie made a face. "I was just extolling your virtues to this nice young woman. Who you haven't introduced me to yet."

Alex laughed. "Birdie, this is my neighbor, Roxy St. James."

Birdie's eyes went wide. "Not *the* Roxy St. James? I heard you were moving into town, but I didn't know you were here already. Well, aren't we lucky?"

Roxy knew the woman was being friendly, but the thought that people knew she'd moved here was a little unsettling. Maybe Birdie knew Delaney and that's who she'd heard from. "Um, yes, that's me. You must be friends with Delaney. Is that how you heard?"

"I know Delaney well enough, but I know Pandora too, and that's who sold you your house, right? Plus, Willa over at the jewelry store is a huge fan of your books. She got me reading them." Birdie fanned herself. "That Wolfgang Blackborne is so hot."

Roxy swallowed. This was so...unexpected.

Birdie seemed to pick up on Roxy's unease. She reached out and patted Roxy's arm. "Honey, it's not like the whole town knows, but you've got fans here. We won't bother you or show up at your door, I swear. This might be a tourist town, but it's also a *small* town, and we're real protective of the citizens who live here. We know what being pestered can be like. I promise, we're not a bunch of crazies either. Well, Martha Vines is a little woo-woo, but you get one of those in every crowd."

Roxy still felt a little side-swiped. "Well, that's good. The protective part."

Alex took her arm. "Birdie, we're going out for lunch." Then he guided Roxy out the front door and onto the sidewalk. "Are you okay? You look like you just got hit by a small truck. Birdie has that effect on people, but she's mostly harmless."

She exhaled slowly. "I'm fine. Just didn't anticipate that sort of reception, I guess. I knew

Delaney wasn't keeping my move a secret or anything, but...I don't know. That was so unexpected."

"You must be used to some of that, right? Fans, I mean."

"Sure. But usually it's at a reader convention or a signing. Some kind of event where I expect it. Not in the town I live in. And really, authors are hardly ever recognized unless they're super famous like Anne Rice or JK Rowling."

"So you didn't even get that sort of reaction where you lived in New Jersey?"

She snorted. "No. My ex thought my career choice was ridiculous. I may have had fans among our crowd up there, but mostly my books were the punchline to every other joke."

"Sounds like your ex was intimidated by you and your success."

She looked up at Alex. "You think so?"

He nodded. "I do. You look really nice, by the way."

She smiled. "Thank you." He looked outstanding. The uniform suited him, especially the way it hugged his biceps and left no questions about how trim and fit the rest of him was. But before her mind went too far down that rabbit hole, she changed the subject. "Where are we going for lunch?"

Alex pointed up ahead. "One of my favorite places. Howler's."

Alex had already reminded himself three times that lunch with Roxy was just his way of repaying her for the speeding ticket. But she looked so pretty and smelled so good, forgetting that this wasn't a date became way too easy.

It would have helped if she wasn't his type, but the petite, curvy brunette was exactly the sort of woman that wound him up. Well, petite, curvy, brunette *supernatural* women. Too bad Roxy was human. He would have been all over her, otherwise.

In a respectful manner, of course.

"Howler's?" Roxy scrunched up her face. "I've seen that place. Isn't that a biker bar?"

"No." He snorted. "It's a little divey, but that's part of its charm."

"Dive bars have charm?"

"This one does. And pretty great food, too."

Her mouth curved in a cute little semi-smile. "It better be, or this will not count as making up for that ticket."

He laughed. "Noted. Hey, how are your fish?"

"No fish yet. Just the tank. But it's going to be awesome. You'll have to come over and see it when it's done."

"Yeah, that would be great. I love fish." What feline shifter didn't? "Do you have any other pets?"

"Nope. I was thinking about getting a dog, though. It would give me a good reason to get outside more."

He frowned. Dogs were not his thing.

She made a face. "You don't like dogs?"

"They're okay."

"Don't you have a K-9 unit?"

"Not in Nocturne Falls." Between the vampires, werewolves and other supernaturals on staff, dogs were unnecessary. "Here we are. Howler's."

They got a table, a booth along the far wall, actually, and settled in.

Roxy looked around. "Okay, it's not as bad as I thought it would be."

"What were you expecting? Harley-Davidson signs and female servers in hot pants and halter tops?"

She shrugged. "Something like that." She pointed towards the bar. "And I do see one Harley-Davidson sign."

Their server, in khaki shorts and a black polo shirt with the Howler's logo on the chest, arrived with menus. "Afternoon. Hey, Officer Cruz."

"Hi, Shanna." Maybe he came here too often for lunch. Might be time to hit Mummy's up a little more.

Shanna smiled at them. "What can I get y'all to drink?"

"Do you have any sparkling water?" Roxy asked.

"We have the local Nocturne Falls spring water, but that's not sparkling." Shanna thought for a moment. "I'll check at the bar, but we might have Pellegrino, too."

"That would be perfect, thanks." Roxy smiled. "With lemon."

"Got it." Shanna looked at Alex. "You want your usual sweet tea?"

He nodded, and she left to get their drinks.

Roxy leaned in. "You obviously eat here a lot."

He lifted one shoulder. "Yeah, maybe too much."

"No, no. I think it's a good sign. You must really like the food." Her brows quirked up in amusement. "And clearly the server really likes you."

"Shanna? She's just a kid." What was she…twenty? Twenty-two, tops.

"A kid with a crush."

"No way." Alex glanced over at Shanna, who was at the server station getting their drinks. She caught his eye and grinned. Oh, crap.

"She welcomed you by name, with a big smile, and she remembers your usual drink. Yeah, she likes you." Roxy held her hands out. "I know what the signs of attraction are. It's my business to know. It comes with the romance-writing territory."

"Maybe she does have a crush. But that's as far as I'm willing to go. I've certainly never encouraged it."

"Hey, I'm not judging. Although she is a little young."

"Because I'm such an old man."

"You said it, not me."

He liked the teasing. Most people treated him with a certain deference because of his job, acting like they had to be serious around him all the time, but not Roxy. She was a refreshing change.

Still smiling, Roxy opened up her menu. "So what's good here?"

"Pretty much everything." He looked at his menu, although he didn't really need to. There were no specials on Saturdays, so he usually got the ribeye sandwich with fries and coleslaw. And sometimes the brownie sundae.

"What are you getting?"

"The steak sandwich with fries."

She looked up. "You always get that, don't you?"

He hesitated. "I get it a lot. Why?"

Her smile bordered on knowing, like she'd just figured him out. "Just a guess. But you strike me as a creature of habit. You always give tourists tickets, but not locals. You drink the same thing at lunch every time you're in here. You go for a run every day after work."

He sat back and shot her a look. "How do you know I go for a run every day after work?"

She suddenly became very interested in her menu. "You go right by my house. That's all."

Had she been watching him? A little thrill zipped through him at the thought that Foxy Roxy had been checking him out. "And you don't like routine?"

That brought her head up. "I live for routine."

Shanna came back with their drinks. "Sweet tea for you, Officer Cruz." Then she put a bottle and a glass of ice in front of Roxy. "And Pellegrino for you. Y'all ready to order?"

Alex looked at Roxy. She nodded. "I'll have the Caesar salad with grilled chicken. Dressing on the side, hold the croutons. Thanks."

Alex ordered the steak sandwich. Roxy might be carb-averse, but he wasn't. He also wasn't going to give her grief about her order. Her figure was amazing. Whatever she wanted to do to keep it that way was up to her.

As Shanna went to put their orders in, Roxy

twisted the top off her bottle of sparkling water. "As I was saying, routine is my thing. Lately, I haven't had much of one because of the move, but I hope to get back to it soon."

He crossed his arms on the table top. "What's your normal day like?"

She twisted the edge of her paper napkin. "Get up, have coffee, do some yoga, shower, eat breakfast while I watch some news, then I'm pretty much in my office all day. Now that I live in a town like this, I might start adding an evening walk."

Might be nice to walk with her sometimes. "You spend all day in your office writing?"

She nodded. "Writing and also handling all the other stuff it takes to put my books out. Talking to my team about ongoing and upcoming work, scheduling promos, checking in on social media, answering fan mail, proofing audiobooks...there's so much to do."

"Your team?" He hadn't realized being a writer involved so much.

"My team is basically my assistant, Emily, my—"

"You have an assistant? Very impressive."

"I've had a few actually. My last one was excellent, but Marissa quit on me a few months ago without much reason. Anyway, Emily has been a great replacement."

"So who else is on your team?"

She ticked them off on her fingers. "My editor, my cover designer, my formatter, my foreign rights agent, all those people. Then Em handles my street team, giveaways, keeping the social media active when I can't, travel arrangements when I have a conference or a book tour coming up, all sorts of stuff."

"Wow. Your job sounds more complicated than mine. I had no idea."

She laughed. "You see why I don't leave the house? I don't have time."

"I get it. But you have to have some kind of life outside of work."

"I suppose." Her smile went a little dreamy. "But I love what I do. I love the stories I tell, the characters I create, the worlds I build…all of it. And I love making my readers happy. I guess sometimes that means I spend too much time doing it."

"They say if you love your work, you'll never—"

"Well, if it isn't my big brother and Little Red Corvette." Diego slid into the seat beside Alex. "Hello, *Roxy*." He stuck his hand out. "We haven't formally met. I'm Diego. You and I have a lot in common."

Alex bit back a snarl. "Diego—"

"How do you figure that?" Roxy stared at him but didn't extend her hand.

He gestured suddenly to cover the fact that he'd been left hanging. "We're both very good-looking, we both like fast rides on big engines, and have I mentioned we're both very good-looking?"

He grinned like he'd just delivered the smoothest line ever. Alex repressed a groan.

Roxy's eyes narrowed for a moment, then she shook her head. "That's so sad. All of it, really. Just so sad."

Confusion filled Diego's eyes. "What's sad?"

Alex had a feeling this was going to be interesting.

Roxy took a drink of her fancy water before she spoke. "First of all, it's sad that you think that kind of bro nonsense would appeal to any woman with a brain in her head. And secondly, it's sad that you don't respect your brother enough not to interrupt him while he's on a date."

Diego gaped at her, silent.

Her mouth pursed with disdain. "Is there some pressing news that brought you here?"

"No, I just—"

"Then if you'll excuse us, we're having lunch."

Alex snorted.

Diego slid out of the booth and stood by the table, looking totally confused.

Alex felt the tiniest bit sorry for him. His little brother had been seriously outclassed. "Why did you come by?"

"I, uh…" Diego looked up. "I have a job interview to tend bar."

"Good for you. That explains why you're wearing my shirt and tie. Is the interview with Bridget?"

Diego nodded.

Alex had never seen him this subdued. "Please don't flake on her. Her brother is my boss. Got it?"

"Got it. I better go." Diego shuffled off.

Alex raised his brows. "Wow."

"I'm sorry." Roxy bit her lip. "I shouldn't have said anything. It wasn't my place. I don't know what got into me."

"It wasn't a what, it was a who. Diego. And I'm the one who should be apologizing for him. You were fine." He laughed softly. "Pretty brilliant, actually."

"You're not mad?"

"No." He lifted his sweet tea to her. "You have a real way with words, Miss St. James. But I guess that shouldn't surprise me, considering what you do."

She smiled, a little self-consciously, but then picked up her water and clinked it against his glass. "Thanks."

Their food arrived and they ate. The conversation turned to Roxy asking him all kinds of questions about how things worked in the sheriff's department. He figured she was using him for research, but at the same time, he'd never known someone so interested in what he did. It was really nice.

Hell, everything about her was really nice.

Except for the part where she was absolutely, positively human.

Shanna came back to clear their plates. "How about some dessert for you two? The peach cobbler is plenty big enough for sharing."

Sharing a dessert was definitely date territory.

Roxy shook her head. "Thank you, but I'd better not. Alex, go for it if you want. Don't let me stop you."

"No, I'm good. Just the check, Shanna." When she left, he looked at Roxy. "So? Did this make up for the ticket?"

She smiled and started to nod slowly. "Yes."

"Really? Even with Diego's interruption? You're generous. I like that."

She laughed, then said, "Oh! I almost forgot. She dug into her big purse and pulled out a book and a pen. "For your mom. What's her name?"

"Carmen. Thanks."

"You bet." She opened the book, scrawled something across the title page, then added her signature underneath. She closed it and slid it toward him. "There you go."

He picked it up. "You have no idea how happy this is going to make her. I might owe you another lunch."

Her cheeks went the slightest bit pink. Was she blushing? "I might take you up on that. Hey, I totally forgot to ask you. Does someone in the neighborhood have a big black cat?"

A warning bell started ringing in his head, then he realized she couldn't possibly know what he really was. "Probably. Why?"

But then Shanna came back with the check, and Roxy never answered. He paid the bill and looked for Shanna to hand the cash back to her. No sign of Diego. He must still be in Bridget's office.

"Worried about him?"

Alex turned back around. "I'm always worried about him. For a former Marine, he's so…"

"Lackadaisical?"

"Now you're just showing off."

She laughed.

He sighed, smiling. "He's my brother, you know? I want the best for him. But he doesn't seem to want the best for himself. He just floats through life."

"And that bothers you because you're a routine guy. Everything is planned and by the book. You say you're going to be there, you're going to be there."

"Pretty boring, huh?"

She winked at him, causing his body to tighten unexpectedly. "One woman's boring is another one's pleasure." Then she sighed, and her gaze shifted to something behind him. "But I suppose the opposite must be true too."

He turned to look. Diego was talking to Shanna. Alex frowned, then glanced at Roxy. "I need to let him be, don't I?"

She lifted her shoulders, her expression placid. "He's a grown man. And Shanna's probably old enough to make her own decisions. Even if they are bad ones."

Alex grabbed the signed book she'd given him. "In that case, I really need to get back to work."

"Sounds good. I still have errands to run."

They walked out together and all the way back to the station, then stopped at the door. "Where are you off to?" he asked.

"In no particular order, the post office, the Shop-n-Save and Delaney's store." She grinned. "Just because I didn't eat dessert at lunch doesn't mean I'm not going to want something sweet later."

He nodded. "I get it." He hesitated, the feeling that he should kiss her battling with the reminder that this was *not* a date. "I guess I'll see you around."

She smiled. "I'll call you when the tank's all done. You can come see the fish."

"Sounds like a date." He paused. "I mean, not a date. A…" What did he mean?

Her grin widened. "I have your number. I'll call you."

"All right. Good." He went inside before he said anything else that made him look like a half-wit. The woman had a strange effect on him.

Birdie waved. "How was lunch, Alex?"

Her voice snapped him out of his thoughts. "It was…" He smiled, his mind returning to Roxy's big, brown eyes and rosebud lips and warm sense of humor. "Good." And it had been. Really, *really* good.

Birdie grinned and started humming the *Wedding March*.

Roxy felt lighter than air. It was the same feeling she got when she released a new book, or got a great, over-the-top review, or knew she'd nailed a scene.

Thomas had never made her feel that way. But Alex sure did. In fact, he was the first man who had.

And it scared the stuffing right out of her. It was an odd combination to be gloriously happy and also petrified of what that glorious happiness meant. What she did know was that she was *not* feeling anything remotely romantic for Alex. Not at all. He was just hot. (*So* hot.) And nearby. And nice.

That was *it*.

Please let that be it. She did not need, or want, a man in her life. She still hadn't technically gotten rid of the one she had. Which reminded her that she needed to nudge her attorney on Monday about what was taking Thomas so long to sign the papers.

She looked in the shop windows as she walked, not really seeing anything.

Maybe she was feeling this way because Alex was the first guy in a long time who'd been so kind to her. He hadn't wanted anything from her. Just to make up for the ticket and be a good neighbor.

She squinted at that thought. That was all he wanted, right? Nothing he'd done had given her any indication of anything else. And he was such a standup guy. It was literally his job to uphold the law. There was no way he was playing some secret game of Let's Be Friends Who Turn Into Lovers.

No, this was just a guy being neighborly. Not a guy. A neighbor. That was a safer way to think of him.

She checked the address of Delaney's shop on her phone, then plugged it into her maps app. She'd thought she knew where she was going, but after walking several minutes with her head in the clouds, she wasn't sure at all.

As it turned out, she was only a block and a half away. She arrived at Delaney's Delectables a few minutes later.

The smell was divine. She paused just inside the door and inhaled, eyes closed. Chocolate was both the fuel for her writer's mind and the bane of her writer's backside. But she'd had salad for lunch. Very low carb. She could splurge a little.

And chocolate was good for the writing. She believed in literally feeding the muse.

"Roxy!"

Delaney's voice rang out over the hum of the shop. Roxy opened her eyes and smiled. "Hey, woman, what's up?"

Delaney came out from behind the counter and greeted her with a hug. "I didn't know you were coming by today. Did you tell me and I forgot? I might be getting pregnancy brain."

"Can you have pregnancy brain when you're not even showing?"

"I'm showing." Delaney leaned back and pulled her apron tight across her stomach, displaying a slight roundness.

"I look like that after a big lunch. Are you sure that's a baby in that little bump?"

Delaney nodded and laughed. "Yep. I'm almost four months now."

"Picked out any names yet?"

"Not really. We talk about them a lot, but nothing's stuck. I'm sure it'll come to us as we get closer." Delaney put her hands on her hips. "You look happy. And a little weirded out. What's going on?"

Roxy shrugged. "I wish I knew. Do you have a minute to talk?" The shop was kind of busy. "I don't want to take you away from your work. Maybe after you close?"

Delaney waved that idea away. "I have all kinds of time for you. We can go in my office. You want a slice of something? Some truffles? Coffee?"

Roxy eyed the display cases. "Yes, definitely. But there are too many options. I need help. Anything new I haven't tried yet?"

"Let's see, what's new... I've got these fireball truffles I just came up with. Plus a new mocha flourless cake. The strawberry champagne bonbons aren't as new but they're a summer only thing and I just started stocking them again. Oh, and adult chocolate-covered cherries. You should definitely have one of those."

"What are adult chocolate-covered cherries?"

"The cherries are soaked in moonshine. I hear they're good, but I haven't been able to try them myself." She patted her stomach. "You'd really be doing me a favor."

Roxy laughed. "Well, if it's doing you a favor, how can I not help out a friend?"

Delaney nodded. "Exactly." She looped her arm through Roxy's. "C'mon."

Roxy let Delaney guide her back behind the counters, and a few minutes later, they were in Delaney's office with two plates of sweets and two small bottles of milk.

Roxy took the chair beside Delaney's desk and

dug into the mocha flourless cake. The coffee-chocolate goodness of it spread across her tongue and raised goose bumps on her arms. "Oh man. I could weep at how good this is."

Delaney grinned and finished the bite of truffle she'd just taken. "You want a slice to take home?"

"Just one?" Roxy laughed, then shook her head. "I don't know if it'll keep in the trunk. I still have some other errands to run. I better not this time. Trust me, this plate will keep me going for a long time."

"Good." Delaney sat back in her desk chair. "So what's up?"

Roxy rested her fork on the edge of her plate. "This is going to sound really strange. It's the stress of the divorce, I know that's all it is, but...I...I'm seeing things. Weird things."

Delaney's brows lifted, but that's where the surprise on her face ended. "Like what?"

Roxy rubbed her forehead. "I thought I saw a black panther this morning. I'm pretty sure that was just a weird shadow, or someone's overgrown house cat, but still. And then when the woman came to install my tank—"

"Undrea?"

"Mm-hmm. I'm embarrassed to even say this, but I could have sworn I saw gills behind her ear. Because of course the woman who owns the fish tank place would have gills." Roxy groaned and shook her head. "I'm sort of worried that all this stress from moving and getting divorced and being behind on my book is making the stuff I write about come to life."

Because that's all it was. Stress. Nothing like what had happened to her mother.

Delaney bit her lip. "Stress does do strange things to people. I don't think you should worry about it too much. Hey, maybe it'll give you some new story ideas."

Roxy leaned in. "Your teeth look odd. Pointed, sort of."

"What?" Delaney seemed to pale a little. She closed her mouth and then, after a breath, said, "I thought the divorce was final. Didn't you say it was just a matter of time?"

"Yes, and when I said that, I thought I'd have the signed papers any day. They still haven't come." Roxy stabbed another piece of cake. Delaney's teeth seemed normal now. Weird. "That jerk. He's really dragging this out. Oh, and get this, because emailing and texting me wasn't enough, he just sent me this creepy little note asking me if I was enjoying my new house."

"What?"

She scowled. "He cannot leave me alone. I can't believe I ever fell for him. He was so different when we first got together. But man, once that ring went on, he changed completely. Absolutely thought that little band of gold made me his property."

Delaney made a noise of disgust. "The sooner you're done with him the better."

"I'll say."

"You know what? You need to get out. Spend some time doing something that will take your mind off things. The book can wait a little bit, right? Your fans aren't going anywhere. Did you get your dad's car yet? Take it out for a drive maybe—"

Roxy started laughing.

"What's so funny?" Delaney asked.

"I went for a drive. And ended up with a ticket."

"Oh no! Do you want me to have Hugh take care of that for you? Because he can. And he will."

"No, no. I already paid it. Plus the officer responsible took me out to lunch."

Delaney's mouth hung open. "What? Why didn't you start with that?" She swatted Roxy's leg. "Now that's news. Who was it?"

"Alex Cruz. Do you know him?"

"Ooo, he's a cutie. I know him a little. Why, you want me to do a little digging on him? Find out how available he is? Help you get to know him?"

"No, no. Nothing like that." Roxy smiled. "He's my neighbor. I think I'll be getting to know him well enough pretty soon."

Delaney ate the other half of her truffle. "You couldn't do better for a neighbor. You'll never have to worry about crime. Not that you would in this town anyway."

Roxy looked at her watch. "I'd better go. I still have to get some groceries, and I really need to write a few pages today. Thanks for listening to me and my craziness."

Delaney put her hand on Roxy's arm. "I'm here any time you need to talk. I can only imagine how nuts this divorce must be making you. Please don't hesitate to come by or call. I am so glad you're here. If I wasn't pregnant, I swear I'd be dragging you out every night."

Roxy stood. "I'm glad to be here. Having a friend in town I can rely on is awesome."

Delaney got up and gave Roxy a quick hug. As she pulled back, she said, "Hey, you want to come over for dinner some night this week?"

Roxy narrowed her eyes. "Is this one of those things where you secretly invite Alex too? Because I'm not looking to get involved. I'm really not. I need time to process this divorce."

"Nothing like that, I swear. Just dinner, and then I'll watch you and Hugh drink all the wine I can't have."

Roxy snorted. "Sounds good. Text me."

"I will. You know what else we're going to do soon?"

"What's that?"

"A spa day. Maybe even before the dinner, because it sounds like you need it."

"No argument there."

"Excellent." Delaney opened the door. "C'mon, I'll walk you out."

On their way back into the shop, Delaney grabbed a bottle of water from one of the big coolers. "Here, take this with you. This isn't like Jersey. You have to stay hydrated in the South."

"Thanks." Roxy stuck the bottle in her purse. "Talk to you soon."

Delaney waved as Roxy left. She walked back to her car feeling better. The divorce would be over soon, and her life would take on a new normal. It was just going to take time. And maybe in time, she'd give Alex a chance to be more than just a friend.

But for right now, Officer Hotness was going to have to settle for being Nocturne Falls' sexiest neighbor. One Roxy was really glad she lived next to.

Alex's radio came to life in a burst of noise. "Alex, this is Birdie. Pick up."

He reached over and grabbed the handset. "Go ahead, Birdie. This is Alex." Birdie wasn't the department's dispatcher, but she did sometimes radio with calls.

"Are you in town? You need to swing by Delaney's shop, pronto."

He changed directions to head that way immediately. "I'm on it. What's the issue? Theft?"

"Not sure. Just get there."

"ETA is four minutes." He laid on the speed a little and made it in three and a half. Black Cat Boulevard was full, so he parked in the fire lane. Patrol cars could do that.

He strode into the shop on full alert, but it looked like business as usual to him. He took his sunglasses off and tucked them in his shirt pocket as Delaney came out from the back room. "Birdie said you needed me as soon as possible. What's going on?"

Delaney shook her head. "That's not what I said at all. But since you're here, come into my office and we'll talk."

Curiosity piqued, he followed her back.

She closed her office door and pointed to the chair beside her desk. He sat there while she took the chair at her desk.

He leaned forward. "Employee problem? Embezzlement? Property theft?"

She sighed. "None of those things. I want to talk about Roxy St. James."

He sat back. "What?"

"You went out to lunch with her today, right?"

"Yes. I'm not sure what that has to do with anything."

"What did she drink at lunch?"

"A bottle of some fancy sparkling water."

"Not the Nocturne Falls stuff?"

"Nope."

"That makes sense, then. She must drink a lot of bottled water. That's all I can figure out." Delaney rubbed her chin like she was thinking.

"I'm not following."

"She's clearly not drinking the Nocturne Falls tap water, or not enough of it, because she thought she saw gills on Undrea and a *black panther* in her neighborhood."

"She did ask me if someone in our area had a big black housecat. She never said panther, though." No doubt Diego out and about. Alex would have a word with him on that subject this evening.

"Well, she said panther to me. And then she thought my teeth looked odd earlier when she stopped by. Fortunately, I drew my fangs up in time, but this isn't good. It's one thing for tourists to think they see supernaturals all around them, but if the human citizens don't drink the water and they start seeing us for what we really are, we're in deep trouble."

The water from the natural springs at the falls

had been enchanted by the Ellinghams' personal witch, Alice Bishop. When humans drank the water, their reality blurred at the edges a bit, helping to keep human residents and tourists oblivious to the supernaturals around them. And because that water fed the reservoirs and was bottled and sold everywhere in town, getting tourists to drink it wasn't a problem.

Until now. "I can't force her to drink the water."

"Neither can I, but I did give her a bottle of it on her way out. Let's hope she drinks it. In the meantime, you've got to cool it around her. No shifting outside your house."

"I promise you, I'm not the panther she saw. It had to be Diego."

Delaney squinted.

"My brother. He's staying with me." Alex's expression was less than happy. "He's not the easiest to rein in sometimes. I'll talk to him. Make sure he knows the deal."

"Good. Roxy and I have been friends since college. She's under enough stress with this divorce. She doesn't need to think she's hallucinating too."

"Why not tell her the truth?"

Delaney's eyes widened slightly. "When Hugh told me he was a vampire, I climbed out a second-story window and ran off into the woods in the dark of night. And I wasn't under the pressure of a deadline or a controlling ex who wouldn't sign my divorce papers. I don't think Roxy needs that kind of reality dumped on her right now."

"Okay." He thought for a moment. "You know, I might be able to help with this. But only if Diego gets the bartending job he interviewed for today and gets out of my house at night."

That perked Delaney up. "If it's a matter of getting him that job, I can help with that. I assume it's at Howler's."

"Yes."

"Good. I'll call Bridget. She'll do it as a favor, I'm sure. Even if he doesn't last, maybe she can keep him busy for a week."

"That should be more than enough time."

"What are you planning?"

He hesitated, then smiled. "Just a little neighborly get-together."

By the time Roxy got home, it was so late in the afternoon it was practically dinner time. She unloaded her groceries and, for a moment, wished she was good enough friends with Alex to make use of his hot tub. A soak would be glorious. She rolled her shoulders, trying to release the tightness in them. She might have to take Delaney up on that offer of a spa day.

But as much as Roxy wanted to loaf, the book called. She grabbed a bottle of water from the fridge, set it on her desk in the office, then went to change.

A few minutes later she was in yoga pants and a Lost Boys T-shirt, sitting in front of her computer and staring down at Chapter Two. She put her hands on the keyboard and thought for a moment about what events needed to happen next. Then she dove in.

Marabella tugged against the restraints holding her. For eight long months, she'd suffered at the hands of the druids, imprisoned in this damnable tower and kept from her beloved, Wolfgang. No doubt he thought her dead. She closed her eyes and a prayer escaped her lips that he didn't think she'd also been the one to betray him.

Did he understand that this was all his brother's doing? She couldn't be sure, but Wolfgang was no one's fool. If anyone could have discovered Ulric's plan, it was him.

She went very still and listened but the hall beyond her chamber seemed deserted. This might be her only chance. Her captors could return at any time. She closed her eyes and, at long last, summoned the witch's power she'd been born with.

All these months, the druids had laced her food and drink with herbs meant to destroy her magic. And they nearly had. But the incessant use of them had begun to create an immunity in her. One she'd kept hidden.

One she'd nurtured. And what the druids in Ulric's control didn't know was that her magic had almost fully returned to her. In a very short time, she would leave this dank prison behind.

Then she would find her beloved and together they would rain down vengeance upon the head of Ulric and his minions.

She concentrated, calling upon her powers to manifest themselves. The magic curled inside her, aching to be free, almost bursting from—

Roxy's doorbell rang, and her head came up. How many times had the chime sounded? Once? Three times? She had no idea. A glance at the window told her the sun was just about to set. How long had she been sitting here? She scrambled out of her chair and made it to the foyer as the bell rang again.

She pulled the door open and smiled. "Oh, hey, Alex."

"Hey. I thought I'd invite you over for some celebratory pizza." He grinned. "Diego got the bartending job."

"That is worth celebrating. And I love pizza, even if it's not really on my diet."

He gave her a little side eye. "You don't need to diet."

She was curvy. She knew that. Thomas never let her forget it. Dieting wasn't something she did, it was a way of life. "Watch what happens when I don't. With my job? It's a constant struggle."

"Well, I think you look great. And I'm ordering from Salvatore's. If you haven't had their pizza yet, you really should. It's kind of legendary." He cocked his head. "Or are you sick of hanging out with me?"

That she was not. "No. I'll come over. One slice won't kill me. Can I at least make a salad or something?"

"So long as you don't mind being the only one

eating it." Then he laughed and held his hands up. "I could try some, I guess. So long as there's a lot of dressing on it. And maybe cheese. And bacon." He shrugged apologetically. "The Cruz men aren't really salad eaters."

"Okay, forget the salad. Are you ordering the pizza now? I'd love to finish this scene I'm working on."

He looked at his watch. "Come over in an hour?"

"That would be perfect."

"I'm also making my mother's famous lemonade. You're not allergic to citrus or anything, are you?"

"Nope. What makes the lemonade famous?"

"Um…" He thought for a second. "I don't know actually. It's just lemonade with some mint in it. She usually adds vodka, too, but tomorrow's a work day, so I'm not doing that."

"Well, I'm game. I've never had lemonade with mint."

"Great." He started to leave then stopped, his hand on the column of her front porch. "Oh, bring your suit if you want. It's a perfect night for the hot tub."

"Sounds good. Will do." She closed the door. Then, realizing what she'd just agreed to, she leaned against it and let out a big sigh. Wear her bathing suit in front of Alex? That shouldn't bother

her. But it did. Her figure was far from perfect. Of course, Diego would be there too, but for whatever reason, she didn't care what he thought.

Then why should she care about Alex seeing her in her bathing suit? He was just her neighbor. Not a guy she was interested in. Was she going to turn down a chance to soak in the hot tub, something she'd just been wishing she could do, because her *neighbor* might think she wasn't in perfect shape?

He'd already said he thought she looked fine. Which could have just been him being polite.

Either way, she was letting Thomas get in her head. It was so hard to shut out the years of living with him. She could hear his relentless criticism about how sitting all day was going to make her fatter, how she needed to get off her butt and work out, how he didn't understand why she wasn't interested in keeping herself attractive for him.

Meanwhile, he went out drinking beer and bowling with his buddies all the time. Like that was the equivalent of time at the gym.

Her chin lifted, and anger filled her belly. Thomas could shove it. She did yoga every day and went for walks when the weather was nice. Could she do more? Sure. Who couldn't? But she wasn't exactly a shapeless blob who lay around the house all day eating bonbons.

Although, technically, she'd had a bonbon

today. A strawberry champagne bonbon. Her mouth watered at the memory of that particular goody sampled at Delaney's.

Then her back teeth ground together. Thomas was not in charge of what she did. She was going over to Alex's, and she was having two slices of pizza, and she was definitely getting into that hot tub.

Because Roxy St. James wasn't about to let her soon-to-be ex-husband ruin any more of her life than he already had.

Alex texted Delaney. *She's coming over.*

A few minutes later, Delaney texted back. *Good. Let's hope this works.*

Then you'd better hope Diego doesn't do anything to get fired on his first night.

I already told Bridget to make sure he stays busy the entire shift.

He put the phone down and sighed. He was lying to Roxy, and he hated the way that felt. Yes, Diego had gotten the job, but Diego wasn't going to be here this evening, which was pretty much what he'd led her to believe. Instead, it would just be the two of them, and his real objective was to get her to drink as much lemonade, made with good old Nocturne Falls water, as possible.

If that didn't stop her from seeing supernatural things, then it was Delaney's problem. In fact, if he had to tell Roxy the truth himself, he would.

He couldn't stand lying in general, but to lie to someone he genuinely liked was an ugly feeling. Sure, it was for her own good. He guessed. But it didn't feel right to him.

On one hand, he understood why Delaney didn't want to tell Roxy about the full reality of Nocturne Falls and the supernatural citizens who lived here just yet. But on the other hand, she seemed like a woman who could roll with it. She hadn't freaked out over the ticket, and to him that was one barometer by which he judged people. Roxy was a pretty cool customer. Would finding out that her college friend had been turned into a vampire really be that odd?

The woman wrote paranormal romance, for crying out loud. She might enjoy knowing that her next-door neighbor was a panther shifter.

That gave him a thought. He picked up his phone and scrolled to his favorite ebookstore, then did a search on her name.

Impressive. She had a decent number of books out. Most of them looked like vampire stuff. Maybe that's why Delaney didn't want Roxy to know what she'd become. Maybe Roxy painted vampires as the villains? But then, his mom read and loved the books, and so did Birdie. And from what Roxy had told him, her hero was a vampire. Or at least part vampire.

Maybe he should read one for himself. He had the one she'd given him for his mom, but he didn't want to break the spine. Instead, he one-clicked the first book in her Blood Moon Brotherhood series and opened it as soon as it downloaded.

He was two chapters in when he realized he hadn't ordered the pizza yet. He swiped back to the home screen, pulled up his contact list and dialed Salvatore's.

When the pies were on their way, he went back to reading. Roxy's work was good. Better than good, actually.

Roxy's writing was dark, emotional, sometimes funny, a little over the top, but really readable. And smart. This was no throwaway story. The heroes and heroines were exactly what they should be. Strong, capable and sexy.

He could see why his mom and her friends were so hooked. He also liked how the hero and heroine of this book knew right away they were meant to be together. He understood that feeling and wanted that for himself. A soul mate.

Did that mean Roxy believed in soul mates too? She must. She wrote about them. But did that also mean she expected the next man in her life to be as perfect as the ones she wrote about? Because Alex knew he wasn't that.

Her hero was flawed, but he was also wealthy and worldly. And Alex was a deputy in a small town. Hopefully a sergeant soon, but even with the decent raise that would bring, he wasn't about to be driving a Ferrari anytime soon. Was Wolfgang the kind of guy Roxy pictured as her soul mate?

Maybe a better question was why Alex cared so much what Roxy thought. She was human, he was a shifter. They weren't meant to be. Couldn't be.

He put his phone down and went out onto the back porch to make sure the temperature in the hot tub was just right. He adjusted it, then stood there for a moment, breathing in the night air.

He hadn't been on a good long run in his panther form since the last full moon. That was too long. Next day off, he'd drive up into the hills and let loose in the acreage the Ellinghams kept for just that sort of thing. He'd drag Diego along with him, too. A run together would do them good. Remind them both of their childhood, when being brothers was all that mattered. He tipped his head back and stared at the rising sliver of moon. Almost two weeks until it was full again.

The urge to shift came over him, but he tamped it down, allowing only a partial shift into his half-form. A full shift and he'd never ignore the desire to run.

A knock on his door brought him back to full human. Roxy.

He glanced down at what he had on, never really caring that much before. His jeans and T-shirt were in decent shape, but they were nothing special. That was okay. This was who he was. Just a regular hard-working, blue-collar guy. Nothing fancy.

"Coming." He got to the door a few seconds later and opened it to find Roxy there.

"Hey."

A blind man could see how attractive she was. A total package. Spending time with her was no hardship. He smiled. "Hey. Right on time. Come on in."

He got out of the way to let her pass. She wore a little polka dot sundress, the straps of a black bathing suit peeking out underneath. "Thanks for coming."

"Thanks for inviting me." She held her hands out. "I feel like I should have brought something, but you didn't seem all that interested in salad, so I'm empty handed."

He grinned. "You chose wisely."

She looked around. "Pizza's not here yet, I take it?"

"Nope. I ordered a little later than I meant to. Got distracted." By her book. Something he wasn't sure he wanted to admit, mostly because it felt a little like snooping. Or checking her out. Why else would a guy read a romance? Although he was pretty sure he'd get a few more chapters under his belt before he called it quits. Or maybe he'd read to the end. Which was more likely. "They should be here soon. Are you starving? I might have a PowerBar or something."

She laughed. "No, I'm good. A PowerBar." She shook her head. "You're such a guy."

He got the lemonade out of the fridge. "Is that a good thing? Because my options are pretty limited."

"Yes, it's a good thing. Hey, speaking of guys, where's Diego?"

And so the lying began. "Oh, sorry, he's not going to be here after all. Howler's called him in. One of their bartenders came down with the flu or something, so they decided to put him to work tonight."

She gave him a look. "So we're celebrating Diego's new job without Diego actually being here?"

Alex nodded slowly. "To be perfectly honest, I'm more excited about him having a job than he is. You know this is the first time I've had my house to myself since he moved in?"

Her brows lifted. "Does that mean you want me to leave?"

"No." He winked at her. "I can't eat all that pizza by myself." Then he realized she might feel uncomfortable alone with him in his house. "That is, as long as you want to stay?"

She leaned against his kitchen counter. "And miss out on that hot tub? No way."

"Good. Ready to try the lemonade?"

"Absolutely. If I'm going off my diet, I might as well have something cold to wash it down with."

He shook his head as he got two big tumblers out of the cabinet. "What's up with all the dieting talk? Seriously, you look fantastic. I hope it's not too forward of me to say, but you have a rocking body."

When he turned around, she was staring at him. He filled the tumblers and handed her one. "Did I cross a line? You look upset."

She took the glass from him. "Not upset. Just…not used to those kinds of compliments."

He frowned. "Are you kidding? You were married."

"*Were* being the operative word." She stared at the drink in her hand, and her gaze took on a faraway haze. "He wasn't…kind that way. He wasn't a lot of things."

The doorbell rang, preventing Alex from asking any more questions. He paid for the pizzas, brought them back to the kitchen and set them on the counter. Roxy still didn't look like her usual happy self, and he felt awful for being the one to bring up bad memories of her ex.

He decided that made it his job to cheer her up. "I'll be right back."

She looked up. "Okay."

He jogged back to his bedroom, threw on his trunks, then took two big towels from the linen closet and tucked them under his arm. Plan in motion, he returned to the kitchen.

Her brows rose at the sight of him shirtless.

He smiled as he strode past her and grabbed one of the pizza boxes and the pitcher of lemonade. "I say we eat this pizza in the hot tub. You in?"

Her slightly dazed expression turned into a grin. "Yeah, I'm in."

"Great. Grab the glasses since I've got the pitcher." It was impossible to be sad in a hot tub eating pizza. He opened the slider with one finger, then shoved it back with his hip. His feline senses picked up her pulse increasing like the beat of a distant drum. He hoped that was because she was happy and not worried about anything.

He guessed he'd find out soon enough.

The lemonade was a great idea, because Roxy needed something to cool down the fire burning inside her. Alex with his shirt off was almost enough to make her pass out. It was like one of her cover models had stepped off of their book. But better.

She stared at the open sliding door, the sounds of sloshing reaching her ears. Alex was already in the water. Waiting for her.

Her heart was racing, her palms were sweaty and she was about to strip down to her bathing suit and get into the outdoor equivalent of a bath with him.

She swallowed. Then remembered the cold drink in her hand. She downed a couple of long gulps, happy to let the chilly liquid take the edge off her nerves. Didn't hurt that it was delicious, too. She could do this. And not just because it was exactly the kind of thing Thomas would think her incapable of.

She grabbed both of their drinks and marched outside, using her hip to close the door just like Alex had to open it.

He was indeed already in the hot tub. He sat at the far side, facing her, the pizza box balanced on the wide lip. Steam rose up around him, glazing him with a sheen that made him even more irresistible.

She might be in trouble here. Then she reminded herself that she was technically still married. And that whatever attraction she might be feeling toward Alex, he was definitely not feeling it for her. This was just a friendly get-together.

And then there was the thing where he was crazy hot, and she was just short, curvy Jane Average.

At least it was a little darker out here. She might be in his direct eye line, but there were enough shadows to give her some comfort at the thought of ditching her sundress.

"I put the towels on the chair."

She set the drinks on the edge closest to her and glanced over her shoulder. They looked like bath sheets. Plenty to cover up in when she got out. That was nice. "Great."

He turned to open the box of pizza.

She took the opportunity to shuck her dress and climb down the steps to slide in. The water was hot, and she would have liked to adjust to it a little more slowly, but cover was cover. She sank in to her chin in the bubbling water and took a seat that put her at a right angle to him.

Little ripples headed her way as he came back around with a slice in his hand. His expression took on a humorous bent when he saw she was already in. "That was fast." He tipped his head toward the box. "Trade you a slice for my drink."

"Deal." Of course, that meant she had to leave her seat. She resigned herself to the fact that he was going to see her in her suit sooner or later and stood so she could make her way back to the lemonade without drowning.

She handed his tumbler to him and put hers closer to where she was sitting.

"Thanks." He lifted the box so she could take a slice.

She did just that, sinking back into her seat, but this time on her knees so the pizza wouldn't get waterlogged. It meant exposing a lot more of herself to him, but the warmth of the water was already relaxing her and making her feel like that wasn't such a big thing to be worried about.

She bit into the pizza and groaned as the saucy, cheesy goodness melted over her tongue. "I know it's not polite to talk with food in my mouth, but this might be the best pizza I've ever had." She finished her bite.

Alex nodded as he swallowed one of his own. "It probably is. You can't go wrong with Salvatore's."

"You eat this a lot?"

"At least one night a week. Actually more sometimes, because we order it at the department, too. And it's all Diego knows how to cook." He stared at what was left of the slice in his hand. "I guess I do eat this a lot."

She pointed at him as she finished another delicious mouthful. "How do you look like that when you eat so much of this? It can't just be the running."

His eyes narrowed, and a sly gleam lit his eyes. "Look like what?"

She picked up her tumbler and drank before answering. "Like you own shares in Gold's Gym." The water bubbled around her, popping and spitting. "Like you've been gifted with Greek god genes. Like you could pose for one of my covers." She took a long, slow sip of the lemonade in an attempt to cool herself off as the water got inexplicably hotter. "You don't look like a guy who eats a lot of pizza, that's all I'm saying."

Something gleamed in his eyes. Almost like...gold. He tossed the crust of his pizza back into the box and stood.

He took her pizza and lemonade and set them aside, then pulled her to her feet to stand in front of him.

That put them face to face. It wasn't a small hot tub, but it wasn't an Olympic-sized swimming pool either. He felt very close. So close the only thing between them was a little air and a lot of temptation.

She tried to back up. And almost slipped.

Alex caught her and pulled her against him, his hands firm but gentle on her arms. "You okay?"

She nodded as she stared up at him, trying not to let his touch befuddle her any more than it already had. "I'm fine."

"Good." His hands disappeared beneath the water to rest on her hips. "Because I'm going to kiss you now. Unless you tell me otherwise."

A tremor ran through her. Maybe from the boldness of his words. Maybe from the anticipation of what he'd just told her he was about to do. Maybe from the weight of his hands on her body. Probably from all three. She shook her head, hoping he understood that meant she wasn't going to tell him no.

He got it. He bent down and put his mouth on hers in a kiss that was strong and sweet and deliciously wicked. She was half-naked, kissing a half-naked man in his hot tub. Her neighbor. The cop. The very sexy cop.

The heat of the water steaming up around them only made the kiss more intense. Her head swam with dizziness, like she'd gotten up too fast. She hadn't been kissed in a long time. And she'd never been kissed like this.

Her hands slipped up to his thick biceps, in part

to hang on to something and in part because she very much wanted to touch him.

His body was gloriously hard. Warmer than even the water should have made him. She sank against him just a little, which was all she dared.

Alex's kiss held no obligation, no sense of duty. It wasn't a token of a lukewarm relationship, it was the branding of something new and needful. Something as hot and urgent as the kisses in the books she wrote.

Kisses she'd always thought were just fiction. But this, she suddenly realized, was a real-life romance novel kiss. She gasped at that thought, breaking the kiss.

He ground his teeth together as if he was trying not to lose control, causing his voice to rasp out of him. "I shouldn't have done that. But I guess if I was one of your romance heroes, I wouldn't care about what I should and shouldn't do."

She shook her head, still lost in the moment. "No, Wolfgang wouldn't have stopped."

His answer held a pang of regret. "But I'm not Wolfgang. And you're not Marabella."

Her mouth opened in surprise. "How do you know the names of my characters?"

He looked a little sheepish. "My mother. And...I started reading one of your books. But the point is, we're neighbors. This can't end well."

"No?"

He smiled sadly. "I guess it can. If we end it now. I'm sorry, that was foolish of me and—"

"I didn't stop you." But she knew he was right. The last thing she needed was to get involved with another man before her divorce was even over. Especially one who lived next door.

He put a little space between them. "It was still my fault. Do you forgive me?"

She laughed it off with a sound that rang false even to her ears. "There's nothing to forgive. It was just a kiss. Nothing more, right?" Except it had been so much more.

"Right." He nodded, the sadness in his smile extending to his gaze. Then his smile widened, obviously forced. "I really don't want this to be weird. I like you. I like being friends with you. But maybe that's not possible between a man and a woman. Platonic friendship, I mean."

"So you don't have any female friends?"

"I do, but..." His gaze fixed on her, and the spark of interest she'd seen before returned. "None that I find as irresistibly sexy as you."

She glanced down at herself. "Are you seeing the same things I'm seeing?"

He sighed and sat back down on his side of the hot tub. "I am. But apparently I have a much greater appreciation for them."

She retreated to her seat, tucking her knees under her.

"What did your ex do to you to make you think so little of yourself?"

She blinked hard as sudden, unbidden tears welled. The fact that her emotions would choose this moment to turn on her made her laugh. She wiped at her eyes. "I don't even know where to start."

"He sounds like an idiot."

She glanced at Alex. "I haven't said anything about him."

"Part of my job is profiling people. And for a man to have made a smart, talented, beautiful woman like you think that you're somehow less than that, he had to be a controlling, narcissistic jerk who clearly didn't appreciate you and most likely couldn't handle being married to a woman who was more successful than he was."

Her brows lifted slightly. Alex wasn't far off.

He stood enough to lean over and grab the pitcher of lemonade. "Am I right?"

She nodded, then realized he wasn't looking at her. Which gave her a chance to appreciate how fine he was this close up. "Yes."

He refilled their glasses. "And that's a big part of why you don't want to get involved again, I'm sure."

"Right again. At least, not until I've had a chance to figure out who the real me is. I'd rather it not be the me Thomas turned me into, but more like the woman I pretend to be when I'm at conferences and fan events. I want to be her all the time. I want to be that confident about every part of my life."

He sat down and took a long drink. "I have to tell you, I don't know what that woman is like, but the Roxy I know is pretty spectacular."

"You're very flattering."

He shook his head. "I'm very truthful. And you probably haven't heard a lot of truth from a man in a while."

She sighed. "No, I haven't. It's going to take some getting used to."

"Then I guess we'd better stay friends."

She smiled. "You realize that means no more kissing."

He snorted. "You're not going to let me forget about that, are you?"

"That's what friends do." She lifted one shoulder. "That and the fact that it's going to be a hard kiss to forget. It's been a while."

His expression turned wry. "For me too." He lifted the tumbler toward her. "To being friends."

She clinked hers against it. "To being friends."

But the truth was, if the kissing happened again, she wasn't going to complain. In fact, she might if it didn't.

Using a level of willpower Alex hadn't known

he possessed, he somehow made it through the rest of the evening without kissing Roxy again. He stood at his door, watching her walk back to her house, her shoes dangling from one hand and her sundress clinging to the dampest parts of her.

If he'd had that same amount of willpower the first time, the kiss never would have happened, but he hadn't. And he was damn glad about it.

Truth was, he'd been powerless against the sight of her. She'd been there in his hot tub, steam curling up around her like she was some mystical goddess, her skin glistening with water, her eyes big and deep and impossible to look away from, her little black bikini hugging curves that could make a grown man weep.

His shifter brain had been focused on one thing and one thing only. Claiming the female in front of him. It was a base, animalistic urge. One he'd barely fought back enough to ask her permission before he'd kissed her. Those urges weren't something he was necessarily proud of, but he was getting used to fighting them when he was around her. And he had no regrets that he'd kissed her.

Even if they were just friends until the day they died, he'd savor that moment. It had felt, for the briefest span of time, that they were meant to be.

He knew that was impossible. She was human, of course. But that feeling had created a spark in him that he would have to work very hard to keep from exploding into a full-blown bonfire. Because he wanted to kiss her again.

He wouldn't. But he wanted to.

As she disappeared into the dark, he closed his door, grabbed his phone off the kitchen counter and walked to his bedroom. He stared at himself in his bathroom mirror, wondering what he looked like to her. She seemed to think he was attractive. He tried to take care of himself. Sure, his shifter genes made that easier, but he liked to think he put more effort into it than the average Joe.

After all, he was a cop, and that meant being stronger and faster than the bad guys. He sighed and rolled his shoulders and tried to stop himself from caring what Roxy thought.

What did it matter? She wasn't meant for him. And even if she were a supernatural, she'd been pretty clear about wanting time to herself. Who could blame her after the nightmare of her ex? The thought of anyone, especially a man who was supposed to love her, treating her that way made Alex's hands curl into fists.

A guy like that needed to learn a few hard lessons about how women ought to be cared for. Alex heard a snarl and realized it had come from him. He'd shifted into his half form without intending to.

He started to shake it off, then thought differently. It was late and plenty dark. Diego wouldn't be home until his shift was over. There was no reason not to go for a run.

Besides, it might be the only way he could get Roxy out of his head enough to actually sleep tonight.

Morning came sooner than Roxy would have liked, but she had too much to do to lounge around in bed. Unfortunately. Because staying under the covers and dreaming about her hot but off-limits neighbor would be a very enjoyable way to spend a day. Though not nearly as enjoyable as spending the day in bed with the actual man.

She got up and got moving, but thoughts of Alex stayed with her throughout the morning, even making her lose track of her yoga routine as she went through her sun salutations. She refocused on what move came next. The man was the most tantalizing distraction she'd run into in a long time.

Her writer's brain couldn't help but think that she'd moved in next door to one of her heroes come to life. Wouldn't that be funny?

Hmm. She pushed back into downward-facing dog. There was a book idea. Paranormal romance writer moves to a new town only to discover the world she's been writing about has become reality. She snorted. Maybe that should be her next series.

She stepped forward into a half bend. Alex would definitely make a great paranormal hero. What kind would he be, though? She didn't really see him as a vampire. A werewolf maybe? She stretched her arms out, swooping them up to come to a standing position.

Not a werewolf. He was too...sleek for that. *Sleek* wasn't the right word, exactly. He had enough of that sexy-feral thing going on to be a were, but he'd be something more slinky. More subtle. Sexier even than a werewolf. But just as dangerous.

She dropped her hands and bent to roll up her yoga mat. She hadn't done a big-cat were in a while. Maybe she'd use Alex as the basis for a were-lion.

She nodded. That would be hot.

Then again, maybe writing what essentially would be fan fiction about her neighbor wasn't the healthiest way to stop thinking about him.

She sighed as she tucked her yoga mat back into the closet and headed to the shower. Kissing him was definitely going to be used as inspiration, but the rest of him...the rest of him would stay tucked away in her head for her private fantasizing only.

That probably wasn't super healthy either, but screw it. After all those years with Thomas, who could blame her for being attracted to a guy who treated her like she was a sexy, desirable woman?

She stripped off her workout clothes and stepped under the hot spray. The water beat down on her, the heat easing the muscles she'd just worked out.

What if the only reason she was attracted to Alex was because he was nice to her? Other than the fact that he was unbelievably sexy. The man was hot with a capital H. Or could her attraction be because he was so different than Thomas? Would she be attracted to any guy who was nice to her? Wasn't there always a rebound guy? That could be all this was. She was getting excited about a nice guy simply because she hadn't been around a nice guy in a long time.

She leaned her head under the spray and realized that was exactly why she wasn't ready to get involved again. She couldn't trust her emotions right now. Everything was still so raw and on the surface.

Being friends with Alex was fine, but that was absolutely where things had to stay.

By the time Undrea arrived, Roxy felt mostly back to rights. She left the woman alone with the tank and went off to the kitchen to fix some coffee.

Undrea walked into the kitchen as Roxy was

putting the creamer back in the fridge. "The water's perfect. I'm going to add some pajama wrasses, and we'll see how they do for a week or so."

"Sounds perfect. After all, I'm basically in my pajamas all day."

Undrea laughed. "I do try to match the fish to their environment. Be right back."

"Okay." Roxy sipped her coffee. That tank was going to be amazing when it was done.

Undrea came back a few minutes later with a large bucket and good-sized box under one arm. "Did you know there's a rose on your car?"

Roxy frowned. "A rose?"

Undrea nodded. "Yep. It's tucked under your wipers." She smiled. "You must have a secret admirer."

Roxy made herself smile back while her belly went cold. "I'm sure that's what it is. I'll go get it."

Undrea headed to the office as Roxy went outside. Sure enough, her driver's side wiper pinned a single long-stemmed red rose against her windshield. There was no note that she could see. She checked the ground to make sure it hadn't blown off, but it wasn't that windy, and she already knew who it had come from.

Thomas.

The how was just as obvious. He must be in town. And he must have come by last night, seen her car in the driveway and done this. The why was a lot less clear. Did he think this kind of crazy was going to win her back?

Because in her mind, their marriage had been over a long time ago. Sure, he still needed to sign the papers to make the divorce final, but nothing was going to change her mind. Certainly not high school stunts like this.

She grabbed the rose and marched it over to the trash receptacle, stuffing it in the big green can.

The garage bay where her hybrid would eventually be parked was still filled with boxes of stuff she needed to unpack. Apparently, this was the universe's way of telling her to get on it. Because there was no way she was parking the Vette outside to make room for the hybrid.

She shook her head at Thomas's nonsense and went back inside.

Undrea stood at the end of the hall. "The fish are getting accustomed. I've got a drip line set up in the bucket. Should take about thirty minutes to an hour and they'll be ready to go in. I've got another job to check on a couple houses over, but I'll be back in time to get them swimming."

"Sounds good. I'll see you when you get back."

Undrea left, and although Roxy really wanted to watch the news while she finished her coffee, she decided to get some work done before Undrea returned. Because there was always something to do. And she needed to take her mind off of Thomas's latest stunt.

But first she checked out her new fish in the big five-gallon bucket where they were getting used to the water in their new home. They were gorgeous—deep blue with brilliant orange stripes. She grinned, totally ready to see them in her tank.

Happy, she sat at her desk and got to work. She began by making a to-do list for the week, which was daunting in its length. Then she started answering the fan emails that had accumulated in the last few days. Twenty minutes later, she was working on another email to her assistant about the giveaway for the week.

She was halfway through the creation of a new teaser graphic when her doorbell rang. She got up from her desk and looked out the office window. Undrea's van.

That had been a quick half an hour, but checking the time told her it had been more like forty-five minutes.

She glanced at the bucket holding the two wrasses. It *was* getting full. She hustled to let Undrea in.

Within minutes, Undrea had the colorful pair swimming in the tank.

Roxy clasped her hands to her chest. "They're gorgeous. I could be happy with just the two of them."

Undrea laughed. "Then you're really going to like it when it's fully stocked, but it's good you like it with those two in there because it'll be at least a week before I come back to add more."

"And all I have to do is feed them?"

"Yep. The folder I gave you has all of that info, but you can always call me if you have any questions."

"Great. Thank you so much."

Undrea collected her bucket and dripline. "No problem. See you in a week."

Roxy locked the door after Undrea left, then went to sit and watch her fish. It was just as peaceful as she remembered, and she smiled wistfully as she thought about her dad. He would have loved this tank.

Minutes slid by with the memories. At last, she got up and went back to work, this time to finally make some progress on her book.

She was just getting into the zone when her cell phone rang. Naturally. She didn't recognize the number, but the area code was local. "Hello?"

"Ms. St. James?"

"Speaking."

"Hi," a very enthusiastic voice said. "I'm Agnes Miller. I own the bookstore in town, Bell, Book & Candle, and I am so excited that *the* Roxy St. James is now a resident of our little town. I hope you don't mind that I bribed Birdie Caruthers into giving me your phone number, but I just had to talk to you and see what it would take to get you to do a book signing."

Roxy was dumbstruck for a moment, then she went into author mode. Business was, after all, business, and booksellers were some of her favorite people. For now, she would overlook what Birdie had done, but made a note to say something to Alex about that not happening again. "I hope you mean Bell, Book & Candle as in the Jimmy Stewart movie."

"The movie! Oh my gosh, I love you even more for knowing that. Please say you'd be willing to do a book signing here."

Roxy took a breath. The woman's enthusiasm was overwhelming, but very sweet. And impossible to say no to. "Of course I would. Did you have a date in mind? I'm still in the process of moving in, so my life is a little hectic at the moment."

The woman let out a small, happy shriek. "That is so wonderful, thank you! I have a huge database of your fans that I can access. I can promise at least a hundred pre-solds, if not more."

A hundred pre-solds? Roxy blinked in awe. "Wow. I had no idea."

"Oh, yes. As soon as you put a new book out, I email my customer list and they reserve one. You know a lot of bookstores don't carry your books."

Roxy sighed. "It's the curse of being indie published. But there's not much I can do about it. Interesting about your list. I've seen big bumps in my print sales after a release. I had no idea that was you." She pretty much had to do the signing now.

"Yep, that's me. I'll get to work on this immediately. As for a date, it'll take me about five days to get the books in, which corresponds nicely with the weekend of the Panic Parade, which is next weekend. The town gets flooded with tourists for that event, so we might as well take advantage of that and really crank up the walk-in sales."

"Okay, sounds good." She vaguely remember Delaney telling her about the parade. "Why don't you email me the details?"

"Absolutely." Agnes hesitated. "Is there any way you could come by today and sign the stock I have on hand?" She laughed nervously. "And so I could meet you in person?"

Roxy bit her lip. That meant another chunk of time she wouldn't be writing. But this was part of the job. And necessary. "Sure, I'd love to. Two o'clock okay?"

"Perfect. Thank you so much. See you then!" Agnes hung up.

Roxy put the phone down and leaned back in her chair, then remembered the fish tank. She swung around and watched the wrasses darting in and out of the coral. Part of being an author was meeting fans and doing events.

But in a perfect world, Roxy would probably never leave the house. Oh, she could rock an appearance. On the outside. On the inside, she was a nervous mess who couldn't wait to be home again, writing her books and living in the bubble of her own making.

She smiled as the wrasses did their thing, oblivious to their human observer. She was definitely more of an introvert than an extrovert, but then, so were most of the other writers she knew. At least today would just be meeting Agnes and signing stock. She'd have time to prepare for the big signing.

She checked the time. Maybe she could get her pages done before she left. She nodded. Sometimes deadlines were a good thing.

And meeting with Agnes would definitely be a good thing. Roxy loved her fans. They were the reason she worked as hard as she did. The reason she'd made enough money to leave Thomas and move here.

In fact, the more she thought about it, she decided a little trip to Delaney's for a gift of chocolate for Agnes would be just the thing.

A little gift of chocolate for herself wouldn't hurt either. Because if she couldn't have Alex, she at least deserved chocolate. Not at all the same thing, but infinitely safer. Although, having Alex *and* chocolate, now that would be something.

And just like that, her mind went to a very different place than the book she was supposed to be working on.

Alex poured the last of the pancake batter onto the griddle as Diego walked into the kitchen. They'd both slept late. Alex because he'd stayed up all night reading Roxy's book and Diego because he'd worked the evening shift at Howler's. "Morning. Such as it is."

Diego scratched his head and yawned, looking about as awake as a bear fresh from hibernation. "Mm-hmm. Coffee," he mumbled.

"In the pot. How was your first night on the job?" Alex checked the pancake for bubbles around the edges. Nothing yet.

"Decent." Diego shuffled to the coffee maker, grabbed a cup from the cabinet above and filled it. He added a couple heaping spoonfuls of sugar before going to the fridge for creamer. He splashed some in, then drank half the coffee in one long gulp. That seemed to fortify him enough to string words together. "Money was on point."

"That's good to hear."

"Let me guess," Diego grunted. "Rent is due."

Alex smiled. "Since you brought it up, that was kind of the point of you getting a job. So you could start paying your way." He flipped the pancake, then took a sip of his own coffee, which was strong and sweet and just the way he liked it. "But hey, I hear Mom keeps your room just the way you left it, so you know, there's that."

Diego rolled his eyes and took his coffee to the table. He lounged in one of the chairs and let out a long sigh. "Don't remind me. I'll get you the rent soon but the Camaro needs an oil change first."

Alex shot his brother a look. "I understand you want to take care of your car, but how about a little something toward groceries at least?"

"Quit hassling me." Diego grimaced. "You're so much like Dad. Trying to parent me."

"If you really feel that way, maybe you need to reconsider what's going on here, because that's not what I'm doing." An ironic statement considering he *had* made breakfast. He added the last pancake to the stack and carried it to the table where the syrup and butter already waited. He refilled his coffee before sitting down across from Diego. "This is my house, after all. I get to say what happens here. That doesn't mean I'm trying to parent you."

Diego forked three of the Frisbee-sized cakes onto his plate. "Look, I get it. You're hot for the shorty next door and I'm wrecking your scene, but I need to build up some scratch before I get out of here. Giving you money isn't going to help my financial report, you dig?"

Alex stopped in the middle of putting pancakes on his plate to stare at his brother. "I don't even know where to start answering that."

He dropped the pancakes onto his plate. "Actually, I do. I'm not *hot for the shorty* next door. I like Roxy. As a friend. That's it." That wasn't it at all, but that was none of Diego's business. "And don't call her shorty. That's disrespectful."

He doused the pancakes with syrup. "Secondly, the only way you're going to rent a place is to save up first and last month's rent or whatever it is they want these days, but it's not going to be a small amount. You understand what that means? Saving? It means you have to put money away until you have enough. If you'd been able to do that in the first place, you wouldn't be living here with me to begin with."

"Yeah, but—"

"No buts. I'm trying to help you here. How much did you make last night?"

"A hundred and fifty."

"Great. Give me seventy-five."

"What? No way, dude."

Alex ate a big bite before answering. "I'm not going to keep the money. I'm going to save it for you. It's that or I'll expect immediate payment for food, utilities and rent. Which right now probably amounts to about thirteen hundred dollars."

Diego seemed to be considering it. "And if I don't pay?"

Alex fixed his face into the same expression he used when dealing with a potential suspect. Firm, all business, don't mess with me. "I'll change the locks the next time you're at work."

"You wouldn't—you would." Diego cursed softly. "Harsh."

Actually, he wouldn't. "Seventy-five. And don't lie about your tips because I can and will ask Bridget."

Diego sighed and muttered, "Fine."

Alex bent his head and smiled. That had been easier than expected. "When do you work again?"

"Tonight. My next day off isn't until Wednesday."

"Excellent. At that rate, you'll be in your own place before you know it. What are you doing the rest of the day then?"

"Laundry. And then I'm going to lay out and get some sun." He grinned. "The babes like me with a tan."

"Nice of you to oblige them." Cats of all sorts loved to lie in the sun. Feline shifters were no different. But Alex raised a skeptical brow for a different reason. "Just don't be bringing any of those babes back here, got it?"

Diego rolled his eyes and ate the rest of his meal in silence, which suited Alex. He was being hard on his brother, he knew that, but if Diego was comfortable here, he'd never leave. Alex loved his brother, but he wanted his house back as much as he wanted Diego to get on his own feet. Alex finished his food, put his plate in the dishwasher and went back to his room to change. He needed groceries. Feeding one panther shifter was hard enough, but feeding two meant trips to the Shop-n-Save were almost bi-weekly. He jotted down a quick list, then grabbed his keys.

By the time he came back out, Diego was already sprawled on a lounge chair on the deck. Alex shook his head. Must be nice to be that carefree.

He went out to his car.

Roxy was backing out of her driveway in the Vette, top down, scarf tied around her hair and looking very much like she had the day he'd pulled her over. Hot as all get-out.

She braked the car and waved at him. "Hiya, neighbor."

He walked over, smiling. The chance to talk to her was an unexpected but welcome pleasure. "Hey. Headed out to get another ticket?"

She snorted in amusement. "Very funny."

Still grinning, he shrugged. "Just wondering if I should see who's on duty and give them a heads-up."

"Aren't you working today?"

"Yes, but not until later."

"How did Diego's shift go?"

Alex glanced at the house. "Good. He didn't get fired and he made decent money. If this keeps up, I'll have my house back in a few weeks."

"That's great. Hey, Undrea came by and put the first two fish in the tank. It's a big tank and only two fish, but it's still pretty cool to see them in there. Swing by before you head to work if you want to check them out. I won't be gone long."

He nodded. "I will if I have the time. Tomorrow might be better. Where are you off to?"

"Bell, Book & Candle. The bookstore in town?"

"Yep, I know it."

"Agnes, the owner, wants to talk to me about a signing. And that reminds me…" She turned off the engine and scooted up to kneel on her seat, which still didn't put her at eye level with him. "I hate to even mention this, because it all worked out, but Birdie gave Agnes my cell phone number. I don't even know how she'd have it, but I'm not crazy about that."

Alex closed his eyes and sighed. "It's my fault in a way."

"What? How?"

"The ticket. You must have put your number on it when you mailed it in. Did you fill out the info on the back?"

"Oh, yes." She slid down in her seat. "I didn't even think about that. And that's not your fault."

He put his hands on the edge of the passenger door and leaned in. "Look, I'll talk to Birdie. She shouldn't have done that. It was all kinds of inappropriate."

"Don't be too hard on her. Like I said, it all worked out, but..." She sighed. "I don't want her to hate me. She is a fan."

"I get it, but she ought to know better."

"Yeah, I guess. You know what, on second thought, don't say anything."

He stood. "You're sure?"

She nodded. "Let it go. I'm sure Birdie isn't randomly handing out my phone number to just anyone. Agnes is a special case. And Birdie means well, I know she does. Just...let it be."

"Okay, if you say so. But if you change your mind, just tell me."

"I will. Thanks."

"Sure. Hey, I'm off to the Shop-n-Save. You need anything?" So long as she didn't ask for feminine products, he was good. Actually, he *could* buy those if he really had to, but in this town, that might start some rumors.

"No, I just went yesterday, but I appreciate the ask."

He almost sighed in relief. "All right, have a good one. Oh, and Diego and I will both be gone all night so if you want to use the hot tub, feel free. The side gate is always open."

"Ooo, thanks, I might take you up on that. See you later." She started up the car.

"Later." He watched her go while wishing he could be home to join her in the hot tub. Getting Diego out of his house would be a very good thing, not only because he'd have his house back, but because he'd have some privacy again.

Privacy that might allow him to get to know his sexy neighbor even better. Sure, she was human. But on some level so was he. And that part of him couldn't deny that he was very attracted to Roxy.

But he understood she wasn't ready for a relationship. She'd been through a lot. Whatever time she needed was perfectly okay. That just gave them a chance to become better friends. To really get to know each other.

If that led to something more, he'd deal with what that meant then. And if it didn't lead to anything, that was fine too. They'd still be friends, and his gut told him that was a position she needed filled in her life more than any other.

Roxy walked into Delaney's and smiled. It was hard not to when faced with so much chocolatey deliciousness. The store was only moderately busy, and another worker was helping the customers at the counter while Delaney sat at a worktable making up boxes. Roxy caught her eye and waved. "Hey, there."

"Roxy, hi!" Delaney grinned. "I didn't expect to see you again so soon. How nice! How are you?"

"I'm good. I just need to get a little box of goodies to take to Agnes Miller, the bookstore owner. She wants me to do a signing there so I'm headed over to talk to her."

"Very cool. Sure, let me fix something up for you. I think Agnes likes the lemon creams and the vanilla bean truffles." Delaney grabbed a box and lined it with wax paper. "How are...things? You know, your stress level?"

"Good. I'm feeling better actually." Especially because she hadn't seen gills on Undrea this morning. Not that she'd really looked. "Clearly I just needed to relax a bit." She couldn't help but smile. "Which I did. In my neighbor's hot tub last night."

Delaney's grin widened. "Are we talking about Officer Cruz?"

"Yes."

Delaney's brows lifted as she filled the box with confections. "Is relaxing all you did?"

Roxy pressed her lips together. No, it wasn't, but she wasn't sharing that kiss with anyone. "We're just friends. I can't be in a relationship right now. For one, I don't want to be. And for two, Thomas still hasn't signed the papers."

"I hope you're calling your attorney tomorrow." Delaney closed the box and sealed it with a gold sticker. "That's ridiculous."

"I know, and yes, I'm calling first thing." She wanted to tell Delaney about finding the rose on her car, but knew that would only make her friend worry. She fished her credit card out of her purse. "Here you go."

Behind the counter, Delaney put the box in a pretty little shopping bag. "Sorry, your money's no good here."

"Delaney, no. That's very sweet, but I have money."

"I know you do, but you're my friend. And this is my shop and what I say goes. Also, you're not supposed to upset a pregnant woman." She handed the bag over.

Roxy laughed and put her card away so she could grab the goodies. "You're going to play the pregnancy thing for all it's worth, aren't you?"

"You bet your lemon drops I am." Delaney rest her arms on the top of the display case. "You sure you're doing all right?"

"I'm fine. I swear."

"Maybe we can do that spa day next week. What do you think?"

"I'd love that." She didn't have the time for it, but that was also exactly why she needed to do it.

"Sweet. I'll see what they have available and email you."

"Sounds good." Roxy held up the bag. "Thanks again."

"You betcha." Delaney waved.

Roxy left with a smile on her face. Thomas might be dragging his feet—and playing games with the note and the rose—but that would all resolve itself soon enough. Life here was good. She had good friends in Delaney and Alex and was about to set up a great new bookseller connection. If that wasn't a fabulous beginning to a fresh start, she didn't know what was.

All those hallucinations she'd been having were clearly stress induced. More proof that she needed to find ways to manage her workload better. Going to the spa would be great.

She glanced at the bag. She just had to make sure Delaney didn't pay. It was sweet of her to give Roxy the sweets for free, but a spa day was going to be significantly more expensive than a box of chocolates.

She hopped back in her car and drove to the bookstore since it was several blocks away, then parked and retrieved the goody bag of swag she'd brought for Agnes. That and the chocolates from Delaney would make a great introduction.

The store was adorable from the outside, with a green striped awning that matched the exterior paint. Bell, Book & Candle was spelled out in gold, and the big window in the front held a lovely display of books and knickknacks, but clearly books were the stars.

Roxy walked in and took a whiff. The smell of books was mixed with other pleasant flowery scents. Probably from the candles that were stacked here and there in small groups. Customers were scattered throughout. A seating area took up the front, which also held a coffee station. Beyond that was a small checkout counter, and then rows and rows of bookshelves.

And all the books were faced out, meaning the covers were on display. Very nice. Roxy liked the place tremendously. It was only medium sized, but well stocked and filled with the right kind of cozy feeling. The wall behind the register held a large bulletin board and on that board were pinned cover flats and a list of new releases for the following month.

"Hi, can I help you find something?"

Roxy turned and smiled. That voice belonged to Agnes. Roxy stuck her hand out. "I'm Roxy."

Agnes made the same shriek she'd made on the

phone and then immediately covered her mouth with both hands. "You're early!"

"Sorry. Is that okay?"

"It's fine, it's fine." Agnes clasped Roxy's hand and gave it a good shake. "I can't believe you're here."

Agnes had a short, chic silver-gray bob with baby bangs and a few streaks of teal and purple. Her big round black-rimmed glasses framed bright blue eyes and her wrists sported multitudes of bracelets in a rainbow of colors that matched her patchwork skirt. She looked like a real character. Roxy adored her already.

She held out the two packages. "I brought you a little something. One's edible, one's not."

"Oh my!" Agnes took the bags and peeked into both of them. More shrieking followed. "I see bookmarks, pens, and magnets. How fabulous! I love them. I'm going to put them out on the counter right now. The magnets I'm going to put behind the counter for special customers. If that's okay with you."

"That's perfectly fine. You can do whatever you like with them."

Agnes patted the bag from Delaney's. "As for these lovelies, they'll be going home with me." She slid the box of chocolates out, then held out the bag to Roxy. "But you keep the bag. It'll make it easier to carry yours."

"Mine?" Roxy took the bag. It still had weight to it. She glanced inside. A smaller box with an R on it in black marker made her shake her head. "How on earth did Delaney get that in there without me seeing?"

Agnes laughed. "Never look a chocolate gift horse in the mouth."

"That's for sure." Roxy slipped the shopping bag handle over her arm. Even if it meant an extra round or three of sun salutations, whatever was in that little box was getting eaten tonight. "So. Let's talk signing."

Grocery shopping hadn't been any big deal. Alex knew his way around the Shop-n-Save, and despite being stopped by several people to chat, he was in and out with everything on his list in about thirty minutes.

Getting the groceries unpacked and put away, however, became a much longer task due to the phone call from his mother. It was more of the same. *When are you getting married? Have you met anyone? I want to see my grandchildren before I die.*

He braced the phone between his cheek and shoulder as he stacked family-sized cans of tuna in the pantry. He could probably record his side of the conversation and play it back without his mother even noticing. Fortunately, he had a secret weapon. When his mother took a breath, he slipped in the five magic words sure to change the topic. "Diego finally got a job."

"Where? When? I hope he's not working too hard. Is he working too hard? My poor baby."

Alex rolled his eyes. "He's bartending at a local place. He just got the job. Tonight's his second shift. And no, he's not working too hard. He's never worked too hard."

"Now, Alex, your brother was in the service. In the desert! That's not an easy job. You need to cut him some slack."

"Slack? Mom, he's lived in my house for almost a month rent-free, utility-free, everything free. How much more slack can I give him?"

"Just be kind to your brother. He's had a hard road."

Alex couldn't stop the growl that built up in his throat. "I'm sorry, a hard road? In what way?"

"Well, he can't seem to find a woman who appreciates him."

The snort of laughter that Alex answered with earned him a long sigh. "Yes, Mom, that's Diego's problem. He can't find a woman. I think he's found too many women, frankly." Alex really didn't want to participate in this conversation. Diego was the baby of the family and always would be where their mother was concerned. He could do no wrong in her eyes. "I love you, Mom, but I need to get ready for –"

"Speaking of women, I understand you've met someone."

She'd obviously been saving that one up, testing him with the initial barrage of questions to see if he'd say something, then yanking that out as a last resort when he didn't. "I suppose Diego told you that." Probably as his own out when the conversation went in a direction he didn't like.

"What's she like, this new chica?"

"She's my neighbor. She's very nice. And I only told Diego I liked her so he would leave her alone."

"That wasn't very nice. What if she's the right woman for him?"

"She's not." But she could be the right woman for Alex. If only she were a shifter too. He sighed.

"What was that sigh? You do like her, don't you?"

"Yes, but not like that. Just as a friend." Because that's all he could be. "She's not a shifter, Mom."

"So? Witch, vampire, whatever she is. No one gets hung up on labels like that anymore."

"Really? Not even the label *human*?"

His mother went silent, a rare and curious moment for both of them. After a long break, Carmen finally spoke. "That's not what your father and I would want for you. A mixed marriage can be very difficult."

Alex doubted his father cared half as much as his mother did. "Slow down with the M word. This isn't even in the same zip code of that ballpark."

"Does she know what you are?"

"No. And it's going to stay that way." At least until Delaney decided otherwise.

"But I thought everyone in your town was some kind of supernatural."

"Not everyone. Most. But there are still plenty of regular humans who live here too."

More silence, but this time the pause didn't last as long. "Do you think she'd understand? If you told her the truth?"

"Not happening."

"But if you like her—"

"I really need to get ready for work."

"I just want you to be happy, Alex. You deserve that. You're a good man, you work hard, you've earned the right to be happy and have a family. I want that for you. Unlike Diego, you've never given me a reason to worry or lose sleep, but my heart aches for you to find the kind of happiness that your father and I have."

"I appreciate that. I'll talk to you soon." He hung up, a small knot in his throat. It was nice to hear his mother say those sorts of things. And to hear her admit that she understood more about Diego than she let on.

Alex knew he deserved to be happy. Everyone deserved that.

Roxy wasn't that happiness, though. And that wasn't a gray area, it was black and white. At least to him. Beyond the fact that she wasn't interested, beyond the fact that she wasn't a shifter or any kind of supernatural, she also wasn't his soul mate.

He'd thought he'd felt that *thing* that he'd expected to feel, but the more he mulled it over, the less sure he was. He needed to have that sense of absolutely knowing the person across from him was his one true match. And so far, he didn't. Maybe if Roxy hadn't been his neighbor, maybe he would have pursued a fling anyway, had some fun and been okay with that.

Except flings weren't his style and she really had become a friend to him. And while the surge of excitement and interest he felt when she was around was fun, infatuation—or whatever he was feeling—wasn't something to build a future on.

With an odd sense of disappointment curling through him, he put the last of the groceries away, then went to get dressed.

He might not have a soul mate, but he had his job. And if no woman needed him, the town of Nocturne Falls did.

For now, that had to be enough.

He got to work a few minutes early, so he headed for the sheriff's office to check in. Birdie was already packing up and getting ready to go home since her day was over.

"Night, Alex." She hoisted her big floral purse over one shoulder. She had the biggest, brightest smile on her face that he'd seen in a long time. And that was saying something, because Birdie was generally one of the happiest people he knew.

"Something going on?"

She giggled. *Giggled.* "Oh, yes, but it's not my place to tell. Everyone will know soon enough, though. No hiding a thing like that."

All right, then. "Well, you have a good night, Birdie." He jerked his thumb toward the sheriff's door. "He in?"

"Mm-hmm."

Alex knocked. "Sheriff?"

"Come in," Hank called out.

Alex opened the door. "Anything going on?"

The sheriff broke into a rare smile. "Sure enough. Ivy's pregnant."

"Hey, congratulations! No wonder Birdie was grinning like that. I thought maybe she'd hit happy hour early. You must be thrilled."

Hank laughed. "Yeah, we're pretty excited." He cleared his throat. "I don't imagine that's what you came in here for, though."

"Just wanted to check in before my shift started, see if anything was going on."

"Nothing much. Quiet day. That'll change soon enough with the parade coming this weekend."

"That's for sure." Alex hesitated. "You mind if I ask you something?"

Hank tipped his head at the chairs across from his desk. "Have a seat."

Alex closed the door and took the chair closest.

Hank leaned forward. "What's on your mind?"

Alex took a breath. "How did you know that you and Ivy were meant to be?"

Hank snorted. "Our marriage was arranged. You know that. We didn't have much say in the matter."

"Yeah, but you're obviously in love with each other now."

"True." He took a moment. "It happened over time, as we got to know each other."

"Would you say she's your soul mate?"

Hank nodded. "Sure, I'd say that. We're bonded. I suppose you cats can do that the same way us wolves can."

"Yes. Doesn't happen to all of us, though."

"Doesn't happen to all of us either." Hank's gaze narrowed. "What's all this about?"

Alex sighed. "What would you have done if Ivy hadn't been a wolf shifter? Would you have been able to stay away from her after you fell for her?"

Hank frowned. "That didn't happen, so what's the point of speculating?"

"I just want to know if it would have been a deal breaker."

Hank seemed to mull that over briefly. "No. Once I fell for her, that was that. She could have been anything—human, bird, mountain lion—and I would have chased her to the ends of the earth. That's what love is."

"I guess."

Hank's face screwed up in disbelief. "You've been in love, haven't you?"

Alex sat back. "I don't know."

Hank snorted. "Then you haven't been. Because when you are, you'll know it. She'll be all you think about and all you want to think about. You'll be happy when she's around and miserable when she's not." He tapped a finger on the desk. "Love is not a feeling you can ignore."

"Good to know."

Hank tilted his head. "This about someone in particular?"

Alex shook his head. "Not really. Maybe. I don't know."

Hank laughed softly. "Sounds like you're off to a good start."

"Thanks for your time, boss." Alex stood, the feeling that everyone around him knew more than he did still clinging to him. Maybe he was overthinking this way too much.

It was time to focus on his job and his upcoming exam and put Roxy, and his feelings for her, out of his head.

Pages done, house buttoned up for the night and light beer in hand, Roxy headed to the couch for some downtime and to catch up on *The Bachelorette*, a guilty pleasure she liked to consider research. (Much like its sister show, *The Bachelor*.)

She was just about to plop down and get comfy when she saw her purse on the kitchen counter, which reminded her about the check she'd meant to send to her narrator for the last audiobook.

With a sigh, she set the beer on the coffee table, ran back to her computer to get the amount, then dashed off the check, popped it in an envelope and stuck a stamp on it.

She was about to put it on the counter next to her purse, when she realized the smart thing to do was put it in the mailbox now. Monday mornings were hectic, and she didn't want to forget until the mailman came by and she ended up running down the street after him.

Flip-flops on, she walked the envelope down to the mailbox. The night was balmy and beautiful. The faint perfume of some night-blooming flower drifted past, along with the gentle hum of insects. She paused to take it all in and enjoy that this was where she lived now. Her own little piece of paradise.

Her gaze shifted to Alex's house. A few exterior lights brightened the outside, but she knew no one was home. His offer to use the hot tub echoed in her head, and as enticing as that was, she was too worn-out to take him up on it.

She smiled, thinking about him. If this were a book she was writing, the heroine would definitely use the hot tub. She'd also forgo a bathing suit, since no one was home.

Of course, then Roxy would give the hero a reason to come home unexpectedly, putting her characters in an interesting situation that would lead to their romance leveling up a notch.

But this was real life. And as much as she liked Alex, friendship was as far as she was willing to go. Her heart just wasn't ready for more. Not yet.

She stuck the envelope into the mailbox, yanked the red flag all the way up and walked back up the driveway.

She took her spot on the couch and started to turn on *The Bachelorette*, but the thought of watching all those men vie for the attention of one woman no longer held any appeal, research or not.

For the first time since she'd left Thomas, a sense of loneliness came over her. It was such an odd feeling that she allowed herself to wallow in it a bit. Sure, she was alone, but was she really lonely? She didn't think so, but then, she'd never felt this way before, hollow and achy for something she couldn't express.

She'd been homesick when she'd been in college, but that had been definable. This was so nebulous and deep that, for a brief moment, she wondered if she was slipping into depression. It happened to writers, creative types more specifically, all the time.

And it had happened to her mother. Among other things.

But this could also be a side effect of her divorce. What was a little depression on top of the hallucinations she'd already had?

With that thought in mind, she turned off the TV, picked up her beer, dumped it in the sink and went to bed.

She couldn't afford this feeling. Not with her book already behind schedule. She was going to get a good night's sleep, then first thing tomorrow, she was getting outside for a long walk and some fresh air.

Right after she called her attorney and told him to get Thomas's signature on the papers immediately.

Because it was high time for Thomas's influence on her life to come to an absolute end.

Alex pulled onto his street after a long but thankfully uneventful shift. All he wanted now was a hot shower and his bed. Thankfully, he had room-darkening blinds to shut out the morning sun.

Then he saw Roxy walking down her driveway in spandex capris and a tank top and his mind turned to other things. He pulled into his own, parked and got out.

"Morning," she called. "Just getting home?"

"Yep. You look like you're off for a walk."

"I am." Her smile was wistful and not full of the usual joy it normally contained. "I need some fresh air."

"You okay?"

She shrugged and glanced away for a second. "Yeah. My ex is really dragging his feet on signing the papers. I left a stern message for my attorney this morning, but I'm not sure how much good that's going to do and…" She shook her head.

"What?"

"I don't know. I'm just in a funk, I guess."

He put his hand on his belt. "You want some company on your walk? Just take me a minute to change."

The light finally showed up in her eyes. "You just got off work. You really want to go for a walk with me?"

He nodded. "I'm always a little keyed up after a shift. It'll help me unwind. If you don't mind me butting in."

She smiled. A real smile. "You're not butting in." She leaned against the mailbox post. "I'll be right here."

He grinned and headed for the house. "Back in a sec."

He jogged inside, not caring if the door closed too hard and woke Diego. Alex actually hadn't been keyed up before, but now he was.

He shucked his uniform and changed into gym shorts and a sheriff's department T-shirt, then went in to brush his teeth. Just because. He caught a glimpse of himself in the bathroom mirror and was surprised by how happy he looked.

He should look tired. But he didn't even feel that way anymore.

Because Roxy did that to him.

He stared at his reflection without seeing it, his mind too focused on the thoughts unfolding there. Thoughts he shouldn't even be having.

Was Roxy the one? Was that what these feelings meant? Hank had said that Alex would know when he knew, but that was easier said than realized.

He leaned on the sink. There was no way this was love. It was much too early for that, and they were still getting to know each other.

But this was *something*. That was for sure. He stuck his toothbrush back in the holder, rinsed his mouth, then went back outside to join the woman he couldn't stop thinking about.

Roxy was staring at her mailbox like it was about to do something interesting.

"What's up?"

She glanced at him, then shook her head. "I put a letter in here last night so I wouldn't forget today."

"And?"

Her mouth scrunched up on one side like she was thinking. "Well, for one thing, I'm sure I closed the mailbox all the way and I just saw that it's barely shut. I'm mailing a check. I wouldn't want anything to happen to it."

The door was closed, but only just. "You think someone tampered with it?"

"I don't know. The flag isn't all the way up either, and I made sure it was."

"Did you check that your mail is still in there?"

"Didn't have a chance yet. It's okay to touch it right?"

He hitched one shoulder up. "It's not like we're going to dust for prints."

"Yeah. Okay." She pulled the door open, looked in, then shut it again. Firmly. "Yep, my envelope is in there."

"It's probably nothing."

She gave a little half nod, then tilted her head to look up at him. "Ready to walk?"

"Let's go."

For the first minute or so, they didn't speak, just found a rhythm. Alex shortened his steps a little so that Roxy could keep up, and after a bit, they fell into a good pace.

When he glanced over at her, she seemed to be miles away. "You don't look like you're here."

She turned. "What?"

He laughed. "I said you don't look like you're here. I doubt the mailbox is bothering you that much so it's got to be something else. The divorce?"

She kept her gaze straight ahead. "That's part of it."

"What's the rest?"

She stayed quiet and he let it be, figuring she didn't want to talk. But then she answered him. "It's a lot of things, I guess. The divorce, being behind on my book, working on my new life…feeling a little lonely."

"Lonely?" He wanted to put his arm around her, but that was probably crossing the line of friendly neighbor.

She nodded. "Yeah, it's weird. I've never felt this way before, but it really hit me last night. I just kind of fell into this dark place. My mom had some issues with stuff like that when I was a kid, so maybe I'm just extra sensitive to it."

Now he really wanted to hug her. "Are you feeling better this morning?"

She made a noncommittal noise. "I guess."

"Very convincing."

She smirked. "Getting out for this walk was part of my 'snap out of it' plan."

"Is it working?"

She smiled up at him. "Maybe."

He changed the subject in an attempt to draw her out a little more. "Do you believe in soul mates? You must, right? You write about them after all."

"I do write about them, but honestly, I think they're mostly fictional." She shrugged. "That might also be my divorce talking."

"You sure this walk is helping?"

"Yep."

But something lingered in her gaze, something he'd come to recognize in his years on the force.

She wasn't being completely honest with him. Something was still bothering her. He held the eye contact for a moment. "If you ever want to talk, I'm a good listener. It's part of my job, you know."

She shifted to look down the sidewalk ahead of them. "Thanks. I'll keep that in mind."

"We should go out."

"What?" There was an edge of panic in her voice.

He put his hands up. "Just as friends. I could introduce you to some people, you know, help you feel less lonely maybe."

"That's really sweet of you. The thing is...I don't really like people that much." She laughed. "That sounds way worse than I mean it. I love my readers. I love the emails they send me and the notes they send via social media, but I'm not great in big groups."

"This wouldn't be a big group necessarily. Just some of the people I work with. Like a happy hour thing. Couple of drinks and that's it. Unless you want to hang out longer. It would be totally up to you."

A couple seconds passed before she nodded. "Okay. I'm sure it would be good for me."

"Your enthusiasm is overwhelming."

She laughed, but it died off quickly. "Bear with me."

"Not a problem." He glanced down at her,

caught her gaze and something passed between them. Something that, to him, felt like a promise.

"Thanks," she whispered, her voice thin with an unnamable emotion.

Whatever was going on with her, he wanted to help. But he couldn't do that until she was ready to talk to him. Until then, he'd just be around for her as much as he could. The shifter side of him was born with a desire to protect, especially those he cared about, and Roxy definitely fell into that category.

The cop side of him felt very much the same way.

He wished he could explain that to her, but he didn't want to complicate her situation with his profession of protection. She didn't need to think her neighbor had just become her self-appointed body guard. Although he sort of had.

No, he'd just stay quiet, doing what he could to watch over her and make sure she had whatever she needed to get through this.

He glanced at her again, and whispered back, "It's going to be okay."

She smiled. And a single tear rolled down her cheek.

The tear fell before Roxy could stop it. Alex's kind words hadn't caused it, but they had brought it to the surface. Everything else had caused it. But the mailbox—and the fact that she was sure that either Thomas, or someone working for him, was spying on her—had been the straw that broke the camel's back. She wiped the tear away as subtly as she could, but Alex stopped walking.

"Hey, what's wrong?"

She shook her head, trying to keep one tear from turning into a full-on crying jag. She hated showing that much emotion. Crying in front of Thomas had always turned into more grief from him, so she'd trained herself to hold back. "Stress," she mumbled.

"You want me to call Delaney? I know you two are friends. Maybe you guys should do a spa day or whatever it is women do."

Roxy laughed, despite the knot of emotions inside her. "Delaney was just saying that."

"Then do it. Your book can wait. And there's nothing you can do to speed up your ex signing those papers, so take a day off."

She nodded. "I will. I'll call her as soon as I get home."

Alex took her elbow and gently turned them back toward her house. "Then that's where we're headed."

"I didn't get much fresh air."

He started them walking. "The spa is full of fresh air. They probably import it from the Alps."

She laughed. She knew he was taking care of

her, and it was sweet beyond words. Thomas had never been that way. Maybe in the beginning a little bit, but it certainly hadn't lasted. Alex was such a different man. If she wasn't careful, she might fall for him.

Without thinking, she looped her arm through his. She stiffened as soon as she realized what she'd done. She started to slip her arm back.

But he tightened his arm against his body, keeping her from completely breaking the connection. He smiled and gave her a look that felt like he was telling her he had her back.

She relaxed and let it be. She realized for the first time that she never felt she had to be on alert around Alex. Her years with Thomas had conditioned her to watch him for mood swings and the telltale signs that a rage was coming on. But Alex was easy to be around, and it was nice. No, it was more than nice, it was like breathing again after being held under water for far too long.

That alone caused some of her tension to slip away. With friends like Alex and Delaney at her side, she was going to be all right. She knew that. The divorce and the book would both be done eventually, and as time went on, she'd get the rest of her boxes unpacked, and life would smooth out. It just would. No one stayed overwhelmed forever.

She hoped.

Part of not being overwhelmed was sharing

some of the burden. It was high time that Roxy learned to let go of some of the smaller stuff. Easier said than done, but Em, her assistant, was more than capable.

Roxy just had to loosen her grip on the things that weren't as critical.

"Lost in thought over there?"

"A little. Sorry." She looked up at Alex. His profile was essentially flawless. Almost feline in the way his cheekbones and brow were shaped. Diego had the same characteristics, so it was clearly a family thing. On Diego, the results were pretty, which probably fed his confidence. Unfortunately. On Alex, they gave him a rugged handsomeness that went from warm and welcoming to guy-you-wouldn't-want-to-mess-with, depending on his smile.

"Don't apologize. I know you have a lot on your mind."

She'd have less to worry about it if she shared with him what Thomas had been up to. And Alex was a cop. He might have some advice on how to deal with all this nonsense. They stopped at her drive. "Can you come in for a minute?"

"Sure." He followed her up to the door.

She unlocked it, let him in, then locked it again.

"What's up?"

Without a word, she walked past him and into the kitchen where she went up on her tiptoes and felt around on top of the fridge until she found the note she'd thrown up there. She snagged the envelope, then plopped it on the counter. "This is what's up. My ex sent this. And yesterday, he left a rose on my car."

In a half-second, Alex went from friendly neighbor to cop on the job. It wasn't something easy to explain, but everything about him went hard: his stance, his expression, the look in his eyes. "When did you get this?"

"You brought it over on Saturday."

"What made you keep it? And the envelope?"

She shrugged. "I'm a writer. We always think in worst-case scenarios. So, you know, in case I turned up dead and you had to dust it for prints or something—"

"Are you serious?" A feral light shone in his eyes. "Do you think that's a possibility?"

"I was joking." She stared at the note. "Kind of. Thomas does have a temper."

"Do you still have the rose?"

Had Alex just...growled? No, of course not. She was just projecting the reactions of one of her romance heroes onto a real man. That was silly. "No, I put it in the garbage can."

"Any note with that?"

"No."

"Why do you think he'd do these things? What's his end game?"

"Maybe he's trying to intimidate me about the divorce. I was the one who left him, so him 'losing control of me' probably did some serious damage to his macho image. If he could get me to drop the divorce, he could spin that into me begging him to take me back because I couldn't live without him...you get the picture."

A growl, a real one this time, rumbled out of Alex's throat and turned into a curse. "Give me his full name, current address and phone numbers. I'll see what I can find out about what's going on with him and whether he's in town or knows anyone in town, other than you. Anything else happens, anything, you tell me okay?"

She nodded, the rare sensation of being protected sweeping through her. He really cared what happened to her. She went up on her tiptoes for the second time that day, but this time it was to reach something far more interesting.

Alex's mouth.

She meant the kiss to be a brief thank-you. But the moment their lips met, the heat of him seared into her, and brief was forgotten.

He sucked in a surprised breath, his hands coming up to grasp her shoulders. The growl she'd heard out of him before resounded, this time deeper and softer, like an engine starting up in the distance.

It was strangely encouraging to have that sort of

effect on a man. She flattened her hands on his chest. His very solid, broad chest. And kissed him harder.

Then reality reminded her she was technically still married. She broke the kiss and went down onto her flat feet to stare at the tile on her floor. "Now it's my turn to apologize. We said no kissing. And I'm not even divorced. I'm sorry."

"Are you really?" His voice was dark and edged with desire.

"Sorry?" She bit her lip. "No, but—"

He pulled her into his arms and kissed her some more, causing her to let out a little gasp of surprise. His mouth moved across her jaw and down her neck with small, feathery kisses and the occasional scrape of his teeth.

"I'm…still…married…" she managed to get out.

"His signature is a formality," Alex growled back.

Which echoed what her lawyer had told her months ago. She started to say something else, but Alex found the soft spot below her ear, and her bones turned to jelly, and she exhaled a long, shuddering sigh that racked her entire body.

Then he broke the kiss. "I'm not sorry about that. Are you?"

She didn't know what she was. Who she was. Where she was. She just focused on breathing and not melting into a puddle. She nodded. That seemed right.

He looked hurt. "You are?"

She shook her head. "No. What was the question? You can't ask me questions after doing *that* to me."

He grinned. "Doing what?"

She gave him a lighthearted smack on the chest. Her fingers bounced off the muscle there. "You know. Kissing me like that."

His grin widened and became very smug. "Like what?"

"Oh, stop it. It's a wonder parts of me didn't burst into flame."

He cocked his head, his expression going serious. "Something to shoot for next time."

"Next time?" She put her hands on her hips. "What happened to no kissing and just being friendly neighbors?"

He stepped back and nodded. "You're right. If that's what you want—"

"I don't know what I want. I like you. Obviously."

"But your life is complicated enough right now. I get it. And so yes, no kissing. I promise to cool it until you tell me otherwise."

His restraint was impressive. "And if I don't tell you otherwise?"

His mouth curved into a casual smile, but it didn't match the lingering smolder in his eyes. "Then we're just really friendly neighbors who've kissed."

Except it didn't feel that way to her. Could it really feel that way to him? She narrowed her eyes at him.

He cleared his throat. "Where's your phone?"

"On my desk, why?"

"So you can call Delaney and make this spa day happen. By the time you get home tonight, I should be able to tell you whether or not your ex is in town."

"Didn't you just get off your shift?"

"Yes. Why?"

"You're not Superman, Alex. You need to sleep."

"I'll be fine."

She put her hands on her hips. "I'll do the spa day with Delaney only if you promise me you'll get some sleep."

He smiled. "Can I at least make a few phone calls first? Get some things working?"

"I guess. Do you really think you can find out something today? Can you get results that fast?"

"Sometimes." The corner of his mouth twitched. "But that doesn't mean I don't know when to take my time, either."

And despite agreeing that there would be no more kissing, a trill of anticipation zipped through her. Apparently, her body hadn't gotten the message.

Or didn't want to.

When Alex left Roxy's, she was twenty minutes from meeting Delaney at the spa. He was glad Delaney had been available and the spa thing had worked out. Roxy would be safe there, and not just because Delaney was a vampire with the strength and speed to overpower any human, but because no one else would know Roxy was at the spa.

Especially her ex. Unless he was watching her. In which case, he also knew about Alex. And that was fine with Alex. He didn't know much about Thomas, but if he was the kind of man who made his wife fear his temper and treated her like a piece of property, then he was probably also the kind of man who thought himself superior to everyone else. If he thought he was superior to Alex, he was in for a big surprise.

Big.

Because when it came down to human versus

supernatural, the odds were not in the human's favor. But Thomas wouldn't know that until it was too late. Until the battle was well under way. Because the other thing Alex knew about Roxy's ex was that he thought he was clever. The note, the rose, checking what was in the mailbox, yeah, the guy thought he was sly. Clearly.

Alex snorted. If the man wanted to play games, he was sorely outclassed. Besides being a cop, Alex had the same skill set that all shifters did. Speed, strength, heightened senses. Being a feline shifter gave him some bonus points in stealth and cunning, too.

The lack of crime in Nocturne Falls wasn't a random occurrence. It was due in great part to its supernatural police force. Human criminals didn't stand a chance. And that kind of word of mouth spread, usually in the form of rumors along the lines of the town having a secret force of vigilantes that roamed the streets at night, or a lot of retired special ops guys on the police roster, that sort of thing.

Whatever. It worked.

But of course, Thomas wouldn't know that. So he'd have to find out firsthand just how dangerous it was to tick off a shifter and go after his woman.

Alex stopped himself. Roxy was not *his* woman. She was just a friend. His friend, but that was it. Even after all that kissing. And he understood.

But it was getting harder to remember that when he was around her.

He shoved a hand through his hair. He didn't have time to dissect what he was feeling. He had to find out if her ex was in town. And if he was, what to do about the jerk.

He grabbed his cell phone and dialed. He'd get one of the deputies on shift to run Thomas' record, but as for locating him, well, if there was anyone who could handle that job, it was Birdie Caruthers.

"Nocturne Falls Sheriff Department, Birdie speaking."

"Birdie, it's Alex. I need your help. Actually, Roxy St. James needs your help. But this is strictly confidential. One word of this gets out, and she'll move out of this town so fast—"

"I won't say a word. Butter my biscuit and slap my face, I swear it. Whatever can I do?"

"She thinks her ex-husband might be in town. I need to know if he is."

"That bugger. How dare he?" Birdie growled softly, her werewolf self clearly aggravated, and Alex knew he'd gone to the right person. "You just give me everything you know. I'll track that lowlife down."

"Sure thing. Then I need to talk to whoever's on duty."

"Jenna's here."

"She'll do nicely. This is what I know about Roxy's ex…"

Ten minutes later, Alex hung up. Birdie was looking for Thomas and Jenna Blythe had promised to email whatever she found out about the man.

Satisfied that he'd have everything he needed shortly, he took a hot shower and then planned on getting enough sleep to make Roxy happy. Then he'd do a little investigating of his own. If Thomas was watching Roxy's place, he couldn't be too far away, and this was Alex's neighborhood. People would talk to him.

Hmm. Pandora Williams might be a good one to touch base with. She was the number one realtor in town and lived just a few blocks away. She was out and about a lot. She might have seen something. Or even had someone inquire about houses for rent in the area. Roxy's ex had to be staying somewhere.

Alex's brain kept running scenarios and processing possibilities as he changed into sleep pants. Then Diego called out his name from the hall.

"Yo, Alex, you still up, man?"

"Yes," Alex called back. He went to see what his brother wanted. Diego stood in the door of his bedroom, dressed in tan pants and a Howler's black polo. A packed duffel bag sat at his feet. "What's going on?"

Diego grinned. "You're getting your wish, bro. I'm moving out."

Alex frowned. "Already? How much money did you make last night?"

"Bank. That place is a cash machine, dude."

Alex shook his head, his focus on Roxy clouding his thought process. "So...you made enough to move out and you already found a place?"

Diego shrugged. "Yeah, something like that. I'm moving in with Shanna."

Alex's mouth fell open. "Shanna? The twenty-year-old server that works at Howler's?"

Diego rolled his eyes. "She's twenty-three."

Better than twenty, but not by much. "And you're thirty."

"So? Don't get all weird. It's cool. We're both adults."

Yeah. They were. And Alex had bigger fish to fry. He nodded. "You're right, you are. I hope it works out."

Diego looked skeptical. "I'm sure."

"No, I mean it. Everyone deserves to be happy."

Diego's expression softened. "Thanks, bro."

Alex jerked his chin toward the kitchen. "Your seventy-five bucks is in the jar on top of the fridge. I'm going to bed."

"You haven't slept yet?"

"No. Roxy's having some issues with her ex."

Diego's eyes narrowed with concern. "Sorry to

hear that. You need me for anything, you let me know."

Alex nodded. "Thanks, I will, but I'm sure it's not going to be a big deal."

"All right. I'll leave my new address on the kitchen counter. And you can keep the seventy-five dollars. I owe you more than that anyway. Now get some sleep, dude, you look like hell."

"Thanks." Alex gave him a wave and went in to bed. He crashed onto it, exhaling in exhaustion as he sank into the mattress. But even as sleep tugged at him, his mind stayed focused on Roxy.

The thought that her ex might be up to something had ignited an urge to protect her unlike anything he'd felt before in his life.

Unless you counted the way he felt toward his family.

If Thomas touched a hair on her body, Alex was going to put him in a world of hurt. The kind that left a lasting impression and made sure the idiot never attempted anything against her again. Alex might be an officer of the law, but he was a shifter first. And his kind had their own laws when it came to protecting those they loved.

Love. Was that what he was feeling? He let the word roll around in his brain as he turned onto his back to stare at the ceiling. His eyes began drifting closed and he stopped fighting it, the last thought on his mind that while Roxy might not believe in soul mates, he did. In fact, he was starting to believe in them more than ever.

"Ooo." Roxy let out a moan that she was powerless to stop.

Delaney snorted. "You sound like you're having a very different massage than I am."

Imari, Roxy's masseuse, laughed softly. "They are both the same, I promise."

"I don't know," Roxy said. "This is pretty good."

Sandrine, Delaney's masseuse, chimed in. "They aren't *exactly* the same. After all, Delaney is pregnant."

"True," Imari answered, digging in deeper on Roxy's shoulders.

Imari's renewed efforts caused Roxy to sigh some more. As best she could anyway with her face plastered into the padded doughnut that stuck out at the end of the massage table. "Forget pretty good, this is heaven."

Delaney was on the table next to her since they'd opted for the Besties Package, which was kind of like a couple's day at the spa, but without romantic overtones. Just a few special provisions for Delaney's growing baby bump. "Why do you think I've been trying to get you here?"

"I was a fool not to listen to you sooner."

Imari moved on to Roxy's lower back. "You should come any time you need it."

"Agreed," Roxy answered. She really ought to make this a more regular thing.

Delaney spoke again. "Why did you decide to finally do it anyway? And with such short notice?"

"Um…" Roxy hadn't had a chance to explain yet. When they'd arrived at the spa, they'd been whisked off to a changing area, given robes, cups of specially blended relaxation tea, and then ushered into the massage room for "meditation time," which was basically listening to pan flute music and whale sounds while not talking. Which, as it turned out, was surprisingly relaxing.

Roxy exhaled another deep sigh as Imari began running her forearm over Roxy's back in big, sweeping motions. "Let's just say Alex talked me into it. I'll explain more later." Like when they weren't naked and being rubbed into jelly. Besides that, Roxy liked Imari and Sandrine, and it felt weird talking like they weren't there.

And just in case they were the chatty type, Roxy didn't want to risk having her business spread all over town any more than it already had been.

Delaney moaned something back that sounded like she understood.

Then they both went quiet and boneless under the hands of the very capable professionals working on them. Roxy decided about halfway through that getting a massage every couple of months had just become mandatory. Sooner if she could swing it.

Sixty minutes later, she and Delaney were left alone to recover enough to get off the tables and then be escorted to the next room for facials. Roxy wasn't making a lot of progress getting upright until she heard movement. If Delaney could do it, so could she. Digging deep, she found a thread of consciousness and pulled herself upright, wrapping the sheet around her as she did.

Next to her, Delaney made a noise like an old man trying to hoist himself out of a recliner, which made Roxy laugh. She looked over her shoulder. Delaney had a serious case of bed head and a nice oily sheen from the massage lotion, but her eyes were heavy-lidded with bliss.

Roxy's brows lifted. "If I look anything like you do, we're both a hot mess."

Delaney grinned. "Do I look like I just had a wild night in the sack?"

"A wild night in the sack that was preceded by oil wrestling."

"That's the sign of a good massage." She slid off the table and tucked her sheet in like a long, strapless dress. "Ready for part two?"

Roxy nodded. "Totally."

"How are you feeling, stress-wise?"

"Stress? What stress? I don't even know what that word means right now."

Delaney nodded with great satisfaction. "Excellent. Also, told ya."

They shrugged their robes on, then dropped the sheets.

Delaney put her hand on the door handle, but didn't open it. A serious light shone in her eyes. "Have you had any more hallucinations lately?"

Roxy shook her head. "Nothing. I think it was definitely stress."

"That's good. That's really good." Delaney smiled. "Hey, you should be able to write today off, then."

Roxy laughed. "Yeah, I don't think my accountant will go for that."

Delaney opened the door. "Doesn't hurt to try."

The facials were followed by pedicures, and then the whole thing was finished up with a half-hour guided relaxation, during which Roxy drifted off into the most luxurious catnap she'd ever had. By the end of the day, she was cocooned in a warm, happy glow.

At the front desk, she and Delaney were handed complimentary bottles of "energizing water" as they were checked out by Imari and Sandrine.

Roxy held hers up. "I'm not sure I want to drink this. I'm pretty happy just the way I am. I don't want to ruin this mellow feeling."

Imari shook her head. "You need to drink a lot of water after a massage. That bottle will get you started. It's got a lot of good minerals in it. Right from the springs here in the hills. Some of the best water around."

"Really?" Roxy looked at Delaney. "Why didn't you tell me? You know I love good water."

Delaney leaned her hip against the counter as she handed over a black American Express card. "Why do you think we sell it all over town?"

Roxy shrugged shoulders that felt like happy mush. "I just thought it was a tourist thing."

"Nope. We all drink it." As if to prove her point, Delaney twisted the top off hers and took a big drink.

"Got it. Lots of water. Starting with this one." Roxy collected her receipt, then she and Delaney walked out together.

They stopped under the awning. They'd been in the spa for almost four hours, and during that time, the sky had gone gray. A light drizzle fell.

"Perfect writing day," Roxy said.

Delaney stretched. "I'm so glad I don't have to go back to the shop today. I love it, but the way I feel, I just want to go home, snuggle up with my husband and continue to pretend the rest of the world doesn't exist."

"That sounds lovely." It did. But it also made Roxy the tiniest bit melancholy. She had no one to snuggle with. Maybe she should get a dog. Or a cat.

Or an Alex.

She shook her head at her own thoughts.

"What?" Delaney asked.

"I didn't say anything."

"No, but you shook your head."

"Just..." No reason not to be truthful. "Just thinking about Alex."

Delaney's eyes lit up.

Roxy raised her hand. "No. Don't even go there."

Delaney pressed her lips firmly together, but couldn't keep herself from smiling. "Whatever you say."

"Good. Because I say I'm not ready. I'm not even officially divorced yet."

"Rox, I gotta tell you. The more you say that, the more it sounds like an excuse. You've been separated from Thomas for almost a year and a half. No one considers you married to him anymore. I think you're scared."

Roxy opened her mouth to protest, but Delaney didn't give her a chance. "And you know what? It's okay to be scared. Who wouldn't be after what you went through? But don't let fear ruin the possibility of what might be. You know what I mean? Alex is not Thomas. He's a great guy. You couldn't ask for better. Just...don't shut him out entirely. I think seeing what could happen with a guy like him, a guy so opposite of Thomas, could be really good for you."

Roxy nodded. "I get it. I do. And I am afraid. But I'm also just not ready."

Delaney smiled, but there was disappointment in her eyes. "You know I just want you to be happy."

"I know." Roxy hugged her friend. "Tell Hugh I said hi."

"Tell him yourself." Delaney tipped her head at the sleek Jaguar that pulled up. "He's here."

Hugh Ellingham, Delaney's gorgeous husband, hopped out of the car, umbrella in hand, and came around to open Delaney's door.

"Must be nice," Roxy said.

Delaney grinned as he helped her in. "It is. Very nice."

Roxy gave Hugh a little wave. "Hi."

He nodded back. "Hello, there. Nice to see you."

"You too."

He shut Delaney's door then turned to Roxy and lifted the umbrella. "Can I walk you to your car?"

"Sure—oh, crud. I just realized I left my earrings on the counter in the dressing room. Thank you so much, but you go ahead."

"All right then."

She waved at Delaney and ran back in. Her earrings were right where she'd left them. She scooped them up and went back outside.

She stood a moment under the awning, waiting for the rain to let up and thinking about Hugh and Delaney. How amazing it would be to have that kind of relationship.

The drizzle wasn't getting any better, so she ducked her head and ran to her car. She got in as quickly as she could, but had to wipe rain out of her eyes. Oh well. She was already covered in a bunch of different lotions and potions, what was a little rain water? And her car could totally use a bath.

Her thoughts went from Hugh and Delaney to Alex. Had he found anything out yet? She pulled her phone out and turned it back on now that she was out of the spa.

While she waited for it to start up, she glanced into her rearview mirror to look for cars behind her and went very still as she saw the back window. The rain had washed some of the words away, but enough of it was still readable, etched into the grime.

Have fun?

Alex woke to the ringing of his cell phone. He grabbed it off the nightstand without opening his eyes, a reflex born of years of being on call. He mumbled, "Cruz," and waited for Birdie to fill him in on whatever emergency required his attention.

"Alex, it's Roxy. Thomas followed me to the spa."

Alex sat up, wide awake. "Are you okay?" She'd sounded stressed. The exact opposite of how she should sound after her spa day.

"Yes, I'm fine. Just shaken up."

"Where are you?"

"Home. I didn't actually see him at the spa. He wrote something in the dirt on my car window." She hesitated, then blurted, "I feel like I'm being watched. That's probably just my nerves, though. This is really freaking me out."

"On my way over. Don't answer the door for anyone else."

"Okay. Thank you. I won't."

"You got it." He hung up and got dressed, glad he'd showered before hitting the sack. He threw on jeans and a T-shirt. For a second, he thought about taking his off-duty weapon, but Thomas was a human. Alex wouldn't need a gun to take the man down. Even if Thomas had a weapon, Alex was a shifter. It would take more than a bullet to stop him. That decided, he raced over.

He stood on her porch and checked the street in both directions. A steady drizzle had turned the day gray and dreary. No pedestrian traffic. No suspicious cars. But maybe the rain had sent Thomas back to wherever he was staying. Alex knocked. "Roxy, it's me, Alex."

She answered the door. "Hey." Her tense expression gave way to a slow smile. Not the greeting he'd been expecting considering how she'd sounded on the phone. Then she pointed at his feet. "You forgot to put shoes on."

He glanced down before answering her. "So I did. Is that a problem?"

She shook her head and stepped back so he could enter. "No, I think it's very sweet that you were in that big of a rush to get over here."

"You sounded worried." And he was grateful that she'd called him. That he was who she'd chosen to reach out to when she needed to feel safe. Sure, he was a cop, she didn't know that many people in town, *and* he lived next door, but he was still glad he was the one she'd turned to.

"I am a little worried." She sighed as she closed the door. "Actually, I'm not freaking out as much as I was before. I don't think I'm in danger, but I'm really ticked off. I just want Thomas to sign the stupid papers and disappear from my life."

"What exactly happened at the spa?" She smelled great and looked...glowy. Must have been the spa treatments.

"When I got out to my car, he'd written on the dirt on the rear window. It said, 'Have fun?' like he knew I'd been in there."

"Did you take a picture to document it?"

She frowned. "No, I didn't even think about that. I just drove straight home. The rain washed it off."

He studied her. "You said you don't think you're in danger, but how can you be sure? He's obviously trying to rattle you. And if he doesn't get what he wants soon, which I assume is for you to retract the divorce, he could escalate." Alex hoped that was all Thomas wanted and not something more sinister.

She wrapped her arms around her torso and took a long moment before answering, her eyes losing some of their sparkle. "His temper can be scary."

Alex took a breath, wishing he didn't have to ask her the hard questions, but he needed to know what they were dealing with. "Did he ever hit you while you were married?"

"No." She bit at the inside of her cheek. "But he put holes in walls. Threw a few things. Raised his voice a lot." She shrugged. "I think he's capable of it."

He reached for his cell phone, then realized he'd left it on the night stand. He started to move toward the phone in the kitchen. "I'm calling the station."

She put her hand on his arm, stopping him. "Please don't. If the police get involved—I mean, I know you're a cop, but the more complicated this gets... I just don't want to give him any more reason to keep sitting on those unsigned papers."

"You need an RO."

"A what? Oh, restraining order?"

"Yes."

"He hasn't really done anything, though."

Alex gave her a stern look. "And it needs to stay that way."

"I'll think about it. It's not like I could get one today anyway."

"You might. I could try to move things along. Plus, you're a friend of Delaney's, and the Ellinghams can make things happen."

She shook her head. "I don't want to ask her

husband for a favor like that. Not yet. Not unless I really need it."

He could have argued that point, but he also understood. He wasn't someone who liked to be indebted to anyone either. "Okay, but you do need some kind of protection until we know for sure what's going on."

"What kind of protection?"

He put his hands in his pockets, the tile floor of her kitchen cool under his bare feet. "Me."

Her brows lifted slightly, as did the corners of her mouth. "My own personal police force, huh?"

He nodded. "Something like that."

"Okay, I'm game. What's the plan?"

He took a breath. "First, I'm going back to my place. If Thomas is watching you, I want it to look like I was here and left. I'll return to my house, gather a few things, then cross over from my backyard into yours. You can let me in through the slider."

Her eyes narrowed. "There's no gate in the fence between your yard and mine. And that fence is at least six feet tall. You plan on getting a ladder out?"

"Something like that." Actually, he planned on jumping it. "Just be ready to let me in."

"Got it. Then what?"

"Then we wait until dark, see if anything else happens. I hope not, but it would be nice if this came to a head sooner rather than later. If it doesn't, I'm going to do some more investigating, see if I can figure out where he's watching from, that sort of thing." He also needed to check in with Birdie and Jenna again.

She bit at her cheek again. Like she was still worried.

"Hey, nothing's going to happen to you. I'm not going to leave you alone until this is sorted out. When I'm not here, I'll have another deputy on watch outside. But mostly, it'll be me. Right here with you."

She nodded, then lifted her head to look at him. "You're going to stay here all night?"

He tipped his head toward the couch. "That's why I'm coming back with a few things. I plan on staying in the house. On that couch. So long as that's cool with you."

She stared at the couch and let out a breath as her shoulders relaxed. She'd been more worried than she'd wanted to let on, that was obvious. "Yeah, that's totally cool with me."

He cupped her elbows and smiled at her. "Nothing's going to happen to you. Nothing. Think of me as your own personal Wolfgang Blackborne."

Her little half smile wasn't that convincing as she muttered, "Thanks. If only you *could* change into a big scary wolf."

He laughed. If only she knew. "I'm glad you think so highly of my ability to keep you safe."

Her smile turned genuine. "No, no, I know you're good at what you do and all that. I just…Thomas can be sort of be a bull dog about stuff like this."

He gave her a wink. "Then maybe it's time he was neutered."

In the twenty minutes that Alex was gone, Roxy checked out her front windows twice, sent a quick email to her assistant, and opened a bottle of wine. Because if she was going to be a prisoner in her house, she was going to enjoy it.

Which was how she finished the first glass before Alex got back. She stood at the sliding door that led into the backyard, glass number two in hand, staring at the fairy house and wondering if her life would ever level out to something normal.

She sipped her wine, then sighed a long, slow breath that fogged the glass in front of her. She wiped it away with the heel of her palm, clearing the spot in time to see Alex appear in her backyard.

She blinked. It had looked like he'd jumped over the fence, but that wasn't physically possible. He must have pulled a ladder up to his side and jumped from there. That's all she'd seen.

He strode toward her door, shoes on this time, and a duffel bag in one hand. The litheness of his movement was fascinating.

A little anticipatory shiver ran through her. Deputy Hotness was sleeping on her couch tonight. If that wasn't romance novel inspiration, she didn't know what was.

She unlocked the slider and pulled it back, careful not to spill her wine. "That was fast." Actually it had seemed like forever.

"All quiet?" He walked into the house.

She raised her glass. "All quiet. You want a glass? C'mon, have a drink with me."

He hesitated. "I probably shouldn't, but I guess one small one couldn't hurt."

She smiled, happy that he was joining her. "One it is." Then she frowned as she got a second glass and filled it with wine. "It's okay that I drink, right?"

"It's fine. If it helps you relax, even better." He took the glass, touching it to hers before lifting it. "I don't want you stressing about this anymore than you already have. I'm going to do everything I can to make this problem go away."

His wording made her eyes widen. "You're not going to...kill him, are you?"

He choked on air. "No. Why on earth would you think that?"

She shrugged. "I'm a writer. Worst-case scenario is kind of my wheelhouse."

"Okay, well, great, but no one is killing anybody. All we want to do is catch him in the act of trespassing or something else that's an arrestable offense. Once we get him in front of a judge, it'll be a lot easier to nip this behavior in the bud. Are we clear on that?" He drank the wine while watching her.

"Yep. Totally clear." She set her glass on the counter. "Let me go get you a pillow and blanket while I'm thinking about it. Be right back."

She left him in the kitchen and went down the hall to the linen closet next to the guest bath. The wine was kicking in a little. She could feel it. But it was also taking the edge off her nerves. She resolved right then not to let alcohol influence her evening with Alex.

Which wasn't really an evening or a date or anything. It was just him watching over her in case Thomas tried something else. Just a friend taking care of another friend.

She pulled out a blanket and pillow, hugged them to her chest and smiled. She'd never really had a friend like that before. Not in New Jersey anyway. Now she had Alex. And Delaney, who she was sure would have gotten her husband to do whatever Roxy had needed, if Roxy had asked.

Despite the nonsense Thomas was putting her through, Roxy had never felt safer. Or more cared for.

Moving to Nocturne Falls had definitely been the right decision.

Alex was closing the front blinds when she walked out to the living room. She set the blanket and pillow on the chair next to the sofa. "So what's the game plan? You said you were going to do some investigating?"

He shut the last set of blinds. "Yes, but not until after dark, so it'll be a few hours."

She glanced at the clock on the cable box. It wasn't even five o'clock yet. "We could...watch a movie. Or something."

"Don't let me interrupt your day. If you need to write or work in your office, go for it. I don't need to be entertained."

That might be, but right now, having a real live man in her house was a lot more interesting than the made-up one waiting for her in the book she was supposed to be writing. "Okay. Hey, you want to see my fish tank?"

He smiled. "Sure."

"It's in my office."

He followed her back. The moment he laid eyes on it, he let out a soft, "Wow. When you said fish tank, I was thinking something a lot smaller. That's your whole wall."

She grinned. "Cool, right?"

"Definitely." His gaze trailed the wrasses. "Very cool." He took a few steps closer, his eyes never leaving the tank.

She pulled her desk chair around. "Sit."

He did, staring into the tank like it held the wonders of the universe. She knew the feeling. She sat on the edge of the desk, enjoying his rapt attention and feeling like he'd just become a kindred spirit. "I love fish."

He nodded slowly. "Me, too."

"Very peaceful."

More nodding. He leaned forward in the chair. "Um-hmm."

She shifted her gaze to the tank then and focused on his handsome reflection. A trick of the water playing behind his image made it seem like gold light gleamed in his eyes. She'd seen that before. In the hot tub. Maybe it wasn't a trick of the water. She glanced at him. The light was still there.

He caught her looking at him and blinked. The light was gone. He stood up. "That's some tank. Can't wait to see it when it's fully stocked."

She stared at him. Was it possible that a person's eyes could reflect light like an animal's? Sure. If she was hallucinating again, anything was possible. She looked away. Was this what it had been like for her mother when she'd first begun her descent into madness? "I'll, uh, let you know."

His butt made a buzzing sound. He reached back and pulled his phone out of his pocket and checked the screen. "I need to take this. I'll leave you alone so you can write."

She just nodded.

He walked back to the living room. "What did you find out?"

She closed her office door and wheeled her chair back in front of her desk, then sat down. She'd been stressed before. Like the time the wrong file had gotten uploaded and her readers were almost sent the keynote speech she'd written for a writers' conference instead of book three in the Blood Moon Brotherhood series. Or the time her first editor had quit the business a week before Roxy had expected her to get edits from the woman.

But she'd never had hallucinations before. Never. And if she was really honest and stopped pretending she didn't know what she was seeing, well, then, the truth was she felt like her writing world and her real world were melting into each other.

How else could she explain seeing fangs and gills and gleaming eyes on people?

This wasn't stress. It was stage one of her losing her mind. She'd never considered herself anywhere close to being like any of the great creative geniuses of the world, but it wasn't unheard of for people in the arts to go mad.

Or people with a history of mental illness in their families.

And Roxy was both.

Her writing career would be over. Medications might take the edge off her storytelling abilities. She could lose her creative edge. Or her drive to write. If there were even drugs that could help. After all, nothing had made her mother better.

What if she lost the ability to write altogether?

She pressed a hand to her head and wondered if maybe the favor she needed to ask of Delaney and her husband was to recommend a really good therapist.

Her laptop was open on her desk. She swiped her finger over the touch pad, bringing the screen to life.

Her Word document appeared before her. There wasn't much choice now, it seemed, except to finish the book as quickly as she could and wrap up the series so that her fans would have the closure they needed before she got carted off to an institution.

Like mother, like daughter.

Then her gaze moved to the closed office door and her thoughts turned to the man beyond that door. She couldn't tell him about this, could she?

No, that would be a new level of weird. At least at this stage in their friendship. But she would tell him eventually. As for tonight, maybe...maybe she should forget work for the day and enjoy one last sane evening while that was still possible.

She stood, staring at the closed door, trying to make a decision. Alex or work?

She almost laughed.

That wasn't really a hard choice to make at all. She needed to live now, before her life was nothing more than four padded walls and a locked door.

15

Alex looked up from his seat on the couch as Roxy walked out from her office. He'd just hung up with Jenna who'd given him her report and Birdie's, who'd turned out to be as good a resource as he'd hoped, even if he hadn't gotten the answer he'd expected. "You're not going to believe this."

"You'd be surprised what I'd believe."

Her response caught him off-guard for a moment, then he shook it off. "The only record your ex has is a couple of tickets. And none of my sources have been able to track him down in town. And they were very thorough."

She put her hands on the back of the couch and leaned against it as she took the news in. "So what does that mean?"

"It means a few things. He's either staying here under an assumed name, or staying outside of town. Both are possibilities, so we're working those angles to see what we come up with. But we also have to consider that he could be paying someone to do his dirty work. Or that it might not be Thomas at all."

"Who's we exactly?"

He lifted his phone. "I have some help at the department."

"That's very nice of them." She sighed. "If it's not Thomas, I don't know who it is. And if it is Thomas, then he's probably using a fake name and thinks he's being all sly and smart."

"Any idea what that name might be?"

"He's a big Jets fan. Maybe he'd use the name of one of the players? I don't know."

Alex nodded. "That's a good place to start." He sent that info in a quick text to Jenna. "Maybe that'll turn something up."

"I hope so."

He put his phone on the coffee table. "Aren't you supposed to be working?"

"Yes." She smiled. "But my head's not in it."

Something did seem a little odd with her, but if Thomas had done something else, she'd have told him. "So what do you want to do?"

"I'm going to fix an early dinner, then maybe you want to watch a movie with me? You've got time before it gets dark, and I'm so behind on new releases that I'd be happy to watch just about anything. You game?"

To spend more time with her? Absolutely. "Sure. But I didn't intend to distract you from your work or for you to have to feed me."

"You're not distracting me." She laughed as she headed for the kitchen. "And I love how you think that dinner's for you."

He grinned at her teasing. "Hey, if you don't want to share, that's fine. I'll just keep the flan to myself."

She stopped and turned around to look at him. "What flan?"

"The flan I made a couple days ago. I brought it over in my bag and stuck it in your fridge. Shame to let it go to waste."

She went in and opened the fridge. "Wow, you really did bring flan." She glanced over at him. "You *made* this?"

"What? You think a guy can't cook?"

She pulled a few things out, then shut the fridge door. "Cook, sure, but flan is sort of…I don't know, that's not beginner stuff."

He got off the couch and joined her in the kitchen. "My mother wanted my brother and me to know how to feed ourselves. I took to it more than he did."

"Clearly."

He leaned on the counter. "So what's for dinner?"

"Shrimp scampi. You cool with that?"

"Oh, yeah. I love seafood. Can I help?"

She hesitated. "Yeah?"

He nodded. "Yeah."

A few minutes later he had a chef's knife in his hand and tasks assigned. He started chopping the garlic and shallots first, reserving the parsley for last since it was more of a garnish. He loved cooking, he loved hanging out with Roxy and he couldn't think of a time he'd been happier. If not for the shadow of her ex hanging over them, the evening would have been perfect. "You sure you don't want me to devein the shrimp too?"

"Nope." She filled a big pot with water for the pasta. "I have to do something or you'll basically be making dinner by yourself."

He smiled as he worked. "I'd be okay with that. You could go get some writing done if you want. I can call you when it's ready."

She put the pot on the stove, then sidled up to him. Her hip against his. "Are you trying to kick me out of my own kitchen?"

He let the knife rest to answer her. "Not at all. Just trying to give you some time to work if you want it." The urge to kiss her rose up within him. She was only inches away. He could just lean down and—he took a breath and forced the thought away. "I mean, my mother *is* waiting for that book."

She laughed.

Then he quickly added. "But I also think she could learn some patience. So…stay."

Her smile softened and the look in her eyes went oddly unreadable. She pivoted away, leaving him to wonder what he'd said that had changed the mood so suddenly. "I should make a salad."

"Only if you want it."

"Yeah, I remember. The Cruz men don't eat salad."

He turned as she went back to the fridge. He couldn't let go of the thought that he'd upset her. "What just happened? We were having a nice moment, then I asked you to stay. Was that too forward of me? Tell me, because I don't understand it and I want to."

She straightened, a head of lettuce in her hands, but she didn't look at him. "I like you, Alex. A lot. You're so different from what I've been used to for so long. I had no idea how much that difference could mean to me. But…"

She shut the fridge, walked to the counter next to him and put the lettuce down. She stared at it for a long time without saying anything.

He went back to chopping shallots, slowly this time, letting her have all the space she needed. Something was obviously weighing on her thoughts. Whether she shared what it was or not was up to her.

"I think I'm losing my mind," she whispered.

He almost laughed, thinking she was making a joke, but the seriousness of her tone stopped him.

He quit chopping. "What makes you think that?"

She laughed nervously and started unwrapping the lettuce. "Creative types are prone to mental stress more than most people, I think. Depression especially. And my mom had some issues with schizophrenia. And I guess that's what's starting to happen to me. I'm just...losing my grip on reality a bit."

"But what, specifically, makes you think that?"

"I've been seeing some things—"

He released the knife to cup her face and gaze into her eyes. He hoped the truth of what he couldn't say came through. "You are *not* losing your mind, Roxy. I swear you're not. Trust me on this."

His heart ached for what she was going through. She must have stopped drinking the town water and was getting glimpses of the local supernaturals again. He wished he could tell her the truth, but he'd promised Delaney he wouldn't. Damn it. He needed to tell Delaney that the time for keeping secrets was over, no matter what she thought Roxy could or couldn't handle.

"How can you be so sure?" she asked. "You barely know me."

He dropped his hands from her face. "I do know you. You're not crazy. I just... I wish there was something I could do to help."

"Just listening is good." The lettuce sat between Roxy's hands, which were now flat on the counter.

"And I wasn't going to tell you, but I like you and I sort of had an epiphany while I was in my office earlier that I shouldn't say no to something that might not be available to me in the future. Carpe diem and all that."

He leaned on the counter. "Are you saying what I think you're saying? I hate to sound full of myself, but is this about me?"

She finally looked at him. "Yes. Well, it's about us." She closed her eyes for a moment and took a breath, like she was steeling herself to say something difficult. "I am so attracted to you that just thinking about you makes parts of me ache. I love your company. You make me happy, as silly as that sounds considering we've only known each other a few days."

Her cheeks went the most adorable shade of pink. "I have never said anything like that to a man. Ever. But if I'm going crazy, I want to enjoy all the sane days I have left. With you. If you're willing. Or interested. Or not afraid to catch whatever crazy I have."

A shot of hot, pure electricity zipped through Alex, filling him with the unquestionable sensation that this woman was absolutely, one hundred percent meant for him. His soul mate. It was that fast and that complete. He just knew. Shifter or not, she was his.

"It's not silly and you're not crazy." He wiped

his hands on his jeans, then threaded his fingers through her hair and kissed her. Hard.

She seemed to exhale into him. As if all the tension that had built up inside of her while she was spilling her heart was now gone, released by his response. Then she kissed him back.

For the next few moments, they were lost to that heated contact, their need for each other overriding all else. Until the pot on the stove boiled over and pulled them apart.

She turned the burner down, then looked at him, her chest rising and falling with the intensity of the kiss they'd just shared. Her eyes were full of light and happiness. "That was a yes, right?"

"That was a hell yes. But you have to know something about me."

"What?"

"I'm sensing that you want—or expect—a temporary kind of arrangement. Something with an expiration date. That's not happening. I'm not that kind of guy. Either we do this with the full understanding that it could be forever or we don't do it at all."

"But I could be in an institution next month."

"Well, that sounds like a wild exaggeration, but as long as I know the address and what visiting hours are, I'm in."

Her eyes narrowed. "You might be the crazy one."

"I might be." He crossed his arms. "But those are my terms. All or nothing."

"I'm not divorced yet—"

"You will be."

"So I was going to say, we can't go public with this until that's finalized."

"I'm good with that. Does that mean you agree to what I said?"

"All or nothing, huh?"

He nodded.

She nodded tentatively. "But what if I get overwhelmed, or can't handle being in another relationship so soon, or—"

"We'll figure it out. We'll slow down or back off or whatever, but if we're meant to be, I don't think either one of us will feel that way."

"I haven't had a reason to believe in soul mates, you know."

He shrugged. "I know. But maybe I can change that."

Her tentativeness gave way to a bright, beaming smile that matched the look in her eyes. "So yeah, I guess we're doing this." She pointed at him. "I'm big on honesty and being upfront and just putting everything out there. I don't want to have to guess what you're feeling or try to figure out if you're happy or if you're not or any of that. I had too much nonsense like that the first go-round. I'm not doing it again."

"I wouldn't have it any other way." Which meant talking to Delaney just got moved up on Alex's list of priorities.

All the way to number one.

Roxy floated through dinner. Alex had responded so much better to her heartfelt declaration that the thought she might be losing her marbles no longer put her in such a state of panic.

Granted, she hadn't figured on him wanting a full-blown relationship, but he'd said all the right things and her reservations had disappeared. Plus, he seemed so willing to let her dictate the speed and intensity of the relationship. How could she not want that? She'd never been in the driver's seat with Thomas. She couldn't miss the chance to try it now, especially with a guy like Alex.

A smokin' hot guy like Alex. It really was like he'd stepped off one of her book covers.

"You're staring."

"Hmm?" She realized he'd said something and she'd been miles away. Thinking about him, but still miles away.

"Do I have parsley in my teeth or something?"

"No, I was just...taking it all in." She laughed, the giggly nervousness of desire and possibility and this new infatuation making it impossible not to.

He grinned. "It?"

"You." She pushed her linguine around on her plate. "You know what I mean."

He put his fork down and sat back. "No, tell me. You're a writer. Use your words. Tell me exactly what you mean."

"Oh, is that how it's going to be? A challenge?"

"You're the one who said you believe in putting it all out there."

"That I did. Okay, then." She'd already stripped her soul bare in front of him once. She was willing to do it again. "What I mean is that I am sitting here reveling in how unbelievably sexy you are. How amazing you are inside and out. And I'm in awe of how the last four abysmal years of my life have led me to a man who could easily have any woman he wanted, and yet, he wants me."

Alex nodded. "True statement. I do want you."

She grinned. "That works out then, because I've also been contemplating how best to make up for lost time."

"Meaning?"

She stared at him. "Meaning all the years I went without. Attention, affection, companionship. *Sex*."

He swallowed, and she thought she saw a hint of color cross his cheeks. "Okay, definitely getting the picture."

She shifted in her chair. "In fact, I was thinking about all the sex scenes I've written over the years. About how I don't even really know if all of them are possible. Like, there's one that takes place in a shed."

His brows lifted, and he nodded. "Or the one on the motorcycle."

Her mouth opened. "That scene doesn't come until almost the end of the first book. Did you really read that far?"

He shrugged. "I read the whole thing. Couldn't put it down, actually."

She shook her head in disbelief. Thomas had never even shown the slightest bit of interest in her work, except to mock the very idea that anyone would want to read about romance. But Alex had read one of her books without her saying anything about it. She'd never felt such utter amazement in her life. Or desire.

She stood up, willing that intense feeling to power her through the next bold move. "Dinner is over. Dessert is being served. In the bedroom. If you're interested. Which I'm hoping you are. The flan we can have later. We'll probably need some sugar to fuel the rest of the evening."

His eyes flashed gold, but she was too happy to care that the crazy had returned. He jumped up and grabbed her hand. "Yes, I'm interested— actually, *interested* isn't a strong enough word, but there are two reasons this isn't going to happen tonight."

She frowned, knowing she looked disappointed, but she'd already told him this was going to be all about honesty. "Which are?"

"One, it's dark now and my first concern is keeping you safe. Which means checking in with my friends who are helping me and heading out to make sure your ex isn't lurking somewhere, plotting to do you harm. Your safety takes precedence. Which is why there will be another deputy parked outside, watching your place while I'm gone."

She nodded reluctantly. "Okay, I understand all that. And thank you. What's the second reason?"

He grabbed her hips and pulled her against him, his eyes blazing as he peered into hers. "I believe in foreplay. Physical and mental, and right now, you're running on impulse, which I appreciate, but waiting a little longer will be worth it. I promise. I want our first night together to be perfect."

She liked the sound of that.

He glanced at the table. "And maybe not after we've both just had large quantities of garlic, either."

She laughed and slid her hands up his chest. "Okay, those are good reasons. How long are you going to make me wait?"

He leaned down and nuzzled her neck, making

her sigh and shiver at the same time. Her pulse kicked up. She was already anticipating what was to come. If only Thomas wasn't out there and Alex didn't have to go look for him.

His hot breath tickled her skin as he answered. "Until you think you can't wait another second."

His teeth scraped her throat. "And then, one second more."

"Coffee? Cookies?" Delaney asked. "I have some salted butterscotch blondies too, if you want one of those."

"No, thanks. I just ate." Alex stood in her kitchen, thankful that Delaney had agreed to see him on such short notice at her home. He'd called as soon as Deputy Lafitte had shown up at Roxy's. Then Alex had driven straight here with the hopes of this being a quick trip. He had no desire to be away from her any longer than necessary.

Delaney took a few sugar cookies out of a jar on the counter, put them on a small plate, then sat at the kitchen table. "You said you wanted to talk about Roxy. What's going on?"

He shook his head. "She's still seeing things she shouldn't. I'm sure of it. For whatever reason, the magic in the water isn't having any effect on her."

Delaney broke one of the cookies in half and

took a bite. She swallowed before she answered. "That shouldn't be."

"But it is. So someone has to tell her the truth. She thinks she's going crazy. Actually losing her mind. Did you know her mother had some issues with schizophrenia?"

Delaney stared at the plate. "Yes. She told me about that when we were in college. Very sad."

"Then you can understand how this can't go on any longer."

"Oh no. Of course not." Delaney put the remains of the cookie down. "That's not good at all. She doesn't need to think she's going mad in addition to all the stress of this stupid divorce. But with her mother's history, you can see why I'm hesitant to add any more stress to that load."

"I get that, but listen, her ex is playing games. Sending her notes, leaving messages on her car, and generally freaking her out."

"What?" Delaney's eyes flashed with indignation, and she snarled, baring her fangs. "That lowlife piece of—are you doing anything about this?"

"I am. I've made the other deputies aware, in fact, one of them is sitting outside her place right now keeping watch while I'm gone, and we've been actively searching for him in town. Nothing yet, but we'll find him. I also plan to stay at her place tonight and I hope to lay hands on the man."

"Are you also going to put a little supernatural fear into him?"

Alex nodded. "When I'm done with him, he'll be begging to sign those divorce papers and leave Roxy alone. Hell, I doubt he'll ever step foot in Nocturne Falls again."

"Good."

"So then we tell Roxy."

Delaney pushed the remains of the cookies around on her plate, her expression tortured. "I just... I don't know how to tell her. I always pictured doing it over a girls' night, after a couple of drinks and when the mood was just right. But thanks to my pregnancy, that hasn't happened. Now there's all this stuff with her ex going on and I worry that I could be telling her something that could do more damage than good."

"She writes paranormal romance for a living. She'll probably handle it better than you think."

"But in her current state of mind?"

"I think she would find it a great relief to know she's not actually having a break with reality."

"Yes, you're right." Delaney tipped her head. "Do you think her job is why the magic in the water isn't working on her? She's already so connected to the supernatural. She writes about it, so she must think about it all the time. Maybe her subconscious already knows better and just won't let the magic take root."

"Is that possible?"

She shrugged. "I'd have to ask Alice Bishop. It's her spell, after all."

Alex thought for a moment. "You've known Roxy a long time. Any chance she has a little supernatural blood in her? That could keep the magic from working, right?"

"It absolutely could. But whether or not her background includes supernatural bloodlines is beyond me. Remember, I was as human as she is when we first met. And if she does have some supernatural heritage, it's so small that neither Hugh nor I have picked up on it."

"Did I hear my name?" Hugh Ellingham walked in, a newspaper under one arm. "Hello, Deputy." His brows lifted. "Everything all right?"

"Everything's fine. I'm not here on official business."

Delaney stood and kissed her husband on the cheek. "He's here about Roxy."

Hugh nodded and slid his arm around Delaney's waist, but his concern remained. "She's not in any trouble, is she?"

Alex frowned. "Her ex is giving her some grief, but I'm on top of it."

Hugh's expression shifted to confusion. "Is there something we can do to help with that? Because we will. Just say the word."

Alex looked at Delaney. He didn't know what

she'd told Hugh and what she hadn't. "That's not really why I'm here. But if things escalate, I may take you up on that."

Delaney sighed. "He's here because he wants to let Roxy in on the truth about Nocturne Falls. The magic in the water isn't hiding the supernatural from her, and according to Deputy Cruz, she thinks she's going crazy because of the things she's seeing."

Hugh's brows knit. "Then by all means, tell her." He shook his head. "I said you should have told her when she first moved here."

She barked out a laugh. "You remember how I reacted when I found out you were a vampire?"

He leaned back. "Very well. You climbed out of a second-story window with your cat in a backpack in the middle of the night and took off." He snorted. "I had to follow you through the woods and convince you that I was telling the truth."

"Exactly. So can you imagine how Roxy will react on top of the stress of her looming deadline and going through this awful divorce? I just don't want to push her over the edge."

Alex cleared his throat softly. "Not telling her is already pushing her over the edge."

"And it's my fault." Delaney put a hand on her belly. "Again, you're right. I need to tell her. I think this pregnancy is scrambling my brain a bit. As much as I'd rather put it off until morning, it needs to be done tonight, doesn't it?"

Alex didn't hesitate. "Yes. I can't keep withholding the truth from her. We like each other, and that's just not a good way to start any kind of relationship."

Hugh nodded. "I agree. And not just for that reason." He looked at Delaney. "I'm sure you're tired, my darling, but your friend obviously needs to understand what's happening around here as soon as possible."

Delaney nodded. "She does. And I think Alex needs to go with me. She obviously trusts him and that way, if she runs off like I did, he can go after her. Are you good with that, Deputy?"

"Absolutely," Alex said. That was exactly what he wanted. "It'll be easier to show her that what we're talking about is real if she sees two of us for what we truly are. And if she runs, which I don't think she will, I'll definitely go after her."

Delaney narrowed her eyes a little. "You think she's going to be okay with this?"

"I keep coming back to what she writes about. Based on those books, I think she could be very receptive to it."

"I hope you're right." She hoisted herself out of the chair. "Fudge balls. I get any bigger and I won't fit behind the steering wheel."

"I can drive if you like," Alex offered.

"No, I can manage. I'm going to swing by the shop and pack up a big bag of Roxy's favorites.

Might help things go down a little better. I'll be there as soon as I can. Half an hour, tops."

Relief washed through Alex. Finally Roxy would know the truth and have peace about what was happening. "I'll see you at her house then. Thank you. Evening, Hugh."

Hugh nodded. "Deputy."

Alex texted Roxy that he was on his way back, and by the time he turned into their neighborhood, he'd pretty much planned what he was going to say. Of course, he'd let Delaney go first, so he realized he might have to modify his words a bit, but that was okay.

There would be no more secrets between them after this evening.

Since he had time before Delaney arrived, and Deputy Lafitte was parked outside of Roxy's house on watch, Alex decided to do a quick drive through the streets around her place.

There wasn't much to see. Pandora Williams's house was dark except for the landscaping lighting. She spent a lot of time at her boyfriend's house these days. The Dravens were away on a tour of Scotland. Freda Stover was visiting her sister in Florida. As he drove around, he realized there were a number of vacant houses Thomas could be hiding out in.

He parked on a side street a few blocks away and sent a text to Lafitte that he was back and

Lafitte was free to return to his shift duties. Alex appreciated the man's help, but he also knew this wasn't officially sheriff business yet. That done, he headed on foot toward Roxy's. He cut through yards and down driveways, keeping to the shadows and using his feline shifter senses to be as quiet as possible and hear every little thing.

Then a familiar scent and the crack of a twig brought him to a full stop at the corner of the Goldburgs'. Their yard wasn't fenced and sat behind his and to the left of Roxy's, meaning the top story of the playhouse in her backyard blocked most of his view of her property.

He leaned against the Goldburgs' house, hidden by a trellis of bougainvillea. His night vision was excellent, so even through the deep shadows he could do more than just pick out shapes and forms.

A figure lurked at the edge of Roxy's fence. A man, by the shape and size. Maybe five-ten, a hundred and seventy-five pounds.

Alex shifted into his half-form and inhaled, mouth open, so he could get a better read on the stranger's scent. Definitely human.

The man rounded the corner of the fence, heading for the front of Roxy's house via the Hadads' side yard. Alex trailed him with the deep quiet only a big cat shifter could manage. He'd gotten to within inches of a perp before without being detected. This guy hadn't hesitated or glanced over his shoulder once. He was making it easy.

He went around the fence and into the front yard. Alex stayed back, watching to see what the guy was going to do. He had some kind of package in his hands. A small box.

Alex inhaled again but smelled nothing suspicious.

The man stopped, his gaze seemingly on the front porch.

Alex moved behind him, repositioning himself in the shadow of a big oak on the Hadads' property.

The guy looked around as he moved toward the gate that led into the backyard. He lifted the locking mechanism slowly, eased the gate open and slipped through, shutting the gate behind him just as carefully.

Alex made his way to the gate, listening closely. The man sounded like he'd moved a few feet away. What was his plan? To leave that package on Roxy's back porch? Then what?

Then Alex heard footsteps on wood. That's exactly what the man was doing—walking up the porch steps.

This had to stop now. Anger wound around Alex's spine, and he decided the best way to get rid of this creep was exactly as planned. Put a little supernatural fear into him. Alex, still in his half-form, leaped over the fence.

He landed on all fours and almost shifted into his full panther form, but he wanted to talk to this guy.

The man was on the porch, bending down in front of the sliders.

Alex lunged, knocking the guy off the deck and into the grass. He landed on his stomach. Alex put a knee on his back, then bent to snarl in his ear, a deep menacing sound that had caused many a tough guy to cringe in fear.

The man stiffened at the sound and stopped struggling. Alex straightened slightly as he heard a car pull up to the front of the house. Delaney had arrived. This business needed to come to a close.

He bent toward the man's ear again. "You're done here, you understand? Done. No more notes. No more roses. No more anything. Sign the papers and leave Roxy the hell alone."

"I-I don't know what you're talking about."

"Liar." Alex let a growl spill from his throat. Time to flip Thomas over and show him exactly who he was dealing with.

Suddenly, the slider and the curtain covering it opened, spilling light into the backyard. "Alex?"

He turned, realizing at the last moment what he looked like. He shifted immediately back into his full human form, but it was too late.

Fear masked Roxy's face. Delaney stood behind

her, looking slightly horrified. Roxy put a hand to her throat. "What…"

Alex stood. "I can explain."

Freed, Thomas scrambled to his feet and took off. Alex glanced after him, but let him go. The man wasn't likely to be much of a threat now, and the woman in front of him was more important. "Roxy, listen—"

"What was that? What *were* you?"

Delaney put her hand on Roxy's shoulder. "We should all sit down and have a talk."

Alex walked onto the porch, stopping to pick up the box Thomas had left behind. "That's a good idea." Although an already difficult conversation had just gotten harder.

Roxy looked at her. "*All* of us? Do you know about this? About him?"

Delaney glanced at Alex, then answered Roxy. "Yes. And it's because of me that we haven't told you yet."

"Told me what?" Roxy looked at both of them, backing away toward the kitchen.

"We're supernaturals." Delaney frowned, then let out a long sigh. "I'm a vampire." She pointed at her teeth, her fangs on full display and gleaming in the kitchen light. "See?"

Roxy stared at her, blank-faced. Her numb expression didn't change as she looked at Alex. "You too?"

He shook his head. "I'm not a vampire, but I am a supernatural. A panther shifter. What you saw just now was me in my half form."

Roxy nodded like he'd just said there'd be rain tomorrow. She put her hand out to grab hold of the kitchen counter, but she was a few inches shy of making contact. Her knees buckled, and she went down.

"Son of a—" Alex threw the box toward the table and caught her before she hit the floor. He cradled her in his arms and shot Delaney an unhappy look that did nothing to adequately convey what he was feeling. This had become exactly the kind of mess he'd wanted to avoid.

Delaney put her hand on her stomach and grimaced. "Go ahead. Say I told you so."

"You already did."

Roxy woke from the craziest dream she'd ever had—and that was saying something for her. *Active imagination* did not begin to describe her brain when it came to dreams. And if the schizophrenia was actually kicking in, there was no telling what her mind might come up with. She stretched and pushed up to her elbows. She didn't feel that rested. What time was it? She glanced over at the clock.

A little after ten at night. She sat up some more

and realized that although she was on her bed, she wasn't under the covers and she was still fully dressed.

She sucked in a shuddering breath, and her gut went cold as she remembered her dream had not been a dream at all.

Alex and Delaney had told her they were supernatural creatures. A were-panther and a vampire. Had that been real? Or had her hallucinations taken a sharp turn for the worst?

She had no idea, but the sick feeling in her stomach wasn't going to go away without some kind of closure. Soft voices reached her from the living room. Delaney and Alex were still here. That was good, right? She could at least go out there and find out what was truth and what was fiction.

At the very least, she'd had some kind of episode and fainted. Then one of them had carried her into her room. Had to be Alex. She couldn't see pregnant Delaney doing that.

She flipped the light on, went into the bathroom, and splashed some water on her face. She stared at herself for a few minutes in the mirror, trying to make sense of all the games her brain was playing on her, but couldn't. She finally walked out to the living room.

Delaney was on the couch. Alex was pacing between the dining room and the kitchen. Both of them froze and turned toward her.

Alex looked awful. Like he'd just found out someone had died. He raked a hand through his hair. "How are you feeling?"

Roxy took a breath. "Not really myself." She went into the kitchen and got a bottle of water out of the fridge. Making eye contact with either of them was proving harder than anticipated. "What happened? Did I faint?"

"Yes," Delaney said. The mellowness of relief filled her voice. "We were telling you about who we really are and—"

"Crud." Roxy leaned against the sink. She felt like dipping her head under some cold running water, but that would really be odd. She wasn't so far gone that she didn't know that much. "That actually happened. Or this is still one giant hallucination that hasn't ended."

"It's not a hallucination," Alex said.

She looked in his direction. "You're telling me this is real. And what happened before I passed out was real."

"All of it is real. There's nothing wrong with you."

She twisted the top off the bottle and took a long drink. The water helped. A little. Maybe this called for something stronger, but she didn't have any hard alcohol in the house. She carried the bottle over to the chair next to the couch and sat down so she could face Delaney. "You're a vampire."

Delaney nodded.

Roxy pointed back at Alex. "And he's a were-cat."

"Panther shifter," Alex corrected. "And yes, I am."

"Your brother too, I suppose."

"My entire family."

Of course they were. She put her water on the coffee table and spoke to Delaney. "And I guess Hugh knows you're a vampire and he's okay with that."

"He's a vampire too. He's the one who turned me."

Naturally. Roxy stared at her. Then burst into laughter. "Okay, you got me. Great joke on the paranormal romance author."

Delaney didn't smile. Roxy looked back at Alex. No smile there either. Delaney's hand on her knee brought Roxy's attention back around. "It's not a joke."

The cold seeped back into Roxy's gut, and a thin ringing filled her ears. She was either going to faint again or throw up. "I don't believe you," she whispered. "Those creatures in my books are just…make believe."

Delaney shook her head. "No, they're not. We're real. This whole town is filled with them. It's what Nocturne Falls is all about. A haven for super—"

"I need you to leave." Roxy stared at her hands.

Darkness wavered at the edges of her vision. This couldn't be true. Because it just wasn't possible that the two people she considered friends had kept something this big from her for so long. And all the while knowing that she'd started to think she was losing her mind.

Alex walked into her line of sight. She kept her gaze on her hands, unable to look at the man she'd tried to take to bed only a few hours before.

"Please, Roxy. We can talk about this and you'll see—"

"Why didn't you tell me before now?" She stared at Delaney. "You're the one who talked me into moving here. Don't you think Nocturne Falls being a 'supernatural haven' should have been on the list of pros you listed? Or cons... I don't even know right now."

Delaney twisted her hands together. "We don't tell people. It's just not done in most cases. Not that you're most cases, but..." She sighed. "I'm sorry."

Alex moved closer. "I wanted to tell you, but—"

"He did," Delaney cut in. "But I talked him out of it. I didn't want to add to your stress, and I knew about your mom and—"

"You both need to leave." Roxy tried to swallow the bitterness coating her tongue. Her best friend hadn't thought she could handle the truth. That her mental state was so fragile she might have a psychotic break just like her mother if Roxy found out. And that's actually what had almost happened.

What Delaney—and Alex—had almost caused. Because he was just as much a part of this as Delaney was. He could have told Roxy at any time. Like right after she'd agreed to date him so long as they were up front and honest about everything.

So much for that.

"Please," Alex said. "Can't we sit down and start over? Just talk it through? This hasn't gone down at all like we intended."

Roxy choked out a harsh laugh. "It sounds to me like you *intended* to keep me in the dark and let me think I'm losing my freaking mind instead of telling me the truth. Would you have even told me if I hadn't seen you just now?"

He stiffened. "Yes, that's why Delaney came back with me. We discussed it earlier and decided—"

"What?" Roxy glared at him. "You discussed it and decided? So you two, the two people in the world I consider my closest friends, maybe my only friends, are making decisions behind my back about what I can and can't know about my new hometown. And my new boy—"

She cut herself off before the word "boyfriend" left her mouth. She was not calling him that now. She pointed toward the door, on the verge of losing it altogether. "Go."

Delaney stood. "Roxy, please."

"Get out." Roxy whispered the words, then cleared her throat and said them again, louder. "Get out now."

"I'll be right next door if you need me," Alex said.

But she was too numb from betrayal to look at him. The door closed and Roxy was alone again.

So very alone.

Alex checked out Roxy's house as he did every day on his way to work. It had become his routine, the slow roll past. In the last three days, nothing had changed. The blinds stayed closed. The house locked up tight.

There'd been no sign of movement, other than the UPS man bringing packages or food-delivery guys bringing food, and from what he'd seen, all of it got left at the door without waiting for the bell to be answered.

He hadn't seen Roxy in all that time either. Not even just to catch a glimpse of her getting her mail.

He'd reduced his calls and texts to once a day. She wasn't responding. And clearly didn't want to. But at least she'd know he was thinking about her and willing to talk when she was. He hoped she was talking to someone. He knew it wasn't Delaney. She hadn't had any more luck than he had.

Roxy had shut them both out.

He'd left flowers (not roses) at her door the first day. Yesterday, he'd mowed her lawn when he'd gotten home from work.

No response to any of it. There wasn't much else he could do but respect her wishes to be left alone. That didn't keep him from being heartsick over what had happened. Especially because it was his fault. He should have talked Delaney into telling Roxy the truth sooner. Argued Roxy's side of it harder.

Or just ignored Delaney and told Roxy the truth right away, consequences be damned.

Now, he had no idea if he'd ever get the chance to talk to her again. If she had been just a neighbor, he could have lived with it. But she was so much more.

She was the woman he'd realized three days ago was his soul mate, something that had since left him with a raw wound. Because if that's really who Roxy was, why hadn't he done more to protect her from this? Why hadn't he listened to his gut and just told her exactly why she wasn't losing her mind?

His only peace came from knowing that Thomas had been dealt with. At least now Roxy would get her divorce and could do whatever she wanted with her life. Hopefully, she'd be happy. He wanted that much for her.

He turned into the parking lot at the sheriff's department and headed in, hoping work would distract him from everything he was feeling. But despite having a pretty active morning at the station, mostly because of prep for the Panic Parade, his mind returned to Roxy at every opportunity.

And then, just as he was about to head out on patrol (where he would *not* be driving by Roxy's house), his mother called. He braced himself with a deep breath before answering. "Hi, Mom. I'm just about to head out, so if this can wait—"

"No, it can't wait. You live next door to my favorite author and you said nothing to me about this? What is wrong with you? Why are you such a bad son?"

"Whoa, hold up. Who told you—Diego." Alex closed his eyes and tried not to imagine murdering his brother.

"Yes, Diego, because he is a good boy and knows that this is information his mother would be very interested to hear."

Alex rapped his fingers on the desk. "For your information, I didn't tell you because I got her to sign a book for you and I didn't want to ruin the surprise."

A shriek answered him, followed by a barrage of happy Spanish. He grimaced and held the phone away until his mother calmed down. It took a minute. Finally, she spoke to him again. "You are forgiven, my angel. Now *mi hijo*, let me hear all about Miss Roxy St. James. Diego tells me you two are seeing each other, so I have to assume this is the human woman you were telling me about."

"Yes, that's who I was talking about, but I'm at work, Mom. I really can't do this right now. How about I call you later?" Like Christmas.

"Oh no, I'm not going to fall for that. You say you'll call and then you don't. I will call *you* later. And you had better answer."

"I will." He'd never been so happy his parents were in Tallahassee. Although he'd be okay if they were a little farther away than six hours. Say, Miami.

"Very good. I love you. And I am so proud of you! Roxy St. James! She must be the most perfect woman in the world!"

She was. Just not for him. "I love you too."

"Be safe out there today."

"I'm safe every day. Tell Dad I said hi." He hung up, then watched his screen until it went dark and his own image reflected back at him.

And what a picture it was. Alex Cruz. Sheriff's deputy. Supernatural. And persona non grata to the most perfect woman in the world.

By the time he arrived home, he was exhausted from work, from the growing weight of what he'd done to Roxy and just as worn down by the inability to make it better. He got out of his car and stood in his driveway, looking at her house for the longest time. There wasn't anything new or notable about it, and yet he couldn't make himself stop standing there, hoping she'd walk out that front door and tell him all was forgiven.

It was such a nice scenario the way it played out in his head.

The purr of an engine brought him out of his thoughts. He turned to see why the sound was so close and let out a long sigh. His evening wasn't going to get any better, but it was right on course for how his life was going.

The car pulling into his driveway was a shiny red Cadillac. And the woman behind the wheel was his mother. She must have left Tallahassee right after she'd talked to him.

Within an hour of being in his house, Alex's mother had started a load of *his* laundry, made a pitcher of her famous lemonade, filled his freezer with casseroles (out of the first cooler she'd packed), tucked a *tres leches* cake into his fridge (out of the second cooler she'd packed) and was currently making him a dinner of pork loin, rice and beans, and *maduros*.

Unfortunately, he had no appetite. Hadn't had one in days. Three days to be exact. He sat in the living room, staring at a baseball game on the television he didn't really care about, and nursing a beer that was growing warmer by the minute. But the living room was a lot safer than the kitchen, and pretending to relax in front of the ball game was a good excuse not to talk. The other option was studying for the sergeant's exam, but he didn't think he'd be able to concentrate. No, the living room was the best place for him with his mother here.

Because Carmen Cruz was a force of nature. There was no point trying to stop her, whatever she was doing. Best to just get out of her way and hold on for dear life.

He sucked down a slug of the beer.

"You want another one, Alexito?" his mother called from the kitchen. She only called him that when she wanted him to do something for her, or she felt sorry for him. He was pretty sure it was the former right now, but would change to the later once she found out what had happened with Roxy.

Because she *would* find out.

He didn't really want another beer. But he also wouldn't mind numbing himself a little. "Sure."

A minute later, she took the warm one out of his hand and replaced it with a cold one in a Howler's neoprene coozie. Where she'd found that in his kitchen, he had no idea. She must have rummaged around. He didn't care.

"There you go." She stood there a moment. Waiting.

"Thanks."

She didn't move. Obviously, he was missing something. He looked up. "Yes?"

"Why don't you invite your girlfriend over for dinner?"

And there it was. He shifted his gaze back to the game. "I don't think so."

"Why not? Are you ashamed of your mother?"

Scared was more like it. He kept his eyes on the television. "Did you come here to see me or meet your favorite author?"

"Alex, that is no way to speak to your mother. Of course I came here to see you, but it would be nice for your girlfriend to meet me, don't you think?" She put her hands on her hips. "And I'm making all this food so—"

"She's not my girlfriend." Might as well nip this fantasy of hers in the bud. He took a long swallow of the beer. The cold brew slid down his throat but offered no relief to the ache inside him.

"What do you mean she's not? Diego said—"

"Diego has no idea what's going on. I told Roxy the truth about me, and she stopped talking to me. If you want someone to eat all that food, why don't you call Diego and *his* new girlfriend, the barely legal waitress he shacked up with, and see if they'll eat it? His address is on the sticky note on the fridge." Alex put his beer on the side table and stood.

His mother backed up, but the gold fire in her eyes hadn't diminished. Her beast was wound up. "Where are you going?"

"To take a shower." He walked to his bedroom, closed the door and stripped down. A few moments later, he stood under the hot spray, letting the water beat on him and wishing he knew how to fix things between him and Roxy.

Or at least, how to make the pain of losing her go away.

Roxy wasn't sure how many days had passed, but she knew it wasn't enough to put a dent in the pain of betrayal and the awful humiliation she still felt. She couldn't remember a time she'd hurt this much or felt this alone. Even marriage to Thomas hadn't affected her this deeply. After all, she'd known before their first anniversary what a jerk he was. She'd expected the kind of treatment he gave her.

But from Delaney and Alex? She'd been blindsided. She wasn't sure which one of them had surprised her the most. Delaney had a lot to answer for because she was the reason Roxy had moved here. And Alex…she shook her head. They'd just agreed to be completely honest with each other, then she'd tried to seduce him, and he still hadn't said anything about Nocturne Falls being a haven for the paranormal or that he was a were-cat and Delaney was a vampire.

She paused on that thought. Was the paranormal real? Had they been telling her the truth? She was inclined to think they had been. Which was good, because it meant she wasn't going crazy. But it also meant she had a lot to wrap her head around and she wasn't even close to being there yet.

What she had fully arrived at was being a hot mess. She knew that. She sniffed and tucked a few stray curls behind her ear. She'd been in the same pajamas for however long she'd been in the house. Hadn't done a single sun salutation in days. Been living off whatever delivery this town had, which was mostly pizza, subs and Chinese. Fortunately, most of those things qualified as comfort foods. She'd even persuaded the pizza guy (with the promise of a big tip) to swing by the ice cream place and pick up a quart of Triple Chocolate Explosion, which was the most chocolaty ice cream they had, according to their website.

But what was worse than how she looked or the direction her diet had taken was that her book was also a mess. She'd tried to write, but every scene ended up going horribly off the rails as her feelings slipped through. Her tale of undying love between two soul mates had turned into a mish-mash of angry diatribes and bitter betrayal.

It would be career ending to turn something like that over to her readers, so she'd stopped trying. In fact, she was seriously thinking about postponing the book indefinitely. Or maybe writing something completely different. The only bright spot in the last few days had been that her divorce papers had finally arrived. *Signed*.

She was a free woman. Also miserable, friendless and woefully behind on her deadline, but free. Maybe Alex had helped that along by scaring Thomas into it, so she might owe him a little credit there. But not enough to answer his calls or texts.

Not yet.

She opened the fridge, not really hungry so much as looking for a way to distract herself. The pickings were slim. Some old house lo mein, a container of wonton soup, half an Italian cold cut and a box that held a couple slices of veggie pizza. Veggie. Because even miserable, she'd been thinking about her weight. A little.

"You are a sad, screwed-up woman, Roxy St. James."

Too bad she hadn't been thinking about her weight when she'd polished off the flan Alex had brought over, or the large box of truffles Delaney had left behind. Both of which she'd eaten in bed while watching old black-and-white movies.

Why hadn't she been born in the age of old

Hollywood? When times were simpler? She sighed and pulled out the box of pizza. She took out a slice, biting the point off the end. Heating it up took too much effort.

Her doorbell chimed. She had no idea what package this was, but she'd been ordering stuff online constantly in an attempt to never have to leave the house again. Hopefully, this delivery was the thirty-two pack of toilet paper, because that was going to become a necessity pretty soon, and running into Delaney or Alex at the Shop-n-Save wasn't something she wanted to risk. They would want to talk—they'd both been trying repeatedly since she'd made them leave. But she wasn't at the talking stage. And wasn't sure she ever would be.

She shuffled to the door, thankful the UPS man had a drop-and-run policy, and opened it to collect her goods.

A small woman with black hair and a bright, familiar smile stood there, holding a large covered dish. "Hello there."

"Hi." If this was one of her neighbors coming to welcome her to the neighborhood, she really hoped that was a cake under that dome. Cake would be perfect right now. And actually, so would a little company that wasn't Delaney or Alex.

The woman lifted the dish. "I'm Carmen. I thought you might like some *tres leches*. Do you know what that is?"

Roxy almost smiled. Almost. "Oh yeah, I know what *tres leches* is." Her back teeth ached with the thought of all that gooey sweetness, and her soul cried out for the indulgence. She opened the door a little wider. "Come on in. I'm Roxy."

"Nice to meet you, Roxy." The woman's voice had a happy little lilt to it. "Are you sure I'm not interrupting something?"

Roxy glanced down at her pajamas. "No, I, uh…I work from home, so these are sort of my work clothes. I wasn't in bed or anything." Although she could have been.

"I see." Carmen came in. "I understand you just moved in not too long ago?"

"That's right." Roxy closed the door and walked with her to the kitchen, which wasn't too much of a wreck thanks to eating so much takeout. "Do you live on this street?"

Carmen's smile faltered a tiny bit. "I live a little south of you. It's very nice of you to invite me in and also unexpected. If I had known you were going to do that, I would have brought some coffee. But I suppose you have coffee. It's just the thing with *tres leches*."

"I have plenty of coffee. Just the stuff you make in the machine, though. The stuff from the cups. Hard to drink a whole pot when you live alone."

Carmen nodded. "My son got me one of those fancy machines for my birthday last year. He's such a good boy. I haven't figured out how to use it yet."

Roxy laughed for the first time since *that* night. She took two mugs from the cabinet. "It's not hard. Look, I'll show you. You put the mug underneath, put the cup with the coffee in it in this part right here, then close the lid and hit Brew."

Carmen paid close attention, then clapped her hands when the coffee started coming out. "That's so easy! I can do that. You're a good teacher."

"There's nothing to it, really." Roxy handed her the second cup. "You make the next one." While Carmen did that, Roxy got out small plates, two forks and a serving knife.

Coffee made, Carmen uncovered the cake, cut two generous slices and added them to the plates.

Roxy took one and her coffee to the kitchen table. Carmen followed. She sat across from Roxy and they both dug in.

The sugary sweetness caused Roxy's cheeks to ache in the best possible way. The cake was a flavor bomb of pudding-moist milky goodness. "Oh man, that is amazing. You're welcome to bring this cake over anytime."

"I'm so glad you like it." Carmen's smile faded. "I have a confession to make. I never thought you'd invite me in. I was just going to bring you the cake, say hello, maybe talk to you a little, but now…"

Roxy sat up a little straighter. "If I'm keeping you from something—"

"It's not that. It's just...I feel like I'm not being truthful with you."

Roxy snorted. Must be a Nocturne Falls thing. "Why? What aren't you being truthful about?"

Carmen folded her hands together on the table, one on top of the other. "I'm not exactly your neighbor."

Roxy frowned. "Then who are you?"

Carmen tried to smile again. "I'm Alex's mother."

Roxy put her fork down, the cake tasteless in her mouth. *Carmen.* Of course. The woman she'd signed a book for. "Did he send you over here?"

Carmen shook her head. "No, he's in the shower. He has no idea I'm here. And he'll be furious with me if he finds out. But when he told me what happened, I just had to come and talk to you. I knew if we could just have a chat, I could fix everything."

Roxy pushed the cake away. "I don't think this is a good idea."

"Please, Roxy, he's a good boy. And he's miserable that you won't talk to him. I just hope you'll give my son a second chance. He's the best man I know."

"Too bad he didn't think I'd be strong enough, or like him enough, or whatever enough, to handle the truth about what he is. He was afraid telling me would stress me to my breaking point." Delaney was really more to blame for that, but Alex had hurt her in a different way. Because she'd thought they had something. Because they'd agreed to be truthful with each other. "He lied to me. After promising me we would be upfront about everything."

She crossed her arms and stared at his mother, almost challenging her to defend him. "I'm sorry, but accidentally finding out the guy you're interested in has been holding back a major secret is no way to build a relationship."

"What?" Carmen scowled in disapproval. "You found out he was a shifter accidentally?"

"Yes." Roxy sighed. "But he was going to tell—"

"Unacceptable." Carmen's eyes flashed gold. "My son knows better than that. I am not happy with him."

A pang of sympathy for Alex shot through Roxy. "It wasn't entirely his fault. A friend of mine made him promise not to tell me." Roxy exhaled and felt the fight—and the anger—go with it. Being this miserable was exhausting. She didn't want to feel this way anymore. "She didn't think I could handle it either."

Carmen sat for a moment. "Then you didn't reject him because he's a panther shifter?"

"No." Roxy leaned her elbows on the table. "But

I'm not entirely sure what that means. In my fictional world, sure, but not in reality. Is he…not human?"

Carmen huffed out a breath. "He should have told you all this."

"I think he tried. But I was too upset. I threw him and my friend out before they could really explain."

Carmen reached over and patted Roxy's hand. "And you had every right. The truth about what we are isn't something that can just be thrust upon a person. It has to be carefully explained."

"We?" Roxy leaned back. "Then you're a were-cat too?"

"I am. We all are in our family." Carmen stood up and smoothed the front of her blouse. Then she took a step back, the air around her shimmering like she was about to combust, and a second later, a large black cat about the size of a Labrador retriever sat on the other side of Roxy's dining room table.

Roxy's hands fell to her sides. She stared, mouth open.

A second later, the cat turned into Carmen again. She ran a hand over her jet curls and carried on like nothing unusual had just happened. "You see? Nothing to be scared of. Same person. Just a different form."

Roxy nodded, not entirely sure what to say or

how to react. It wasn't every day someone brought you delicious cake, then turned into a panther right in front of you.

Carmen took her seat at the table. "You know, my Alex has never told a human girlfriend that he's a panther shifter. It's not an easy thing for any of us to do. People are afraid of us. Or they treat us like animals. Or side-shows."

Roxy tried to imagine Alex's side of things and what it would be like to reveal something so unbelievable about yourself.

"You and Alex have only known each other a short time. I'm sure you have some things you haven't told him yet."

"Yes, but being a shifter? That's sort of a big detail to hold back."

"It is. I agree." Carmen moved her fork around on the plate. She smiled but it didn't quite reach her eyes. "Not once did I see Alex mope about a girl when he was a teenager. In fact, I've never seen my boy heartbroken before. But he is desperately heartbroken now."

Roxy swallowed. She knew the feeling.

Carmen's brows arched. "Remember when Marabella left Wolfgang because she thought he would be better off without her? The pain he was in? The way he suffered?"

Roxy nodded. "I do."

"Alex is your Wolfgang. You're his Marabella.

Please talk to him. Let him explain. You can come over to the house and have dinner with us."

"I don't know."

Carmen glanced over at the pizza box. "Homemade pork loin with rice and beans and sweet plantains."

Roxy's stomach growled. She couldn't avoid Alex forever. They lived next door after all. She glanced down at herself. "Okay. But not like this."

Alex finally got out of the shower, dried off, then threw on clean shorts and went back to the kitchen to apologize for being short with his mother. He knew she only wanted to help, and she only wanted to do that because she loved him.

But his mother wasn't in the kitchen. Nor was she on the back porch. Or getting anything out of her car. She wasn't anywhere that he could see. He checked the counter for a note, but there wasn't one.

It wasn't like her to walk away from a full oven.

He went to the bedroom to grab his cell phone and check to see if she'd texted. He was just unlocking the screen when he heard the front door open.

"Alex, are you decent? We have company for dinner."

Had she gone to Diego's? That was impossible.

She hadn't had enough time. Alex had been in the shower a long while, but not enough for her to go to Diego's and back. She could have called him, though. And Diego could have driven over.

She must have been outside somewhere waiting for him. Alex walked down the hall to see if Diego was going to get any grief over his new girlfriend or if that was just reserved for—Alex stopped as he entered the living room.

Roxy stood in the foyer with his mother. Her hair was damp and twisted into a loose bun, a few tendrils springing out around her face. She wore another pretty sundress like the night she'd come over to have dinner with him and sit in the hot tub. "Hi." There was no smile, but there was no indication she was unhappy either.

"Hi," he said back. A thread of hope unwound in him.

She didn't quite make eye contact. "Your mother brought me cake. And then she turned into a were-cat in my dining room."

"Panther shifter," Alex and his mother responded in unison.

"Panther shifter," Roxy corrected. "I'm not here because everything is automatically forgiven. We need to talk. But your mom promised me a home-cooked dinner and I've had a lot of takeout lately. I hope that's okay."

"That's very okay." He took back every grumpy

thought he'd ever had about his mother. Who was currently giving him a look he knew very well. She wasn't happy with him.

"Alex, go put a shirt on."

"In a second, Mom."

Before she could say anything else, she threw her hands in the air. "My pork loin!" She rushed into the kitchen, leaving Alex alone with the most perfect woman in the world. He took a few steps toward her. "I'm really glad you came, and I'm so sorry I didn't tell you sooner."

She bit her lip. "Me, too. We have a lot to talk about."

He nodded. "I'm all answers. Whenever you're ready."

"Not over dinner. Not in front of your mom."

"Understood. Thank you for coming."

She shrugged. "Your mother's pretty hard to say no to."

He smiled. "Welcome to my life."

The little half-smile he got in response was perfect. "You really should go put a shirt on. It's very distracting looking at all…" She waved her hands at him. "This."

"In a second." The thread of hope unwound a little more, buoyed by her presence. Things weren't back to normal by any means, but at least he and Roxy were speaking again. He took another step toward her. She smelled like flowers and soap. It was a good smell. He lowered his voice. "But first, I have to tell you that you're one of the strongest people I know. You made your own success and you left a man who didn't treat you right. That takes guts. I will never underestimate you again. And I don't blame you for being mad at me. I was an idiot."

She sighed and nodded. "Thank you. I appreciate that."

He lifted a finger. "Shirt."

He raced to his room, grabbed the first clean T-shirt he saw and dragged it over his head. Then he returned to her, so wishing he could touch her cheek or take her hand or make contact with her somehow, but that was too much to ask of her in this moment. "Do you think we could talk now? At least enough to make you comfortable? We could go sit on the back porch. Have a drink. My mother brought sangria."

She glanced toward the rear sliders, then nodded. "Okay."

That single word sent a new burst of happiness through him. "Great. C'mon." He headed for the porch, opening the slider to let her through. Then he went to the fridge, pulled out the sangria and a fresh beer for himself, and poured Roxy a glass of the fruity wine his mother loved so much. "Mom, we'll be outside. Call us when dinner's ready."

She wiped her hands on a towel and smiled at him. "You take all the time you need."

"Thank you." He hesitated. "For everything."

She lifted her chin proudly. "No one can resist my *tres leches*."

He winked at her. "I'm sure that's what it was." He slipped outside and closed the slider with his elbow, minding the drinks in his hands.

Roxy was sitting on the love seat that faced the yard. She seemed pensive. A mood he well understood.

He took the chair next to the love seat, handing her the glass of sangria as he sat. "This is my mother's version. Fair warning, she spikes it with more brandy than is actually called for."

"Good to know." Roxy just stared at the glass but didn't drink. "I don't know where to start."

He sipped his beer, then nodded. "I cannot imagine what it must feel like to find out that everything you've ever thought was make-believe is suddenly real."

She stared out at the yard. "It's overwhelming. And a little scary. And it makes me feel like…a fool."

He jerked back. "How so?"

She laughed sadly. "I don't know if I can really put it into words. It's sort of like I've been caught imitating something I have no right imitating. What do I really know about the supernatural world? Nothing. Nothing beyond what I've made up in my books. And who knows how much of that is completely wrong or utterly ridiculous or if the supernatural creatures of the world think I'm making fun of them or—"

"I don't think you should feel that way at all. My mother and her friends love your books. So do half the women in this town. I don't think that would be true if you were writing stories that didn't do...our kind justice. From what I read, you did a great job with the supernatural stuff."

She smiled a little, like she'd forgotten he'd read one of her books. "Are all your mother's friends panther shifters too?"

"No. Two of them are witches, one's a nymph and Mrs. Irving is a ghost."

Roxy turned her head to blink at him, open-mouthed. She stayed that way for a few long seconds. "I have no idea if you're joking or not."

"In light of recent events, I don't think joking about any of this is a good idea. At least not for a while."

She took an extended sip of her sangria, then held her glass in her lap and took a deep breath. "So ghosts are real. Are there ghosts in this town too?"

"We have a few."

"What else? How many vampires?"

"A good number. I don't know for sure. That's something you should probably talk to Delaney about."

Roxy put her hand to her forehead and sighed. "I really need to talk to her. In fact, I should text her right now. See if we can get together tomorrow, maybe, if she's free."

"That's a great idea." He waited a moment while she put her wine on the small center table, then pulled her phone from her pocket. "This is all going to be okay, you know."

"I'm glad you think that."

"But you don't?"

She looked at him. "I want it to be. But I don't know yet. I can't shake the feeling that I'm an outsider looking in. Does that make sense?"

"Absolutely. But I hope you don't feel that way for long. Delaney wanted you to move here, so she had every intention from the beginning of telling you about all of this. She just didn't right away because you were already under so much stress."

Roxy opened her mouth, then closed it again and shook her head. "I owe you a thank-you."

"For what?"

"For tackling Thomas in my yard that night. My divorce papers arrived by FedEx yesterday. I feel pretty certain your intervention helped that along."

He smiled, and the hope growing in his gut turned into anticipation. Roxy St. James was a single woman. "If I did, then you're welcome. Hey, what was in that box he brought? Or did you just throw it away?"

"What box?"

"I put it on your dining room table. Or I thought I did."

She shook her head. "I don't remember seeing it. But then I haven't paid attention to much these past few days. I'll have to look for it when I get home." Her mouth curved into a funny little half-smile. "I owe you a second thank-you, actually."

"Really? What's this one for?"

"That flan. That probably saved you from being killed off in a book."

He laughed, a loud burst of sound. "Do you do that a lot? Kill people off in books?"

She shrugged coyly, and it felt like they were back to being okay. "Sometimes. It's a great way to get your frustrations out."

"I would have thought yours was driving fast."

Her smile took a wistful bend. "I need to get back in that car, that's for sure."

Silence passed between them, then she tipped her head and gave him an odd look. "That Sunday that my fish tank was being installed, I thought I saw a black panther in your backyard. Was that you?"

He sat back, resting his beer on the arm of the chair. "First of all, how can you see into my backyard?"

She pointed a little reluctantly to the playhouse

visible on the other side of the fence. "That thing has a loft. Where those windows are. Looks right over the fence. I go up there to write sometimes."

He smirked. "I'll have to remember that next time I go commando in the hot tub."

She rolled her lips in and blushed a little. "Anyway, was that you?"

"No, I was at work that day. That had to be Diego." Alex shook his head. "It's generally understood that blatant supernatural activity is not supposed to take place within range of human citizens."

She shrugged. "Technically, he wasn't, what with the fence and all."

"I suppose."

She stared at the phone on her lap. "Would it be okay if I...saw what you look like when you shift? I mean, if you're willing. Or if that's even allowed."

For the second time since he'd known her, she caused a shot of electricity to zip through him. "You want to see my panther form?"

She nodded. "If that's okay with you. I already know you're not like a wild animal that could hurt me, since your—"

"No, it's nothing like that. It's a lot like your books, actually."

She looked up. "Yes, your mom, uh, showed me that side of her at my house. Wanted to show me it was safe, I guess."

"My mother shifted in front of you?"

"She did. It was very impressive. But I'd still like to see you."

Wonders never ceased. "Okay then. Just so you know, I can't speak in that form, but I'm just as aware and in control of myself in that form as I am in this one." He stood and moved the table out of the way. "Ready?"

Her eyes shone with pure curiosity. "Right now? Yes."

"Here goes." He called to the beast within him, and the magic of his kind rushed through him as the change overtook his body.

Roxy jerked back in her seat, her eyes widening as her soft lips parted and a gasp escaped. "Oh. Wow. You are one big kitty."

Roxy's first instinct was to tuck her legs under her to put a little more space between herself and the enormous creature now sitting across from her. She'd known what Alex was, but seeing him in his panther form this close was not a sight that anything could have prepared her for.

He was as tall as she was sitting down. Taller maybe. His eyes were as gold as the sun and his fur the most gorgeous blue-black she'd ever seen. His paws were nearly the size of bread plates.

She swallowed, realizing as she did that she'd been holding her breath. "Alex?"

The big cat's head nodded. Alex's head. But it was really weird to think of him that way. She lifted her hand to touch him, then on second thought, let it drop back to her lap.

He responded by butting his big head against her knee. The move rocked her back on the love seat. There was no mistaking the power within him.

She raised her hand. "It's okay if I touch you?"

Again, he nodded.

She reached out, still tentative, but the moment her fingers made contact with the top of his head, she relaxed. There were no words to describe how silky his fur was. It was almost liquid. She scratched and his eyes closed.

He rested his head on top of her leg, the weight substantial.

"This is unreal," she whispered.

A low, rumbling noise vibrated out of him. The sound jolted through her, tripping a response in her that was as primal as the sound he'd just made. A longing filled her. For what, exactly, she couldn't say, but part of her felt a little sad that this wasn't something she could ever be part of.

"You're so beautiful." She smoothed her hand down his head and ran her fingers over the muscles of his back. Power seemed to thrum within him. "I wish I could know what it feels like to be such a magnificent creature."

He opened his eyes, snorted softly, then backed up. A shimmer of magic, a second of time, and Alex stood before her again. Human, except for the lingering gold gleam in his eyes. "I wish you could too."

"Thank you for showing me that side of you."

"Of course. Anytime." He glanced at the window into the kitchen. "I'm sure it's time for dinner. Are you ready to go in?"

She got the sense she'd said or done something to make him uncomfortable. She hoped that wasn't the case, but after the last three days without him, she didn't have the energy to dig into it. She lifted her phone. "Let me send a quick text to Delaney and I'll be right in. You might want to fix your shirt. It's on backwards. I noticed it before but we were sort of busy."

He looked down, then pulled the shirt off, giving her an up close view of his incredible body. She sighed loudly, unable to help herself.

He got the shirt on the right way and looked at her. "Everything okay?"

She smiled. After days of no Alex, this was Alex overload. In a good way. Mostly. It was just a little awkward ogling him with his mother in the other room. "Everything's fine. I mean, it's not that that I didn't enjoy that, but there's just so much a girl can take. I am only human, you know."

His smile faltered for a split second. "I'll, uh, see you inside then."

"Okay." As she texted Delaney about meeting the next day, Roxy couldn't help but wonder if Alex was disappointed that she wasn't a shifter too, or if it was something more. Was there some kind of shifter law about humans and shifters interacting? Or being involved? Or maybe something else that might be required of her now that she knew his secret?

Could be a vow of secrecy that she'd have to take. A meeting with the pack? Pride? Clan? Whatever his group was called. Her writer's brain spun out a thousand different scenarios. Would she have to swear some kind of blood oath? Make a sacrifice? Perform a ritual? Hmm. Could humans and panther shifters mate? And if they did, would she have a baby? Or a litter of kittens? Her phone chimed, and she jumped.

Delaney had responded. They were on for tomorrow.

Roxy took a breath and stuck her phone back in her purse. She picked up her glass of sangria and headed inside. Maybe just for tonight, she could stop letting her brain get the best of her and let her heart do the thinking.

Because her heart wanted more time with Alex. Whatever the consequences.

Three hours later, Alex walked Roxy to her door. She was a little tipsy, perfectly full, and abundantly happy. After the last three days she'd just had, she'd needed a night like tonight. She was in a state of pure bliss, and a very welcome one at that. She started to reach for her house keys, then stopped, wanting more than anything to keep him at her side a little longer. She turned to face him. "You want to come in?"

Gold flared in his eyes. He put a hand on the door behind her and leaned in. "Yes. But my mother's here."

"I know." She wanted to touch him. Again. And with the sangria in her system, there was nothing to stop her. She reached up and trailed a finger down his chest. Too bad he was wearing a shirt now. "But I'm not ready for tonight to end."

He bent a little and brushed his mouth across

the line of her jaw. "Neither am I. But all things considered, rushing the next step might not be the best idea. As much as it kills me to say that."

She laughed softly, but the scrape of his teeth on her skin turned the laugh into a sigh. "Then you should probably stop doing that."

"Okay." His hands went to her hips, pulling her in for a long, slow kiss that took her already-Zen mood to a new level.

Desire wound through her in languid spirals, curling around her limbs in a warm, easy way that caused all other thoughts to leave her head except one. She wanted Alex. Plain and simple.

"You make me crazy," he whispered against her mouth.

Her hands lifted and her fingers threaded into his hair. A real live shifter. And he wanted her just as much as she wanted him. "Better you than me," she whispered back.

He laughed softly, breaking the kiss, but not the contact of his hands on her body. "I can't believe I'm saying this, but I should get back. If I leave my mother alone in my house too long, she starts rearranging things."

"I understand." She stared up at him, taking him in. Now that she knew what he really was, so much about him made sense. She could see the panther in him, in his eyes, the lines of his face, the graceful movements of his body. She'd seen it before, even decided he'd make a great big cat shifter hero, but to know that's actually what he was…was amazing. "How long will she be here?"

"Not sure. But if she doesn't go home tomorrow, you can anticipate another dinner invite. Or maybe we'll all go out to eat. That might be good. Just don't make plans, because she'll expect you to be there."

"I do have a book to write, you know." And now that she wasn't consumed by anger and humiliation any more—and that she knew the supernatural really existed, she felt totally energized to get it done.

"That's probably the only excuse she'd take." He gave her hips a little squeeze. "But I'd love for you to be there too."

She wanted to be with him just as much. But work was work. And she was so behind it frightened her. "Let me see how many pages I get done tomorrow after my meeting with Delaney."

"Deal." He kissed her once more, quick and easy. "Night."

"Night."

He walked off the porch, but waited at the end of the drive until she'd unlocked and opened the door. She gave him a wave and he took off toward his house.

She went in, locked the door and grinned. It was wild how fast things could turn around. How you could go from wallowing in a miserable funk to floating on happiness. How you could think you were genuinely losing your mind, only to find out that you'd actually stumbled onto the most amazing secret in the world. How you could be married one second then single but involved the next. Life was funny.

Life was *good*.

She went over to the kitchen counter. The divorce papers were still lying there by the phone with the take out menus. She picked them up to take them to her office, then she remembered what Alex had said about Thomas having a box with him the night of the incident. She looked around but didn't see anything on the counter or the dining table.

She walked around the table and spotted something peeking out from under the curtains at the farthest side of the sliding doors.

A small cardboard box. Barely the size of three paperbacks stacked on top of one another. She picked it up. No labels or markings, just clear tape keeping it shut. Not much weight to it either. She put it on the table and stared at it.

She wanted to ignore the stupid thing, but her curiosity won out. Well, what did it matter? The divorce was final. Nothing inside the box was going to make any difference.

She got scissors and slit the tape, then cautiously opened the flaps of the box. It was stuffed with white tissue paper. Underneath that was a black velvet jewelry box.

The only jewelry Thomas had ever given her was her wedding ring set. Whatever this was, he'd probably be wanting it back.

Couldn't hurt to see what it was she'd be returning.

She took the box out, opened it and sucked it a breath.

It was a gold locket, shaped like a book. The letter R was engraved on the front. She pried the two halves open with her fingernail. The slots on either side for pictures held a photo of her—her official author headshot, actually—and the cover of the very first book she'd ever published.

She squinted at the gift, trying to figure it out. It was kind of perfect except for the headshot. She'd never wear her own picture in a locket. It was also so incredibly unlike Thomas, it was baffling. Had he thought this would be enough to change her mind about him? To get her back? Clearly he'd known better than to put his own photo in there.

So strange. No matter how spot on the locket was, this was a definite case of too little, too late.

Maybe she'd take out the book cover and add a photo of Alex. She snorted. That would be karma, wouldn't it? Using her ex-husband's gift to keep her new man close? Sweet justice was what that sounded like to her.

Although maybe it was a little early to have a picture of Alex in a locket. She didn't want him to think she'd turned weirdly possessive the moment she was single. No, that was too much. For now, the locket would be put away. Or maybe she really should just return it to Thomas's lawyer and let him handle it. She nodded. That was the best solution.

Decision made. She snapped the velvet box closed and put the cardboard one and the tissue into the recycling bin. As she was doing that, she noticed a folded note card stuck in the bottom flap.

She pulled it out and unfolded it.

Saw this, thought of you.

The handwriting seemed like the same scrawling style as the other note Thomas had sent, and neither one was a perfect match for his penmanship. But in this age of emails and text, how often did she really see his handwriting anyway? And it wasn't like she had a treasure trove of cards and love notes from him to compare it to.

She tossed the note in the recycling bin too. Again, what did it matter? The papers were signed and the Thomas chapter of her life was over.

She walked to her bedroom, smiling and ready

to crawl under the covers and dream. Let the Alex chapter begin.

The buzz of insects filled the sweet evening air with a soft hum, and Alex wondered if Roxy was listening to it too, or if she'd already drifted off to sleep. The fence between their houses blocked his view from the back porch, but he could imagine her fast asleep, a peaceful expression on her beautiful face.

Which led to him wondering what it would be like to be curled up next to her, holding her in his arms. He smiled at the thought. If only his mother knew what was going through his mind. He glanced at her on the love seat next to his chair. Maybe she did. "What do you think of Roxy?"

Carmen lifted her glass to no one in particular, almost sloshing the sangria out of it. "I like her very much."

Alex grinned into the darkness of the evening. His back porch was lit only by a single candle, something else his mother had brought along with the food and sweets and wine. She loved to add decorative touches to his house. This one was at least tolerable. And the solitary flame was more than enough for their feline eyes to see by. "Of course you do. You're addicted to her books."

Carmen swallowed another sip of sangria. It was the last glass from a very large pitcher and she'd done more than her share to empty it. "That has nothing to do with it."

He gave her the side eye. "Nothing?"

She laughed. "Well, it's not the main thing. It's a definite bonus, that's for sure." His mother's expression turned serious. "Oh, her books, Alex, they are so good. All that angst and romance and the terrible things that her characters overcome for love." She sighed and clutched a hand to her heart.

He kicked his feet up onto the coffee table. "Yeah, I read the first one. It was pretty good. Really good, actually. I like my books with a little less kissing, but I can see the appeal." The kissing he liked was *with* the author, not on the pages.

Carmen stared at him, her eyes wide and glimmering gold, more from the alcohol she'd consumed than anything else. "You read one?"

"Don't act so shocked. I read. Not sure about Diego, but—"

"Oh, let your brother be."

"You know he's living with a girl he just met. A much younger girl. I'm surprised that doesn't concern you more."

She sighed. It was a long, practiced sound that he'd heard many times before. "Will you take him back in when she kicks him out?"

Alex stared at the porch ceiling. "I don't want to.

I want my own life." With Roxy. "I'm a grown man who needs his space and his privacy."

She nodded. "Especially with your new chica." Another soft exhale came out of her. "I don't know where we went wrong with him. I thought after the Marines..." She tapped her painted nails on the wine glass, sending a crystalline ringing into the air. "I wish that boy would get his act together."

He glanced at her. The expression on her face was more appalled than disappointed. "Maybe someday."

"I'm going to see him tomorrow. Talk some sense into him."

Alex grunted softly. "Good luck."

"Pfft. What he needs is a swift kick in the *culo*. And you." She pointed at Alex. "Don't let him move back in here."

Alex's brows lifted and he repressed a smile. It wasn't like his mother to use saucy language. But then, that was probably the sangria talking. "I won't, but you realize that you'll be his next stop."

"No, he knows better. Your father won't have it."

"All right, then. We'll see what happens. But he'll have to go somewhere." Alex's thoughts turned to his father. "What do you think Dad would think of Roxy?"

"He'd like her very much. You know he respects anyone who makes their own way in the world."

Which was why he wasn't about to let Diego move back in. "I do know that, but what would he think about her being human?"

Carmen shrugged. "It happens. Your great-aunt Alita was human."

He sat up. "No, she wasn't. I saw her shift when I was a kid."

Carmen's eyes widened, and she rubbed her nose, a sign that she was holding something back. It was her tell, and everyone in the family knew it. "Oh, no, that's right. Never mind."

He stared at his mother. "You rubbed your nose. You're hiding something. Spill it."

She frowned. "You're a bad boy."

"Yeah, yeah, out with it."

She grimaced. "Aunt Alita was human, but she loved your uncle Santino so much that she went through an old ritual for him that would allow her to live as one of us, but it's an awful thing. And it's why she died so young. It takes a terrible toll on the human body. Don't even think about it, Alexito. Let Roxy be."

He nodded and slouched back down in his chair. "Just curious, is all. What happens? How does it work?"

"*Alex*. Leave it."

"I wouldn't put her through that. I just want to know. Aunt Alita did it, so why not tell me?"

Carmen sat quietly for a moment. "It takes a

willing human and a powerful witch. It's old, old magic. And it doesn't really turn the human into a shifter, it just puts a spell on them that allows them to shift. It's not the same thing as being born one. But the weight of that spell, that's what does the damage. Humans aren't meant to carry that much magic for too long. After a while, it wears them out."

Aunt Alita had been forty-three when she died. But she'd looked like a woman in her seventies. That much he remembered. He shook his head. "I would never want less time with Roxy. Only more."

Carmen nodded. "That's right. Remember that. And don't let her know that such a thing is even possible. Uncle Santino spent the rest of his life regretting what she'd done and wishing she was still at his side. It's not worth it. For either of you."

"I agree." He glanced toward Roxy's house. The thought of her as a shifter, running wild beside him was a very intoxicating one. But not at such a cost.

It added to his worries about her. Now that she knew Nocturne Falls was a supernatural haven, she'd probably go into research mode to find out everything she could about the town and the people who lived here and how the real supernatural world compared to her fictional one. What if she stumbled onto information about what his mother had just told him?

He promised himself that he would find time to

talk to one of the most powerful witches in town about this as soon as possible. Pandora Williams. She knew Roxy and she'd understand Alex's concerns. She could spread the word that no one was to give in if Roxy were to request such a thing.

A soft snore broke through Alex's thoughts. His mother had fallen asleep. He smiled and took the wine glass out of her hand, then scooped her into his arms and carried her into the guest room.

After he laid her on the bed, he pulled a blanket over her and shut the door.

He ought to go to bed himself, but he wasn't sleepy. In fact, he was restless. What he needed was a run. Normally, he'd drive up to the land the Ellinghams reserved for such use, but he didn't want to take that much time. And the two women he cared about most were right here. Leaving them for that long wasn't something he cared to do either.

For tonight, the neighborhood would have to do. He'd stay in the shadows and make sure he wasn't seen.

With that settled, he slipped out the front door, locked it behind him, then leaped off the front porch and shifted mid-air.

It felt good to be in his panther form. Not as good as when Roxy had run her nails through his fur and stared at him with amazement in her eyes, but close.

He took off in a long, loping run, working out his muscles and disappearing into the dark, a blur of sleek black, a shadow of a creature so large that no one would have believed what they were seeing anyway.

By the time he got home, he was ready for bed. Worn out in a good way. His head was empty of almost all the days' worries and concerns. Except for the thought of Roxy at his side. It was just a dream, though. Maybe even *dream* was too strong a word. A lingering idea. Nothing that was going to influence his decisions.

He could happily live the rest of his life with a human woman. He knew that much. Roxy was enough. More than enough.

But could she spend the rest of her life with a shifter and be content? He'd seen the longing in her eyes as she'd looked at him. Would she come to resent his abilities? Would that imbalance grow into something that would eventually tear them apart? And what if it meant they couldn't have kids? Would that be a deal breaker for her?

That all remained to be seen. And solidified his determination to talk to Pandora. Protecting Roxy had to come before all else.

Roxy was up early after the first decent night's sleep she'd had in four days. She stretched lazily in bed, a smile on her face as thoughts of the night before took over. Alex. That man was reason enough to smile.

She slipped out of bed and into some workout clothes. There were a thousand and one things to do, but a little yoga was first. Her body protested after her spell of inactivity, but it was good to move and stretch.

Coffee was next, followed by a quick text to Delaney so Roxy could plan the rest of her day. *Morning! Where do you want to meet?*

While she waited for Delaney's answer, Roxy tried to figure out what in the world she was going to eat for breakfast. Her grocery supplies were in sad shape. Almost depleted actually. That meant she needed to add a Shop-n-Save run to her growing list of to-do's.

She finally settled on one last slice of cold pizza. Not what she wanted but better than going hungry. As she ate, she thought about heading over to Alex's, pretty sure Carmen was making him a full spread. She seemed like that kind of mom. But heading over there would undoubtedly mean giving up an hour or so that could be spent working, something Roxy desperately needed to do.

Ignored emails didn't go away, they multiplied like spring bunnies, and she hadn't touched her inbox in three days. No doubt it was overflowing.

Roxy's phone chimed with Delaney's reply. *I'm sure you're swamped. Why don't I pick up lunch and bring it over? If that's cool.*

That would be great! I could use the extra time to work.

Perfect. What are you in the mood for?

Something healthy. A big salad with chicken. Or something like that. You decide. I'll be happy with whatev.

Okay, sounds good. See you noon-ish.

Noon-ish. Bye. Roxy put her phone on the counter. Having Delaney come here was an excellent solution. It meant instead of spending time getting ready to go out and then driving into town, Roxy could work this morning. It was sweet of Delaney to suggest. Of course, Delaney may have really just wanted to talk in private, and considering what they were going to discuss, Roxy could understand.

And then, after that discussion, she'd go get groceries. Enough that she didn't have to leave her house for a solid week. Except to see Alex. Because other than that, she needed to chain herself to her keyboard.

With the goal of pages in mind, she fixed a second cup of coffee and headed back to her office. "Morning, fish." She wiggled her fingers at them as she sat at her desk and opened her laptop. New words were about to happen, and it was high time. Poor Wolfgang and Marabella, stranded on the pages of their unfinished story.

"You two will be together soon enough," she told them. "But first...email."

She fired up her inbox and let out a groan as the screen came up. Twelve hundred and thirty-one emails. She scanned through them looking for anything that might pop out as urgent, but her eyes started to blur. There were too many.

Instead, she started by deleting mass quantities of advertisements from places she didn't need to be shopping at anyway, and writers' loop digests filled with info that was pretty much guaranteed to be something she already knew or not that important.

Then she filed away the various statements and

newsletters that had come from the retailer vendors that sold her books. She told herself she was filing them to be read later, but she also knew that was very unlikely. At best, she'd be forwarding the important ones to her accountant come tax time.

Responding to fan mail came after that. Not all of it. That would be an hour. Maybe two. Instead, she answered the oldest ones, buying herself a little time. But reader notes had to be answered. Readers were everything. If they'd taken the time to write to her, then she could certainly take the time to write back.

Almost done, she looked through what was left, picking out the easiest to answer. Some got forwarded to her assistant to deal with. Em was good at that. Maybe her responses weren't as elaborate as Marissa had been, but Em's concise style did the trick.

Roxy kept going. Some emails took a simple yes or no to be handled. Some were invoices to be paid, promotions to approve, and interview requests that got politely turned down, an unfortunate necessity when she was this far behind on a book.

Only a few more emails remained, all from senders she didn't recognize. Then one subject line caught her eye and made her suck in a breath.

Signing this Saturday

Those words made the identity of the sender, AMiller@BBCShop.com, as clear as crystal. Agnes.

And the signing at the Bell, Book & Candle. Roxy had completely forgotten. With a groan, she clicked on it.

She read the short note twice to make sure she understood what she was reading. Agnes had presold two hundred and fifty books and had another two hundred on hand for the signing. Which she expected to sell out of.

Holy bookseller of the year.

Roxy started typing an enthusiastic reply to make sure Agnes knew how much she appreciated the hard work, as well as an apology for not responding sooner. Roxy also promised to bring lots of swag. She finished with more thanks and a happy emoji.

As she hit send, she realized she wanted to bring Agnes a little gift on Saturday. Something special to really show her how blown away Roxy was by her efforts.

Roxy smiled and her thoughts turned to the book locket. That would be perfect. Except she couldn't give Agnes that one. Not only would that be weird, but that locket had an R engraved on it. And it was going back to Thomas.

She rolled her eyes, realizing that meant a trip to the post office. More wasted time thanks to that man.

Shaking that off, she went online, did some searching and found the same locket. Overnight delivery was pricey, but worth it.

Finally, she opened her Word doc and got to work. She read through the last chapter she'd written, pleased to see it wasn't entirely dreck. She did a quick edit on it to bring it up to par, then finally began new words. Her fingers flew over the keyboard with speed and intent, and she was happy to be making progress at last.

Wolfgang and Marabella were on the verge of seeing each other for the first time in eight months when her phone rang.

"Ugh, not now." But she picked up the phone anyway to see who was calling. Delaney. Roxy answered. "Hey."

"Hey. I was going to ring the bell, but—"

"Are you here already? What time is it?"

"It's twelve fifteen. Too soon?"

"No, I was just in the writing zone." She checked her progress. Almost twelve pages. Perfect. "I lost track of time is all. Why didn't you ring the bell?"

"Yeah, I think maybe you should come to your front door."

Roxy hit save, then got up. "Okay, on my way. You sound weird. Is something wrong?"

"Sweet crispy crackers, yes, something is wrong. Something is very wrong."

Roxy raced down the hall as she hung up the phone. She opened the door, her focus on Delaney first.

Then Roxy saw what Delaney was talking about.

One of Roxy's books was spread open and stuck to her door with a knife. The blade went straight through the book's spine and on the exposed pages of type, the word *traitor* was written in red marker.

Delaney's brows were knit together in clear concern. "Does stuff like this happen to you a lot?"

Roxy shivered. "No. That is really creepy."

"Majorly creepy. I thought Thomas had been dealt with."

"He was. In fact, I finally got the divorce papers. He's officially out of my life."

"You sure he knows that?"

"I need to call Alex."

"Agreed. This is too much." Delaney slipped into the house, keeping a wide distance from the knife. "But I'm so glad to see you. You look like you're doing pretty good. I wasn't sure if you'd ever talk to me again."

Roxy smiled. "You can thank Alex's mother."

Delaney squinted. "Not sure I follow."

"I'll explain later." She lifted her phone. "Let me call him first."

"Yes, absolutely." Delaney lifted the takeout bag in her hand. "I'll go put lunch in the fridge."

While Delaney did that, Roxy dialed Alex's number.

He answered on the first ring. "Hello, beautiful."

She smiled. That was an especially nice way to be greeted, given the circumstances. "Hi. I need you."

"Straight into the dirty talk, I like that."

She laughed. "That's not what I meant." Her smile faded. "I have an issue. Like a knife stuck in my door issue."

"What? Are you home?"

"Yes. Are you?"

"No, I'm at the station. Don't touch anything. I'll be right there. I'm bringing Sheriff Merrow with me. Enough is enough."

She thought about the strange handwriting and the unusual gift of jewelry. "Alex, I don't think this was Thomas. In fact, I'm not sure it was ever him."

Alex arrived at Roxy's with Sheriff Hank Merrow in tow as promised. They parked their cars and walked toward her front porch. Roxy and Delaney came out to meet them.

Roxy raised her brows and tipped her head toward the front door, where the vandalism was in plain view. "Nice, huh?"

Alex shook his head. "We're going to figure this out." He jerked his thumb toward Hank. "This is my boss, Sheriff Merrow. Hank Merrow, this is my neighbor, Roxy St. James."

He nodded at her and Delaney. "Nice to meet you, Ms. St. James."

"You too, Sheriff. Thank you for coming."

"Uh-huh." He looked at Delaney. "I take it you two are friends?"

Delaney answered. "We are. And I'd consider it a personal favor if this matter could get some priority attention."

"That's not necessary," Roxy said.

"No," Hank responded. "It is. And we will. The safety of our citizens is something we take very seriously."

"Don't worry, Roxy, we're gonna be all over this." Alex gave her a wink, hoping to reassure her.

Hank shot him a look. "You two more than neighbors?"

"I, uh…" Alex glanced at Roxy.

She smiled. "We're more than neighbors. Not exactly public about that yet, but yes. Is that a problem?"

"No, ma'am." Hank turned to Alex. "So long as it's not an issue for Deputy Cruz."

Alex shook his head. "It won't be."

"All right." Hank started up the steps to the porch. "What time did you notice the knife stuck in your door?"

"I didn't, actually. Delaney saw it when she came over with lunch."

Hank nodded as Alex joined him on the porch. "What time was that?"

"About twelve fifteen," Delaney answered.

Roxy glanced at Alex. "I guess the door was fine this morning when you went to work, huh?"

"I got a call about a fender bender on Route 17 so I left in the opposite direction, but nothing caught my eye."

Hank got closer to the knife. "This could have been here awhile."

Roxy bit her lip. "I locked up around ten last night. There was nothing on the door then."

"What's going on?" a voice called out.

They all turned toward Alex's house to see Carmen standing in the yard between the two homes. She had a kitchen towel thrown over one shoulder.

"I'll tell you later, Mom," Alex answered.

Carmen walked closer. "Is that a knife stuck in Roxy's door? Oh my. What on earth happened? Hello, Sheriff Merrow."

"Ma'am." Hank moved to the edge of the porch. "Did you see any suspicious characters in the area between ten o'clock last night and noon today?"

Carmen shook her head. "No, but then, I've been in the kitchen most of the day making black bean soup and picadillo." She smiled. "Got to keep Alex fed."

Alex leaned out. "Didn't you go to the store this morning?"

"Oh!" She put her hand on the side of her head. "Yes. But I still didn't see anyone."

"Okay, but Mom, did Roxy's door have a knife sticking out of it when you left or came back?"

She grimaced in apology. "I didn't notice. I'm so sorry."

"It's all right." He rubbed the back of his neck. "I'll come see you before I leave."

"Okay, honey." She waved at him, then Roxy before heading back to his house.

"So much for that," Alex said.

Hank shifted closer to the knife again. "Well, at least we have an approximate window of opportunity." He studied the book. "Ma'am, any reason why someone would write the word traitor on this book?"

"It's my book. And I'm not sure."

Hank pushed his sunglasses onto the top of his head. "You mean this book was stolen from your house?"

"No, I mean I wrote that book."

He made a small noise of understanding. "This particular passage mean anything to you?"

"I haven't looked at it actually. If you tell me the page number, I can grab a clean copy from my office and look it up."

He peered closer. "One ninety three."

"Be right back." Roxy disappeared into the house.

Hank looked over his shoulder at Alex. "I'll get a kit from the car and bag this all up. No point in leaving it here any longer than necessary."

"You want me to do that, boss?"

"No, I want you to take her statement. She's more comfortable with you."

Alex nodded, appreciative.

Roxy returned, book in hand, a wide frown on her face. "It's a passage where the hero sees the heroine kissing another guy. It's all a big misunderstanding, but that's what it's about."

Hank looked at Alex again. "Any chance someone might have seen you two kissing?"

Alex crossed his arms. "Yes."

Roxy wrapped her arms around her torso. "Are you telling me I have a whacked-out secret admirer stalking me?"

Hank scratched his head. "Appears that way, ma'am. Any idea who it might be?"

"Not a clue." Roxy sighed. "This is just what I need."

Delaney's mouth came open. "This is unacceptable. You've got to give her some protection. A patrol car in front of the house. A deputy on watch. Something."

Hank raised his hand. "I'm sure Deputy Cruz can help out in that department, but Ms. St. James,

I'm also going to advise that you stay put in your house for the next few days. We can set up a stakeout that way, hopefully catch this stalker while keeping you safe at the same time."

"I can't stay put. I have a signing at the Bell, Book & Candle on Saturday."

"That's the same day as the Panic Parade. The town will be utter chaos." Hank shook his head. "You'll have to cancel that."

Roxy straightened. "Not happening."

"Ma'am, I don't think you understand the seriousness of what we're—"

She stepped into his personal space and stared up at him. "I hate personal appearances. I get nervous. My hands sweat. Sometimes I feel like throwing up. Once I actually did. But you know what? Agnes Miller has pre-sold over two hundred books. That means a minimum of two hundred of my fans are coming to her store on Saturday expecting to meet me and have me sign a book for them. There is no way I'm canceling on them or her. No way. Because the only thing I hate worse than personal appearances is disappointing my fans, of which Agnes is one. So this Saturday? It is absolutely, positively, unequivocally happening."

Alex bit back a grin. It was a rare individual who stood up to Sheriff Merrow that way, not in small part because he was a werewolf. Which, granted, Roxy might not know. Either way she was a brave soul with a real knack for putting her words to good use.

Hank sighed. "You're not going to give in on this, are you?"

"If I was the kind of person who gives in, I'd never have gotten published. And I'd still be married to the biggest mistake of my life."

Delaney snorted.

Hank looked at Alex. "Consider yourself on personal protection duty until further notice."

"You got it, except—"

"Alex." Carmen waved from his driveway. "How many people for dinner tonight?"

"Except my mother's still here." Alex shook his head slowly. "I shouldn't leave my mom in the house by herself tonight. She's going home tomorrow, but until then, this is going to be tricky."

Delaney put her arm around Roxy's shoulders. "How about Hugh and I be her personal protection this evening, then Alex takes over tomorrow?" She nudged Roxy's hip with her own. "Can't get much safer than in a house with two vampires."

Alex bristled with the need to protect Roxy himself, but Delaney was right. This way was easier. He nodded reluctantly. "Agreed. Then tomorrow, she's all mine."

And hopefully, for a long time to come after that.

Roxy looked around at Delaney's house with new eyes. The house was just as gorgeous and just as beautifully decorated as it had been on her last visit, but everything seemed different now. "It's so weird being here."

Delaney's brows pulled together. "Roxy, you've been here before. Several times."

"Yeah, but I didn't know vampires lived here then."

Delaney laughed. "And that makes a difference?"

"Totally."

"Hello, Miss Roxy." Stanhill popped out of the kitchen. "I understand you're spending the night. I'll be happy to take your bag up to the guest room."

"Hi, Stanhill. Thanks." She handed her overnight bag to him, but kept her laptop bag slung over her shoulder. "Hey, are you a vampire too?"

He stiffened and looked at Delaney.

She waved it off. "Roxy knows. It was time. Past time."

"I see." He relaxed. "No, miss. I'm a rook. It's sort of in between a vampire and a human."

"Cool." Roxy nodded at Delaney. "I want to know more about that. I could totally put one of those in a book."

Stanhill's gaze took on a calculating gleam. "So long as the rook in question is roguishly handsome, you've got my blessing."

Roxy and Delaney laughed, causing Stanhill to grin. "I have a reputation to maintain, you know."

"I'm sure," Roxy said. As Stanhill carted off her bag, she looked around. "Where's Hugh?"

"Right here." He strode out from the living room, a ready smile on his face. "Hello, my darling." He leaned in and kissed Delaney, giving Roxy a pang of longing.

She'd never been greeted like that in her marriage, not even once. She made herself smile as Hugh wrapped his arm around Delaney's waist and greeted Roxy.

"Nice to see you again, Roxy. I'm sorry to hear about the troubles you've been having, but I'm glad we can provide you with a safe place to stay while Deputy Cruz is occupied with his mother."

"Thanks." Roxy shrugged. "It was just a little

complicated with her in town." Roxy totally understood that Alex needed to be with his mom—if the stalker had seen them kiss, there was no telling what the guy might do—and yet, she missed him. Which was nuts because there was no reason for her to miss him since she'd just seen him. But she did.

Stanhill came back downstairs. "Dinner's not until seven. Should I fix hors d'oeuvres? Some cheese and crackers, perhaps?"

"I'm fine," Roxy said. She and Delaney had eventually gotten to eat lunch at her house before they'd come here.

"I'm good too, Stanhill," Delaney said.

"And I'm headed out," Hugh added.

Roxy hoped he wasn't leaving on her account. The last thing she wanted to be was an intrusion. "I don't want to interrupt anyone's routine. I'm happy just to sit in a corner somewhere and work for a few hours, if that's okay."

"Take the library," Hugh said. "Seems an appropriate place to write a book."

Roxy nodded. "Sounds good to me."

He smiled. "I'll see you both for dinner, then. I'm off to Sebastian's for a meeting." He kissed Delaney again, then left.

"C'mon," she said. "I'll show you the library. You sure you don't want a glass of wine or something? After the day you've had, you've earned it."

Roxy walked with her. "Alcohol and writing don't mix for me, but I'll definitely have some at dinner."

Delaney pushed open a set of double doors ahead of them, and Roxy sighed. "Oh, this is gorgeous." She inhaled. "I love the way libraries smell."

"If you like this one, you'll have to see Sebastian's someday. That's the brother Hugh went to see. His library is easily twice this size. You'd love it. Two stories and filled with rare books and antique weapons."

"Really? Yeah, I'd definitely like to see that. In fact, it sounds like potential research with all those weapons."

"You'd like his girlfriend too. Tessa. She's a valkyrie. And a librarian."

Roxy squinted. "You mean as in the Norse mythology valkyrie?"

Delaney nodded. "Yep. Her sister, Deputy Blythe—I don't know if you've met her yet—but she's a valkyrie too. Everyone I know in the sheriff's department is a supernatural."

"Really? What's the sheriff?"

"Werewolf."

"Wow." Roxy bit her lip. "I don't know if I would have stood up to him the way I did if I'd known that."

Delaney smiled. "He's got that whole gruff, non-smiling thing going on, but he's really a big teddy bear. You should see the way his aunt talks to him. Birdie. Now there's a character."

"I met Birdie. Wait. If she's the sheriff's aunt, is she…"

"A werewolf too? Yep."

Birdie was a werewolf. That might take some getting used to. Roxy settled on one of the oversized couches and balanced her laptop bag on her knees. "I need to write, but there's so much I don't know and so many questions I'd like to ask. I have a feeling our talk over lunch only scratched the surface."

Delaney nodded. "There are scads of fascinating people that live here and so many interesting things to learn about this town, I feel like I find out something new every day myself."

The writing could wait another hour. Roxy patted the couch next to her. "Tell me all about it."

Delaney took a seat. "What do you want to know?"

Roxy opened her mouth, then closed it again, thinking.

"You can ask me anything," Delaney added.

"I guess what I most want to know isn't really about the town. It's more personal. Is that okay?"

"Absolutely."

"In that case, how did you decide to become a vampire? What was it like? Were you scared?"

Delaney sat back, her hand on her belly, and stared into the room for a moment before answering. "I was...in love."

Roxy could relate to the sentiment if not the exact feeling.

She looked at Roxy. "That colored everything, you know? I knew it was a serious decision and my life would be very different, but I also knew it would mean having forever with Hugh. It didn't take me long to make up my mind. It just felt like there was no question about whether or not I should do it. It was simply the next step in our relationship."

Roxy wound the laptop bag's strap around her hand. "Do you think...that maybe I could become a vampire?"

Delaney's mouth dropped open. "What? Why would you ask me that? I mean, I get wanting to be a vampire. It's incredibly cool, and given what you write, I can see the added appeal, but I thought you were interested in Alex."

"I am. That's why I asked. I thought it would put us on more equal footing."

Delaney reached out and squeezed Roxy's arm. "I don't think he cares one bit that you're human."

"Maybe not so much that he'd say anything, but the imbalance remains. He's a shifter. I'm human. I can never really be a part of his world the way a supernatural woman could."

Roxy let out a small sigh before she continued. "I feel a bit like an outsider looking in. This town is amazing. And the people who live here? It's just beyond exciting. But I also feel a bit like I've just been told I've won the lottery, except I can't spend any of the money. Just look at it. And watch other people spend it."

"Oh, Roxy. That must be so hard. But wouldn't you rather be a shifter like Alex?"

Roxy turned toward her, eyes rounding slightly. "Are you saying that's a possibility?"

Delaney shrugged. "I have no idea. But I know someone who might."

Alex stood in the sheriff's department conference room, staring down at the table and the bagged evidence collected from Roxy's house. Not a single useable fingerprint on any of it. "Whoever's doing this is smart enough to wear gloves and wipe everything down."

Hank nodded. "Which makes me think our perp has a record."

Jenna Blythe stopped clacking the keyboard of her department laptop long enough to look up. "Your girlfriend is pretty active on social media."

"She's a public figure. And a popular one." Just

how popular Alex was starting to understand. "What's your point?"

Jenna turned the laptop around. Roxy's Facebook page was on the screen. "My point is that she posted Saturday's signing as an event. The whole world knows exactly when and where to find her tomorrow."

Alex let out a soft curse. "That complicates things."

"Just a bit."

Hank leaned on the table. "I've already got Nick Hardwin and Greyson Garrett working crowd patrol for the parade, but I can deputize a few more. That would free up another deputy to help keep an eye on Ms. St. James. Of course, if she'd just cancel the signing—"

"You heard her," Alex said. "She won't. And I don't need extra help. In fact, I think it's a good chance to catch this guy. She won't ever be out of my sight, so the minute he shows up, it's over."

Jenna frowned. "You say that like you know what the guy looks like."

"I know his height. And I know his scent. He's human, but I can pick him out. And most of Roxy's readers are female. This guy is going to stick out like a sore thumb."

She pushed her chair back. "Good point. But I still think you should have backup. And I think I should do it. I'll blend in with the demographic."

Hank tapped a finger on the table. "That's a good idea. In fact, why don't we get some of the other women in town to assist?"

Alex liked that idea. "You think Ivy would help?" Hank's wife was a werewolf just like he was.

Hank shook his head. "I'm sure she would, but she's already scheduled to work at Delaney's."

Alex looked at Jenna. "Okay, then how about your sister?"

The valkyrie snorted. "She's not exactly the bodyguard type."

"But she's a valkyrie like you and knows how to protect herself. And she's a librarian. A book signing would be right up her alley."

"True," Jenna replied. "She's probably already planning on being there, so helping out shouldn't be an issue. So long as she doesn't have a commitment immediately afterwards. But I'll find out."

Alex glanced at Hank. "Two valkyries and I should do it. Plus, isn't the woman who owns that shop a witch?"

"Agnes?" Hank asked. "I think so. Maybe she and some of the other coven members could give us some magical aid. A little spell of protection or some such."

Alex nodded. "I'll talk to Agnes about it. I want to go over to the shop anyway, get the layout, see where the exits are, check if she has any kind of security system in place."

"You going to tell Agnes what's going on?" Jenna asked.

"I have to if I'm going to ask for her help. Besides, it's her shop. She has a right to know. And an extra set of eyes can't hurt."

"Agreed." Hank stood. "Whatever needs to happen to keep Ms. St. James safe, we'll do it."

"Thanks, boss. Jenna." Alex gave a wave and left.

Ten minutes later, he'd parked in the public lot on Broom Avenue, a block away from the bookstore, and was walking into the Bell, Book & Candle. There were a few browsers and a clerk behind the counter, a young man with pointed ears. Alex didn't recognize him, but Roxy's stalker definitely wasn't fae, so whoever the clerk was, he was cool.

Agnes Miller was crouched in the front window, working on a display of Roxy's books. He'd never formally met Agnes, but he recognized her from around town. He leaned over the small partition. "Ms. Miller?"

She looked up, a trio of straight pins sticking out of the corner of her mouth. She put down the book that she was holding, took the pins out of her mouth and smiled. "That's me. Can I help you, Officer?"

"I'm a friend of Roxy's and I'm also going to be

handling security for her signing tomorrow. I was hoping you could show me around and we could have a little talk."

Her expression took on greater concern. "I didn't realize she had hired anyone. I can assure you, my events are very well run."

"This doesn't have anything to do with you or your store so much as..." He lowered his voice. "Roxy has an overeager fan that we're concerned may show up. In fact, we're anticipating it. So if we could talk in your office, maybe?"

She nodded. "That's not good. I had no idea. We can absolutely talk." She stood, then opened the small door that closed the window partition off from the rest of the store, and jumped down. "Follow me."

For an older woman, she was certainly agile, which was made even more impressive by the fact that witches never looked their age. They had their spells and potions and magic to hold back the hands of time. If Agnes appeared fifty, she might be seventy. Or older. But she'd act thirty. The streaks of color in her hair were evidence of that.

"Lead the way."

She started off and he fell into step behind her. She pointed at the young fae man behind the counter. "Leo, mind the shop, I have a meeting."

Leo's brows rose and he smiled. "You got it, Agnes."

Her office was in the back and had a small one-way window. The space was tiny and made even more so by the stacks of books, magazines and papers. She scooped a pile off one of the two chairs. "Have a seat."

Then she put that stack on her desk chair and sat on the desk. "What do you need me to do to keep Roxy safe?"

He took the chair. "I'm glad you asked. Do you have any kind of security system? A closed-circuit camera set up?"

She shook her head. "In Nocturne Falls? Nope."

"Not a big deal. I'll be here tomorrow and I'll have at least one other deputy with me, possibly two." He wasn't going to explain about Jenna's sister just yet in case Tessa had other plans. "We'll all be in plainclothes. The women should blend in well with the crowd. I know I won't be able to do that, so I'll probably pick a spot where I can see as much as possible and do my best to disappear while generally keeping an eye on things."

"You can have the run of the place if you like."

"Thank you. I was hoping maybe you and some of your friends from the coven might be able to cast some kind of protection spell over the place?"

She grinned. "I already have an anti-theft spell in place. I can whip up something for tomorrow. It would be easier for me to do something specific for Roxy, but I'd need something of hers."

"Such as?"

Agnes tipped her head back and forth. "A lock of hair, some eyelashes, fingernail clippings...you know, spell ingredients. But I suppose that would be a strange thing for either of us to ask her for. Especially since she's human and doesn't have any clue what this town's about."

"No, she knows. She didn't, but she does now."

Agnes grimaced. "How'd she take that?"

"It was a little tough, but she's adapting quickly."

"Good to hear. Does she know I'm a witch?"

He shook his head. "Not unless Delaney told her. Roxy is at Delaney's now. She's spending the night there as a safety precaution."

"The stalker is that serious, huh?"

He gave her a brief history of what had happened so far.

"Okay, that is serious. Hey, if you have anything physical from this guy, I could scry for him, see if I could find out if he's in town."

Alex sat back as best he could in the small space. "We don't even have a fingerprint. So far, he's a ghost."

"Literally? No, you said you actually had him pinned to the ground, so that can't be." She made a face. "This guy is not going to disrupt tomorrow's event. I'm going to call a few of my coven members and seed the crowd with some extra help. We've got a few who can read auras, and picking out a guy in a group of woman won't be hard. Then it's just a matter of reading his aura to see if he plans to do harm."

"That would be great. Who do you have in mind?"

"Right now, Kaley Van Zant is our best aura reader. Pandora Williams is her mentor."

"I know Pandora. In fact, I've been meaning to talk to her, but I don't know Kaley. Is she new?"

Agnes nodded. "She and her dad moved to town last year. He inherited the old Pilcher manor."

"Wait a second. Kaley is a kid. I don't know if her father would appreciate her being involved in this."

"There won't be any danger to her. If Pandora can't be with her, we'll find someone else. She's just the best aura reader we have."

"All right, but make sure her father's in the loop."

"I will. I suppose you want to have a look around the store now. Besides the sales floor, there's a storeroom in the back. It's where I keep stock, but also the magical books that I deal in. Those aren't out in the open, for obvious reasons."

"I do want to see the rest, but..." He hesitated. "There's one more thing."

"Sure."

"There's a spell that can allow a human to live as a shifter. It's old magic and very—"

"No." Agnes' gaze turned cold. "That spell will ruin any human it's placed upon. I don't do that kind of magic. I won't."

"Good," Alex said. "That's exactly the response I was hoping for. If Roxy brings it up, which is more likely something that would happen in the future, I hope you'll explain to her why it's such a bad idea."

Agnes' expression softened. "You think she might ask me?"

"If she finds out about it, and knows you're a witch, yes. Right now, she doesn't know such a spell exists. I'd like to keep it that way, but in this town..." He sighed.

"She sweet on you? Is that why you think she'd want the spell? Or some other shifter?"

"You know what I am, huh?"

She grinned. "Honey, my first husband was a tiger. Literally. Too bad he'd used up eight of his nine lives when I'd met him. May he rest in peace. Anyway, I know you big cats when I see you."

Alex smiled. "We're sweet on each other. Which is why I can guarantee you nothing's going to happen to her tomorrow." He stood. "I'll go have my look around now. If I see anything out of the ordinary, I'll let you know. And thank you for the spell thing."

"You got it, Officer. See you tomorrow."

Roxy shook her head in amazement. All Delaney had done was offer Pandora Williams a slice of her Tall, Dark and Handsome chocolate cake and Pandora had shown up thirty minutes later. Now the three women sat in Delaney's kitchen, ruining their appetites for dinner and talking around the reason Delaney had invited Pandora over.

Roxy couldn't take it anymore. "So now that I know what Nocturne Falls is really about and I'm starting to find out who people really are—like you being a witch, Pandora—it's making me feel...I don't know, sort of like I'm standing on the outside looking in."

"I get that," Pandora said. "Being a witch isn't that far removed from being human. In fact, being a witch is pretty different from being a vampire or being able to shift into a different shape. Although we can do that too, if we have enough magic and the right spell. Of course, that shape carries the limitations of the spell, which includes an expiration date, but it's still a possibility."

"I'm glad you mentioned that," Roxy said. She couldn't have asked for a better segue. "That's kind of why Delaney asked you here. So I could talk to you about a spell."

Pandora swallowed the cake she'd just eaten. "Oh? What can I do for you?"

"First of all, I should ask what you charge. I have money, but as you know, most of it has gone into the house and that aquarium. So if this is going to be a lot of money, it'll have to wait a while for my bank account to recover."

Pandora scoffed. "I'm not going to charge you for a spell. I mean, if the ingredients are super expensive, then we'll have to talk. But seriously, I'm so happy to finally be able to do magic again that I'll do just about anything for free."

That was a curious thing to say. Roxy squinted at her. "What do you mean about finally being able to do magic again?"

Pandora finished the last of her cake. "My magic only recently started working again. All my life, my gifts were so unreliable that they were worthless. Nothing I did went as planned. I pretty much gave up using magic altogether. Then I met my boyfriend, Cole, and everything changed. Turned out he's a human familiar. Long story short in terms a normie can understand, his presence makes my magic work. And work well."

"Wow, that's really cool." Roxy looked at Delaney. "Did you know about that?"

"A little." Delaney smiled. "Nothing stays secret in this town for long."

Something to remember. "Well, I'm really glad you got your magic working again. And not just because I'd love your help. But I would."

"All right," Pandora said. "What kind of spell do you need?"

Roxy took a breath. "I don't know."

"And neither do I," Delaney said.

"But," Roxy went on, "Delaney said if anyone would know, it would be you because your mom has a pretty intensive library of spell books, and because you're mentoring a young witch, so you must be pretty knowledgeable."

"I like to think so." Pandora smiled. "I spent years trying to figure out why my magic didn't work, so I've done my time with those books. And now I'm super curious to hear what you're after."

Roxy sat up a little straighter. "I want a spell that will turn me into a shifter. Specifically, the same kind as Alex Cruz. A panther shifter."

"Oh, fun." Pandora's eyes sparkled. "I'll have to do some research, but I'll see what I can come up with. In fact, I'll swing by my mom's on the way home and have a look through that library."

"Really?" Hope rose through Roxy's body like a current of spring air. "So you think it's possible?"

Pandora chewed on her bottom lip. "I think it might be. I feel like I've heard about a spell like that, but let me do some research before I give you a firm yes. Hey, maybe I can tell you tomorrow at the signing. I plan to swing by anyway. I'm going to bring Willa Iscove with me. But be prepared. She's probably going to go total fangirl. She loves your books. She got me reading them."

Roxy smiled. "I love her already. Is she a witch too?"

"Nope. She's fae. And legitimately the most beautiful woman I've ever seen. It's a fae thing. They're like unnaturally pretty. Totally not fair to the rest of us, but there you have it." Pandora's phone buzzed, and she glanced at the screen. "Huh. Speaking of witchy things, Agnes Miller just texted me to call her about tomorrow."

Roxy tilted her head. "Is Agnes a witch?"

"Yep. Besides the regular books she carries, she handles a lot of grimoires and spell books too. I should call her real quick." Pandora looked at them. "Do you mind?"

Roxy and Delaney shook their heads at the same time.

"Great." Pandora dialed. "Hey, Agnes, what's up?" She listened intently as she ate the remaining crumbs on her plate. "Uh-huh. Really?" Pandora glanced at Roxy. "No problem. I'll ask him, but I'm sure it'll be fine. Okay. See you then." She hung up.

"Everything all right?" Delaney asked.

"Not exactly." Pandora looked at Roxy. "You didn't say anything about having a stalker. What the heck is going on?"

Roxy explained as briefly as possible. "But why would Agnes call to tell you about that?"

"Alex Cruz was in her shop doing some recon, and Agnes offered to have me bring in Kaley, my boyfriend's daughter, to read the auras of any male customers who show up to see if they mean you harm."

Roxy flattened her hands on the table. "I had no idea that was even a possibility. But I really hope this guy doesn't show up tomorrow. I don't want any trouble. It'll be chaotic enough with the signing and the parade."

Delaney patted her hand. "It'll be fine."

"I agree," Pandora said. "One guy against an assorted bunch of supernaturals? He's got no chance." She stood. "And now I better get going. I have a lot of work to do before making it to Cole's at seven. Thanks for the cake, Delaney."

Delaney started to get up. "I'll walk you out."

"Rest, mama-to-be. I know where the door is." Pandora waved as she hiked her briefcase strap onto her shoulder. "I'll see you guys tomorrow."

Morning came bright and early, and as Alex was carrying his mother's things to her car, a gleaming black Bentley pulled into Roxy's drive. Roxy got out of the back, an overnight bag in her hand. Stanhill, Hugh Ellingham's rook, was behind the wheel. She waved to him, then walked over to Alex. "Hiya."

"Hi. How was your night at Delaney's?"

"Oh, you know. Full of girl talk."

He popped the Caddy's trunk. "You two all right now?"

"Yep. We talked it all out. She told me about the history of the town and the Ellinghams and everything. Even about the water and the spell that's in it to keep humans from figuring out the truth about this place."

"You really did talk it out. Did you get any writing done?"

"A little." She leaned against the car. "Kind of sad your mom's going home today. I haven't eaten that well in a long time."

"She's not happy she's missing the signing, but I told her I know people. And my freezer is full of meals. You're welcome to join me anytime." He put his mother's bag and cooler in the trunk and shut it.

Roxy smiled. "I like your mom. If you give me a few minutes, I'll go sign a set of books for her to take home."

"You don't have to do that."

"I know." She lifted one shoulder. "But I want to. She's the mother of the guy I'm crazy about. I need her on my side. And I have to come over and say goodbye."

He laughed, warmed by her words. "She's already on your side, trust me."

"I do." She stared up at him.

He tried to read her expression. "Are you worried about today? Because you shouldn't be. It's going to be fine. Even if this guy shows up, I've got it covered."

She nodded. "I know. I'm not worried. And I think I'm going to be too busy to get worried."

She continued to study him, but he couldn't read her. "There's something on your mind. I just can't figure out what."

She pursed her lips. "I was thinking that you could kiss me hello from now on." She ran her fingers along the line of the car's trunk. "If you wanted to, that is."

Hell yes, he wanted to. He leaned in and laid one on her. "Does that answer your question?"

She laughed. "Very well." She took a step back toward her house. "I should go get ready."

"What time do you need to be at the bookstore?"

"The signing is from one to four. I told Agnes I'd be there at twelve thirty."

"Okay. I'll drive you. If you want, you can come over here and have lunch, then we can go."

"I might be too nervous to have lunch." She fiddled with the earring dangling from her right ear.

"You have to eat something. That's too long to go without food."

She laughed. "I can tell your mother's been visiting. Okay, I'll come over. In fact, let me go grab those books for your mom and then I'll come say goodbye to her."

"Excellent. I'll keep her occupied until you show up."

She turned to go, then stopped. "You didn't see anything going on around my house last night, did you?"

"No, and I did a perimeter check this morning. Nothing out of the ordinary."

"Good. Thanks. See you in a bit."

He watched her go, distracted by the sway of her hips and the flavor of her berry gloss on his mouth. He was still smiling as he went inside.

"That happy I'm leaving, huh?" Carmen turned back to the sink and put the last of the breakfast dishes into the drainer.

"You know I have a dishwasher."

"Eh, this is faster."

He doubted that, but if she wanted to hand-wash his dishes, he wasn't going to put up too much of a fuss. If there was anything he knew about Carmen Cruz, it's that she liked to feel useful. "I'm not happy because you're leaving."

"Then why were you smiling?"

"Because I'm a happy guy."

She turned to face him again. She leaned against the sink, taking off the rubber gloves she must have also brought with her. "You're in love."

"I'm not in love." No way. Not yet. It was too early for that. Much too early. But if Roxy really was his soul mate—

"You smile like a man in love. Your father gets the same look every now and then. Mostly when I make flan."

"I like Roxy a lot, but our relationship is very young, Mom. I'm happy to just let it happen right now."

She pointed at him. "You'd better protect that woman. Whoever this nut is that's after her, you find him and put him in jail."

"I'm working on it. And I will. Promise."

"Don't leave her side today."

He wouldn't actually be at Roxy's side, but he wasn't going to explain the details of the operation to her. "I won't, Mom."

"Good." She put the towel down and sighed. "I

suppose I should get ready to go. The car is packed?"

"Except for your toiletry case, your purse and you, yes."

She pushed off the counter and headed for the guest room. "I'll be out of your hair soon enough."

"Mom." He rolled his eyes. There was no winning this conversation.

A knock at the door claimed his attention. Roxy waved from the other side of the sidelight.

He let her in, barely waiting until she'd crossed the threshold to kiss her again.

"What was that for?"

"You said to kiss you hello from now on. So I am."

She grinned. "You're a quick study. I like that." She hefted a dark red tote bag with her name and logo—a sly smile with fangs—printed on the side. "I brought the goods in one of my signature book bags."

"My mother's going to love that."

"What am I going to love?" Carmen walked out of the hall, fastening a bracelet around her wrist. "Roxy, hi! I didn't think I'd see you before I left. Alex told me all about your troubles. I'm so sorry. But he'll take care of it, you'll see."

"I have no doubt he will." She lifted the bag again. "I brought you a little gift since you can't make the signing today."

Carmen clapped her hands. "What have you done?"

"Just the first five books in the series, all signed to you, plus a bunch of swag for you and your book club."

More hand clapping ensued, this time accompanied by shrieks of happiness and a few exclamations in Spanish. Then Carmen hugged Roxy. "Thank you. You are a dear girl. I'm so glad someone so good and kind has come into my son's life. It's about time."

Roxy laughed. "Good thing I bought the house next to him, huh?"

"It was fate," Carmen said, nodding. "You two are meant to be."

Roxy glanced at him. "I guess time will tell."

"That's what I told her." Alex took the tote bag. "I'll go put this in the car with the rest of your stuff. Roxy needs to get ready for her signing, so why don't you say goodbye and we can let her get back to her day. Plus, you need to get on the road, Mom. It's a long drive. I don't want you driving after dark."

Carmen rolled her eyes. "My son, the worrier. Fine, I'm saying goodbye and getting the rest of my things. Thank you again, Roxy." She hugged Roxy. "I'll see you soon."

"You're welcome." Roxy hugged her back, grateful for the woman's efforts to bring her and Alex back together. "Have a safe trip home."

"I will."

Carmen went off down the hall again, and Roxy took a few steps toward the door. "Alex, I'll see you in a bit."

He nodded. "Thanks again. That was really sweet of you. I'll be the favorite son for a long time now."

Roxy winked at him. "And if you don't want to lose that status, you'd better keep me happy."

He laughed. "I'm aware."

She left, smiling, and a few minutes later, he had his mother in the car and on the road. It was good to have his house to himself again. He stretched. Today was going to be intense. Roxy might not think her stalker was going to show, but Alex did. He needed to be sharp and focused. The crowd at the bookstore and in town would only make things more difficult.

With that in mind, he started to change into shorts and a T-shirt for a run to clear his head and use up some of the pre-game energy coursing through him. Then he stopped. What was he thinking? He couldn't leave Roxy alone.

He jogged to her house instead and knocked on the door.

Roxy answered a few minutes later in a robe and with her hair wound up in a towel. She was bare-faced, and her skin was pink with heat. She looked beautiful. "Hey. Out for a run?"

"Not really. I was going to, but then I realized I can't leave you alone. In fact, you really shouldn't be here by yourself right now."

"You're too late."

His hackles rose. "For what?"

She cocked her hip to the side. "To join me for my shower."

He grinned, the imagined threat gone. "Clearly, I suck at my job."

Her brows rose and her mouth bent in an amused line. "There is so much I could say to that, but I'm not going to because we might not make it to the bookstore."

He laughed. "Save that thought for the end of the day."

"Will do." She opened the door a little wider. "Coming in?"

"Yes, if you don't mind."

"Nope." She tightened the sash on her robe. "I'm sure it's easier to protect me from here than your house."

He came in, shut the door and locked it. "Abundantly. Just pretend I'm not here. Do whatever you need to do. When you're ready, we'll go back to my place, eat some lunch, then head over. Good?"

"Good. I'm going to finish getting myself together, then I need to pack up some stuff for the signing and if I have time, maybe write a little."

"How's the book coming?"

"Slowly. But it is what it is."

"Can I do anything for you?"

"Not really, unless you can whip out the last twelve or so chapters of this book."

"That's probably best left to the professional."

"In that case, I'd better get moving." She put her hands on his chest, went up on her tiptoes and kissed him, giving him a whiff of her clean scent.

It shot through his blood like a drug, ramping up his craving for her. "Yeah," he mumbled.

She patted his chest and trotted back to the rear of the house. "Make yourself at home."

"Uh-huh," he answered. A brilliant response. He shook his head, grinned at his unbridled infatuation with her and went to do another perimeter check.

He might not be able to write the chapters she needed, but he could damn well protect the woman who could.

At a quarter after twelve, the size of the crowd already assembled in the bookstore was astonishing. Roxy peered out the one-way window in Agnes's office. People were everywhere. Most were in line to buy one of her books, since Agnes had made it clear that supplies were limited and no one was getting anything signed unless they had a receipt for at least one book purchased at Bell, Book & Candle.

Roxy let out a soft whistle. "That's quite a crowd out there. I don't think I've ever seen so many people in one place because of me."

Agnes nodded as she fastened the locket Roxy had just given her around her neck. "It's going to be a good signing. Don't worry about the crowd. Leo will get them organized. He's got tickets to hand out with the times they're to come back to get their books signed. That way we don't have a mad rush of people. After they get their books, that is. The crowd will be spaced out pretty evenly over the event."

"Well done." Roxy smiled. "This isn't your first rodeo, is it?"

"No, it isn't." Agnes looked proud and pleased. "But this might be the biggest one." She lifted her chin and patted the locket. "How's it look?"

"Perfect."

"Thank you again. I love it."

Roxy was about to reply when Alex came in. "It's a madhouse out there, but everything's secure. Agnes, please make sure the alarm's set on the back door."

"It is," Agnes said.

Alex frowned. "Don't you need to check a panel or something?"

"No." Agnes pulled a thin silk cord from under her green and purple tunic top. At the end dangled a silver disc with some symbols marked on it. "The alarm is magical. Anyone comes through that door and this amulet vibrates to announce it."

"That is so cool," Roxy said. The more she knew about this town and the people who lived here, the more she fell in love with it.

Alex's mouth stayed pressed in a hard line. "That's great for you, but I'm not going to know if someone comes through there. Do you have a physical alarm you can set?"

"Yes, but I don't usually set it during the day."

"Can you make an exception today? For me. And Roxy."

Agnes tucked the amulet away. "You got it." She typed in a code on a small touch pad by the door. "There. All set. Now if you'll excuse me, I need to get out there and make sure everything's going according to plan. Leo's good. But he's not me."

"Understood," Alex said.

"Thank you," Roxy added.

Agnes left them and Roxy sighed as the door shut.

Alex took her hand. "You feel cold. Are you okay?"

"Nerves." Which she knew were reflected in her smile. "I'll be fine."

"Can I get you something? Coffee? A soda? A shot of whiskey? Anything. Just name it."

She laughed and shook her head, her smile growing more genuine at his eagerness to help. "Save the whiskey for later, but the caffeine will just make me jittery, and Agnes has water out there. I appreciate the offer, though. And I really will be fine. This is just my process."

"Nerves, huh?"

"Yep."

"About the signing or your unknown stalker?"

"The signing. The stalker is your business to worry about. Plus, with the backup you've got here, why should I worry? In fact, I hope he shows up so we can put an end to this."

"I'm glad you feel that way. I'm hoping he shows up too." Alex glanced out the window. "Jenna and Tessa Blythe just arrived. Pandora and Kaley shouldn't be too far behind them. Yeah, if this guy shows up, not only are we going to know about it the second he steps through the door, but he's not going to know which way to turn."

Roxy's phone buzzed. "Speaking of Pandora and Kaley, they're here and Kaley wants to meet me." She put her hand on the doorknob.

Alex covered her hand with his. "You're going out there?"

She laughed. "Well, I have to at some point."

"You'll be mobbed. Ask them to come back here."

She held her hands out. "Have you seen the size of this office?" Adding two more people would mean someone would have to stand on a chair. Or the desk. If they could find a spot that wasn't covered in paperwork.

He grinned. "Good point. I'll go get them and send them back. I need to talk to Deputy Blythe anyway." He opened the door, then paused and leaned in to kiss her. "You're going to do great."

"Thanks." Then she held on to his shirt to keep him from leaving and kissed him back. "See you out there."

"You need anything, you just look at me. I'll be in your sight line the entire time."

"Got it." She liked the idea of being able to see him anytime she wanted.

He left, and a few minutes later, Pandora and Kaley showed up. They squeezed into the office, and Pandora let out a, "Wow. It is packed out there."

"I know. But that's a good thing."

"That's for sure. I'd love to have an open house with this kind of turnout." Pandora gave Kaley her attention as she held a hand toward Roxy. "Kaley, this is Ms. St. James. She's the author we're going to help today."

Kaley was a cute thing with long brown hair and big eyes. She stuck her hand out and looked about as impressed as any teenager could. "I've never met a real live author before. Nice to meet you."

"You too, Kaley. And I've never met a real live aura reader before." Roxy shook her hand.

"Do you know JK Rowling?"

Roxy bit back a laugh. "No, sadly, I do not." She released the girl's hand. "It's such an honor to have someone with your abilities here to help me today. Pandora has done nothing but sing your praises about how skilled you are."

Kaley grinned. "Thanks. It's the first time I've ever gotten to use my abilities in a professional way."

Roxy smiled, tickled that the girl was taking it so seriously. "So tell me, what do auras look like?"

Kaley shrugged. "They're all different. But there are similarities among them that tell me things like if people are telling the truth or not, what their mood is, how they're feeling. All kinds of stuff like that. Like, you're nervous, right?"

Roxy's mouth fell open. The kid was spot-on. "Yes. You can see that in my aura? What else can you see?"

Kaley looked at Pandora. Pandora nodded. "Go ahead. She asked." Pandora glanced at Roxy. "It's not good aura-reading etiquette to just blurt out what you see around a person. Not everyone wants the world to know they're not feeling so well or whatever."

Roxy nodded. "Sure. Makes sense."

Kaley squinted at Roxy. "You're falling in love with someone."

Roxy sucked in a breath. "Whoa. You can tell that?"

Pandora's brows went skyward. "Well, now, that's interesting. Might it be someone I know? A very hot someone who carries a badge?"

Roxy shot her a look. "I don't think I'm ready to call it love, but we definitely like each other. And with my divorce being final, why not?"

"Exactly." Pandora looked at Kaley. "Anything else you want to tell Miss Roxy about her aura?"

Kaley shook her head, her mouth bending slightly in disappointment. "Not really because I can't tell what kind of supernatural she is."

Roxy laughed. "That's because I'm not one. I'm human."

The teen wound some hair around her finger. "Not totally you aren't. There are too many swirly blues and greens." She pointed at the air around Roxy. "And that purple is definitely not a human color. That's totally witchy."

Roxy knees went a little wobbly. She reached behind her, found the one empty chair and sat. "That can't be. Are you saying I'm a witch?"

Pandora put a hand on Kaley's shoulder. "She's saying that you have some supernatural bloodlines, and one of them looks like witch, yes. Right, Kaley?"

"Yeah," Kaley said. "You're a lot human. But not a hundred percent."

"This is *such* good news." Pandora grinned like they'd just won the lottery.

"It is?" Roxy asked. Her heart was pounding. And not because of the signing. "I don't know how I feel about it. Maybe you should tell me more."

"Sure," Pandora said. "You know the spell you asked me about?"

Roxy nodded. She could manage that much.

"I was about to tell you that it couldn't happen. I researched it and found out the physical cost for a human is far too high. There are some witches who would do it, I'm sure, but I won't, and neither will any of the witches I know. In fact, Alex called me to let me know you might ask about it and he wanted to make sure we both knew how dangerous it would be. But now that I know you're not entirely human, this changes everything. Especially the witch genes. Those are big."

Roxy looked up. The fact that Alex had talked to Pandora about the spell was interesting, but not as interesting as Pandora's obvious excitement about Roxy having witch in her system. "They are?"

"To borrow a word from Kaley, totally."

"Okay, that's a good thing, then." She blew out a long breath, her head still swimming with the news. Witch genes. She was part witch. And some other stuff. It was boggling.

Pandora looked concerned. "I thought you'd be more excited, but you seem upset. I'm so sorry. I had no idea—"

"I didn't mean to make you feel bad." Kaley moved closer to Pandora's side.

"Oh, no, Kaley, this isn't your fault at all. You did exactly what I asked you to. You did great." Roxy made herself smile. "It's just that..." She looked at Pandora. "If I have all these supernatural bloodlines, it means my parents had them too. Where else would I have gotten them?"

"Right. Did you ever suspect your parents were...something else?"

"That never even occurred to me. Definitely not my dad, but my mother…" Roxy took another breath before giving voice to the one thing that had haunted her all her life. "My mother was institutionalized when I was very young. She heard voices. Saw things. *Knew* things." Roxy shook her head. "Do you think…"

Pandora kneeled down beside the chair and put her hands on Roxy's knees. "Oh, honey. Yes, I do think these bloodlines were the reason for all those things. I'm so sorry."

Roxy rubbed her hand over her mouth. "So my mother wasn't really crazy."

"Probably not." Pandora sighed. "But sometimes, having all these little bits of different kinds of supernatural inside you can make a person feel that way. It definitely happens."

"I've always feared I might have inherited my mother's mental health issues." Roxy sniffed. "But she might not have been schizophrenic at all." The relief she felt for herself made her feel sadder for her mother. Maybe she hadn't known she had witch blood, like Roxy hadn't until now. Maybe she died in that institution thinking she really was crazy. Or maybe she did know, but no one believed her. No matter what had happened, knowing what Roxy knew now put an entirely different spin on her mother's illness. She wondered if she'd ever find out the truth of what happened back then. Or even if her father had had some inkling. "I guess being part supernatural is why the water didn't work on me either."

"The town water? No, that wouldn't work on someone with this many strands of supernatural in them."

Roxy stared at her hands, imagining this strange new blood flowing through her veins. "Why can't I do anything magical? Or turn into anything? Shouldn't I have some kind of powers?"

Pandora shrugged. "We don't know that you don't. It could be that you've just never tapped into what's there. Or it could be that you don't have enough of any one kind to be able to manifest it. This is new ground for me. But you know, I've read your books. I wouldn't say you're without gifts."

"That's very kind of you, but I wish I could know more."

"I might be able to help. Run some test. Can you spare a few strands of hair?"

"Sure." Roxy grabbed the scissors off Agnes' desk and handed them to Pandora as she turned and lifted her curls. "Just don't leave a hole."

Pandora snipped. "You won't even notice it."

Roxy turned around to see the witch pocketing a thin hank of curls. "That wasn't much at all."

"Nope."

"You sure you're not upset with me?" Kaley

asked softly. She was biting her lip and staring at her feet.

"Not at all, Kaley. I promise." Roxy's heart went out to the kid. "I'm actually really excited to find out that I'm not entirely human."

Kaley's head came up. "For real?"

Roxy smiled. "For real. I really am. I want you both to do me a favor, though, okay? Let me be the one to tell Deputy Cruz, all right?" She looked at Pandora. "I want to figure out what this means for me and the spell we talked about, first. If you need to talk to someone else about it who might be able to help, I'm fine with that. But I don't want to give him any kind of hope when there might not be."

Pandora stood. "You got it. I'll let you know what I find out as soon as possible."

A knock on the door interrupted them, and Agnes stuck her head in. "It's almost show time. You ready?"

Roxy got up and smiled. The possibility that she might be more than what she'd thought she was filled her head, making no room for nerves. Besides, that crowd was here for her. These were her people. She could do this, and do it well. "I can't wait."

Alex found a spot against the far wall where he could see Roxy and the front door. He couldn't see the rear of the store, but Jenna was positioned in the storage area at that door, and with the alarm on, he doubted that would be the entrance the stalker chose.

Jenna's sister had been given a name badge and was playing the part of an employee, which was more than Alex had expected her to be up for, but apparently Tessa felt strongly about someone threatening an author. And her librarian job made her a natural as a bookstore employee.

Pandora and Kaley had been given two reserved seats in the small front lounge. No one could enter the shop without going by Kaley, who was showing the kind of earnest effort that made Alex think the kid had a future in law enforcement if she wanted it.

Every time the door opened, the noise outside from the parade—and the crowd filling the streets of Nocturne Falls because of it—filtered in, adding to the already significant hum in the building. Alex tuned out the noise, though, and tried to keep his focus on two things: the door and the crowd in the shop.

It was hard not to watch Roxy, however. She'd had a big smile on her face from the start, and not a hint of nerves. She gave time to every reader who stood in front of her table, talking to them and asking them questions, standing for hugs and pictures, accepting the gifts they brought. She greeted everyone with the same enthusiasm, never showing the slightest trace of exhaustion. She was amazing. A rock star.

And he could see exactly why her readers loved her. Her books were great. But as a person, she was a friend to everyone.

A few of the women who came to see her even broke down in tears, but they all left smiling, clutching their books in their arms and practically glowing with the experience. Here and there, he caught snippets of conversations as the attendees wound past him.

"She's so nice. I can't believe how nice she is. I love her!"

"She signed the book I bought *and* every book I brought with me."

"I got my picture with her! I'm totally making that my new profile pic."

And then there were the happy shrieks and endless smiles. It was a love fest and he couldn't help but smile too. Roxy St. James was a freaking phenomenon.

Over the course of the next few hours, several men came in. Some with their wives or girlfriends, some alone, but still with books to be signed. Each time one entered the store, Alex glanced at Kaley, who'd peer at them very intently, then look at Alex and indicate what she'd read. Each time it was a shake of her head no.

None of the men showed signs of meaning harm to Roxy.

By the time the signing was over, Alex was happy the stalker hadn't shown, but frustrated that whoever this jerk was, he remained at large. Roxy was standing at her table now, a crowd of readers surrounding her, asking questions, chatting her up. That went on for fifteen minutes, at which point Agnes announced Roxy had to go and escorted her to the office.

As the fans filtered out, Alex walked over to Pandora and Kaley. He addressed the teenager. "Good work today. Absolutely outstanding."

She grinned. "Thanks."

"You're welcome. You and Miss Williams can head on home." He nodded at Pandora. "Thank you for coming. Really helped."

"No problem." She stood and gathered her things. "Can you believe how many people showed up?"

"Very impressive." He glanced toward the back of the shop. "I have to check in with Deputy Blythe. You two have a good night."

"You too. And tell Roxy we said goodbye."

"Will do." As they left, he headed to Jenna's post in the storage room. He pushed through the door and saw her sitting in a chair against the back wall.

She stood and stretched. "Everything over?"

"Yep. And not a sign of him."

"Nothing back here either. Not even the rattle of someone trying the door. You think he's gone? Given up maybe?"

Alex shook his head. "No. Maybe he wants us to think that, though."

She nodded. "Could be. You need Tessa and me anymore?"

"No. I'm going to take Roxy home. Thanks for your help today."

"Sure thing."

They walked back into the shop together, then Jenna collected her sister, they said their goodbyes and they were gone.

Leo was at the counter when Alex walked up. "If you're looking for Agnes or Roxy," Leo said, "they're still in the office."

"Thanks." He went back and knocked on the office door.

Agnes opened it. "Roxy just finished up."

"Finished up what?"

Roxy was sitting at the desk, which had been cleaned off a little. Several stacks of her books sat to one side and there was another carton of books on the floor. Roxy had a black Sharpie in her hand. She lifted it. "I was signing the books that were ordered. Books that have to be mailed to the customers who couldn't make it in today."

"That's nice." He looked at how many books there were. Then he shifted his gaze to Agnes. "How did these customers find out about being able to order a signed book?"

"Mostly my mailing list. Those are my regular romance readers." She pointed at the computer. "But I posted on the store's social media too."

"The regulars, do you know all of them?"

She nodded. "Absolutely."

"What about the requests that came in through social media? Do you know them?"

"No. But there weren't as many of them."

"Can you email a list of those names and addresses to Birdie?"

Roxy's brows lifted. "Birdie? Where are you going with this?"

"I think it's possible your stalker didn't show today because he knew he'd get caught, but I also think he would have wanted a signed book from you. I'm going to get Birdie to run that list through our system. See if anyone who wanted a book has any priors that fit our suspect."

Roxy nodded. "You really think my stalker could be on the list?"

Alex nodded. "Maybe. And if he is, he just might have given himself away."

Roxy smiled up at the stars as she trailed her fingers through the water of Alex's hot tub. It had been a week since the signing and there hadn't been a peep from her stalker. She was convinced the guy had realized she was with Alex now and had given up.

Alex wasn't so convinced, even after the list of book buyers from Agnes's shop hadn't turned up anything, but that was his job. Well, his job right now was getting her a glass of wine. He'd just gone in to open a bottle for them, then he'd be joining her.

Things between them were so good. Easy and uncomplicated and just what she needed, even with them being intimate. Which was amazing. The writing was finally back up to speed, and she was happy with it. And Pandora was hard at work on something to do with the shifter spell they'd talked about. It had required a few items from Roxy's past, things near and dear to her, but Pandora had promised Roxy it would be well worth it and ready very soon.

Roxy was curious, but content to wait, because at long last, she was caught up on all her obligations. Alex had even helped her unpack the boxes in her garage so she could park her hybrid in there. For the first time in what felt like forever, she could breathe. And relax. A huge improvement over the last several long months.

Life hadn't been this happy in forever.

The doorbell rang faintly, followed by a louder voice as Alex called out, "Just a sec."

Whoever it was, the interruption wasn't going to ruin her night. Her mood was too good and Alex would deal with it. This was *his* house.

She closed her eyes, spread her arms out along the edge of the tub and awaited Alex's return. She sensed movement near her, just the shift of air, really. She smiled. "Who was at the door?"

A hand covered her mouth as an arm snaked around her body and hauled her backward out of the tub. Her heels bumped along the deck and hit grass.

Her gasp and her scream were two parts of one muted noise. She flailed, kicking and striking back at whoever had grabbed her, but was unable to get her feet under her. A man, based on his strength and the woodsy smell of him. She caught a little of the man's palm between her teeth and bit down.

He grunted, but didn't let go. "Hold still," he hissed, hovering above her kneeling form. "This is for the best."

"Let her go, or I will kill you."

Roxy went still at the sound of Alex's voice. The man holding her did too.

He answered Alex. "And risk hurting her? I don't think so. Unless you don't love her as much as I do."

She tried once more to get to her feet, but the water dripping off her had made the grass slippery. Then something sharp and metal pressed against her neck. Had to be a knife. She stayed on her knees, unwilling to make any movement that could dig the blade in deeper.

Alex was standing on the deck now. His eyes were glowing. And he looked very, very angry. "Last chance. Let her go."

The man started yanking her backward again. "We're leaving."

"Roxy, run." Alex leaped off the deck and flew across the yard. He caught the man around the neck, tearing him away from Roxy. She heard a dull thump and a strangled sound behind her, then a low growl rumbled over the noise of the bubbling water. She crawled away as fast as she could. A louder snarl followed, then a very human yelp. She got to the deck and turned.

Alex was crouched over a dark figure. His eyes

still glowed gold in the soft light, but now his canines were long and deadly, and sharp claws jutted from his fingers. He was in his half-form, the same one she'd seen the night she'd found out the truth about this town.

The same night he'd also had a man pinned to the ground.

"Stay down," he snarled. Then he looked at her. "Are you all right?"

She nodded, not quite up to words.

"You sure you're not hurt?"

"I'm sure, Alex. I'm fine." She stared at the man on the ground. A black hoodie obscured his face and in the darkness of the evening, it was hard to make out much more. Black jeans. Black sneakers. All nondescript.

"Good. Do you feel up to getting my handcuffs and my phone?"

"Yes." She could do anything if it meant putting an end to this.

"They're on the dresser in my bedroom."

The stalker squirmed. "Get off me, man."

Alex leaned down. "Move and I'll break you in half."

The man went still as she got to her feet and climbed the stairs to the deck. She picked up a towel to wrap around herself. She stared at the guy on the ground. "He was going to kidnap me."

Alex nodded. "I wouldn't have let that happen."

"You kept saying he'd show up sooner or later. You were right." She shivered and pulled the towel around her, but she wasn't cold. Just shaken by the enormity of what might have happened. This man, whoever he was—she tried again to make out his features in the shadows—had tried to abduct her. But he hadn't. Because of Alex. "Is that who rang the doorbell?"

"Yes. I knew as soon as I opened it and there was no one there."

"I can't believe you took him down so fast."

"I wasn't going to give him an opportunity to hurt you."

"Thank you." She swallowed as a thousand scenarios of what could have happened spun through her head. "Be right back." She ran into the house to get the things he'd asked for, still trembling with adrenaline.

When she returned, Alex's half form had given way to his human one. He took the cuffs from her, then secured the guy and hauled him to a sitting position. Alex yanked the man's hood back. "Do you recognize this guy?"

She racked her brain for some memory of seeing the man before. He was young, his hair black and stringy and hanging over his face. But nothing about him seemed familiar. "No."

The guy muttered something that sounded like a curse. "Don't say you don't know me."

Roxy stepped back. "I don't." She looked at Alex. "I have no clue who he is."

"That's okay." Alex held his hand out. "Phone."

She gave it to him as a sudden surge of weird giddiness welled up in her. It was finally over. She was safe. Thanks to Alex. Her shifter. Her protector.

He tapped a few buttons. "It's Cruz. Roxy's stalker just showed up. Yep. Yep. Thanks." He handed the phone back to her. "Deputy Lafitte is on his way with a car."

"Lafitte? Are there pirates in this town too?"

Alex smirked. "No. He's a Cajun. Remy's his first name. New hire a few months back. Good man. But he's strictly a night-shift guy."

Her mind was happy to contemplate a new subject. What did Alex mean by that? Was the new guy a vampire? Because that was the only supernatural thing she could think of that would make someone strictly night shift. Not that the Ellinghams had to deal with that, thanks to some old family magic that Delaney had mentioned was a big secret. "Is there anything else I can help with?"

Alex shook his head. "Just let Deputy Lafitte in when he gets here and then he and I will take care of the rest." He re-adjusted his grip on the stalker, but his gaze stayed on Roxy. "You sure you're okay?"

She nodded. "Yes. A little weirded out by him touching me, but really glad this is over."

"Me too. You positive you don't recognize this guy?"

She studied the man in Alex's control. He was young, scruffy and pale. But no one she knew. "No."

Alex leaned toward him. "What's your name?"

The man stared at Roxy, creeping her out even more. "You're ruining everything for us."

She grimaced. "I don't know what you're talking about."

"Yes, you do," he said.

She glanced at Alex. "I swear I don't."

"I know." Alex pulled the guy to his feet. "Your prints are probably on file since you were so careful to keep them off everything you left. Or maybe you were stupid enough to carry ID. Or leave it in your car. Or wherever you're staying. You might as well help yourself. It's not going to stay a secret for much longer."

The guy's eyes narrowed. "Jacob Cranberry." He glared at Roxy. "Don't pretend you don't know me. That insults everything we have."

"Everything we have? You are so delusional, I don't know where to start." Then Roxy thought back as she stared at him. "Wait. Are you related to Marissa Cranberry?"

"See?" the guy said. "You do remember me."

Alex lifted his head to look at her. "Who's Marissa Cranberry?"

"Marissa was my first assistant. She was great. Very thorough, totally on top of stuff. But then she up and quit with no real explanation after just a couple of months. The only thing she'd tell me was that her life had gotten complicated and she was pulling back. I let it go. What else could I do?"

She stared at Jacob. "You're her brother."

"You and I could have been happy together," Jacob said. "I know everything about you. I told Marissa not to quit. She didn't listen to me either."

"Looks like you're not as persuasive to women as you think you are." Alex tipped his head like he was listening. "Lafitte's here."

"I'll go let him in." She hadn't heard anything, but then, she hadn't heard Jacob creeping up on her. So much for her supernatural bloodlines.

"Thanks."

She left them and went to the front door. A patrol car was pulling into the driveway. She stood there until the deputy got out and walked up to the porch.

He nodded. "Ma'am. You must be Roxy St. James." His voice carried the soft lilt of Louisiana.

"I am. And you must be Remy Lafitte."

"One and the same and at your service. Where's the perpetrator?"

Deputy Lafitte had two things in abundance: Southern charm and good looks. "Alex has him cuffed in the backyard. I'll show you."

"Much obliged." He came up the porch steps.

She didn't move entirely out of his way.

"Ma'am?"

"Alex said you were strictly a night-shift guy. Is that in all aspects of your life?"

He studied her a moment as if trying to guess what she was after. "Yes, ma'am."

"Does that make you what I think it does?"

He smiled, showing off fangs. "I'm guessing it does."

"How about that? I'm getting pretty good at this." She gave herself points for guessing vampire. "Follow me."

After it was all said and done and Jacob Cranberry was being loaded into Deputy Lafitte's patrol car to be hauled off to one of the holding cells at the sheriff's department (with the help of Sheriff Merrow, who had also shown up), a wave of exhaustion hit Roxy. She slumped against Alex as they stood together on his front porch, happy to have him at her side.

He kissed the top of her head. "I have to go back to the station with Lafitte and take care of this."

"I know."

"I called Pandora to come over and stay with you."

She glanced up at him. "You didn't have to do that."

"Well, I figured I ought to let Delaney sleep, seeing as how she's pregnant and all."

"Speaking of Delaney, Remy just told me he's a vampire too. And you weren't kidding. He sounds one hundred percent Cajun."

"Yep. He's on furlough from New Orleans."

She looked up. "What does that mean?"

"It's hard for vampires sometimes. At a certain point, people notice they don't age, so every so often, they have to move on for a while. He'll be here until he can go home again."

"You mean until everyone who knew him is gone? That's sad."

"It is, but it's a part of a vampire's life. Unless they live in a place like this where magic blurs the edges and makes moving unnecessary."

She thought for a moment. "So if he's that old and he's from New Orleans...could he be a descendant of the famous Jean Lafitte?"

Alex grinned. "You nailed it. He's actually the legendary pirate's grandson."

She frowned. "Wow, so when you say he's old, you're talking, like, two hundred years old?"

Alex raised his brows. "Who says writers can't do math?"

"You hush." She tapped his arm playfully. "That's amazing." Then an unhappy thought occurred to her. "Will Delaney and Hugh have to move on too?"

"No. That's the whole point of this town."

"Good." That was great news. "But back to Pandora, you didn't really need to call anyone to stay with me. It's safe now. And I'm fine."

He squinted at her. "You're not a little shaken up by what happened tonight?"

"Yes, but I'll be okay. I'll sleep easy, I know that much."

"Humor me." He slipped his arm around her waist. "Pandora's going to set a ward of protection around your house, that's it."

"Oh. That's cool." She needed to catch up with Pandora anyway. See how things were going. Pandora had been very secretive about the work on the spell, but maybe Roxy could leverage the evening's events into some sympathy. "Hey, why didn't she do that sooner?"

"We thought it might have been a little tricky explaining why she was burning sage in your house and chanting in front of your windows and doors."

Roxy laughed. "Yeah, I can see that."

A late-model Mercedes turned down the street. Alex pointed. "There she is."

Roxy turned to him. "Go ahead to the station. I'll lock up here and then head to my house."

"I appreciate that." He put his hands on her

shoulders and gave her a soft kiss. "I'll see you in the morning, babe."

She grinned. That never got old. "See you in the morning. I—" She realized the word love had been about to slip out of her mouth. She swallowed it down. But soon enough she was going to say it. "I can't thank you enough for taking care of me."

He smiled. "Happy to do it. Happy to keep doing it."

He headed off, and she went back inside to lock the sliders, then the front door before making her way to her house.

Pandora was just getting out of her car. She greeted Roxy with a gentle smile. "You okay? Alex filled me in when he called."

"Yes, I'm fine. Alex might be overreacting a little. I mean, sure it was scary, but he acted so quickly it was over in a flash. I'm sorry you had to come out here at this hour."

"It's no bother. I live five minutes away."

"But it's late and this isn't really necessary. Like I said, he might be overreacting a little. The threat is gone."

"It's not that late." Her smile widened. "And he's a shifter. Their instincts to protect those they love are not something I'm going to argue against. They can be fierce about it. Especially when things get elevated."

"Elevated?"

"You know. When you're mated or married or whatever shifters consider bonded these days."

"Is that so?"

"That is so." She grabbed a tote bag, then shut her car door. Her eyes twinkled. "Besides, I have something for you."

Roxy clasped her hands in front of her. "It's done?"

"It's done. Let's go inside and you can change out of your swimsuit while I put this ward on your house and then we can get to the fun stuff."

Thirty minutes later, Pandora was seated across the table from Roxy, who was now wearing yoga pants and a tank top. The house smelled faintly of smoke from the sage and two glasses of wine sat between them. Roxy rubbed her hands together. "Let's see it."

Pandora pulled a small box from her purse and set it on the table, but didn't open it. "Based on what I discovered from those strands of hair you gave me, I can confirm you positively have a little witch in you. You also have two different types of nymph and one kind of dryad, which, if you want to get technical, is really a third kind of nymph."

Roxy took that in for a second. "What does all that mean?"

"It means you probably have a love of trees and a real affinity for water."

Roxy nodded. "I'd say that's true. And I

certainly do love my fish. What about the witch part?"

Pandora smiled. "The witch part means you'll be able to handle this." She opened the box she'd brought and pulled out a length of delicate silver chain with a curved, hollow claw hanging on it. "This was a joint effort between Willa and me. We designed it together. She did the metal work, and I built the main spell, and then we both put our different magics into it. Willa added in your parents' wedding rings as your sacrifice, and I used those strands of hair you let me snip as part of my spell. This won't work for anyone but you. Granted, we've never done anything like this before, so I hope this does what we planned it to do."

"Is there a downside if it doesn't?"

Pandora handed the silver piece over. "We're out some time and money and you're still basically human, but there's no chance of you accidentally turning into a toad or spontaneously combusting or anything like that."

"Good to know. And it's going to transform me into panther like Alex, right?"

"Yep. The magic contained in that metal won't change you into anything else."

Roxy studied the claw. It had a spring clip on the back that made it easy to take on and off t he chain. The body of the claw was open. Like a ring. "So what do I do? Wear it around my neck?"

"The chain is just so you can keep it on you all the time. The real magic doesn't happen until you put the claw on."

"Speaking of which, that thing looks pretty real." The end of the claw was sharper than she'd expected. "Other than it being silver, of course."

"It was molded from one of Alex's."

Roxy looked at Pandora in amazement. "How'd you manage that?"

"Birdie."

"The receptionist at the station?" Roxy shook her head. "I still don't get it."

"Every supernatural who comes to work for the department and has fangs or claws that can be considered lethal weapons must have them imprinted." Pandora shrugged. "Birdie snuck me Alex's molds. There's not much she wouldn't do for you."

"Wow." Roxy smiled. She'd drop off a signed book for Birdie next time she was in town. "I like it even more now. So, what, I just slip it on my finger?"

"And say the word *verto*." Pandora looked optimistic. "I hope that's easy enough to remember, but we figured that it'd be better to use good old Latin rather than an ordinary word you might say one day accidentally. You won't say *verto* unless you mean to change your shape."

"No, I like it. I'll remember." She laughed. "This isn't something I'm about to forget, trust me." She stood. "Can I try it out?"

Pandora nodded. "You need to. If it doesn't work, we're back to the drawing board."

Roxy walked to the open space of the living room. Nerves tripped through her. Happy, excited, uncertain nerves. "Just put it on and say the word?"

Pandora got to her feet. "That's it."

"Wait," Roxy said. "How do I get back to being human?"

"Think the word *verto*. It works both ways."

"Okay." She really hoped she remembered that if she actually turned into a cat. "Here goes." She put the claw over her pointer finger, making sure it was snug. It fit perfectly. She held her hand out. Took a breath. And spoke the word. "*Verto.*"

The air wavered and her muscles tensed at the same time that a flash of light filled her vision. When it was gone an instant later, Roxy glanced down. Two furry black paws sat on the floor in front of her. Her paws. She lifted one and flexed it. Long, sharp claws extended from her new toes. *She was a panther.* She looked at her friend.

Pandora's mouth was open and her eyes were wide with astonishment. "Holy cats," she whispered. "It worked."

Roxy stood. Her line of sight was a few feet

lower and a host of different aromas filled her senses. The air seemed crisper. There was an urge to run, too, a desire to use the speed and power this new form had to offer.

But there was joy within her as well. Pandora and Willa had done it. Roxy tipped back her head, opened her throat and let out a growl of happiness.

She couldn't wait to surprise Alex.

Nearly sixteen hours after leaving his house, Alex was home again. He hadn't anticipated spending that long at the station, but since he'd had to do the paperwork for Jacob's arrest, he'd decided to stay and had swapped shifts with Jenna.

The day, such as it was, had been long, but worth it. Jacob Cranberry had been taken care of and was on his way to the country jail. Alex was happy about that, but felt bad for his sister. Marissa had called and explained her side of things. How she'd quit working for Roxy because she'd worried her brother's interest was too intense, and how he'd disappeared a few weeks ago after she'd begged him to leave Roxy alone.

Jacob had been determined to make Roxy his.

Fortunately, Alex had intervened. And now, best of all, Roxy was safe. A deep, primal part of him took great satisfaction in that.

He'd talked to Diego today too, and so far, his kid brother and Shanna were doing all right. That was good news. Alex wanted his brother to be happy. He also liked having his house to himself and the ability to have Roxy over whenever he liked.

He tossed his keys on the kitchen counter and smiled, then immediately wished he could see her. He thought about calling her to see how her night had been and if she wanted to come over, but she must have heard his car. She knew he was home.

She was probably wrapped up in her writing. That was good. He wanted her to get her book done. She put a lot of pressure on herself and while he understood, he didn't want her to work so much that she never had time to relax and unwind.

Or maybe she wanted a little time to herself. After all, he'd been with her, keeping an eye on her, almost constantly since the day they'd met.

Could be that she needed a break. He grabbed a beer out of the fridge. He could understand wanting some alone time. He was tired, but he also knew he should use the afternoon to do some more studying. The sergeant's exam was only two weeks away now and with everything going on with Roxy, studying had fallen to the wayside.

But the truth was, he'd hoped she'd be here. Or would maybe come over when he got home. Text, at least. But those were his expectations and he could be alone in thinking that the last week together had taken this relationship to a new place. A place where things felt more solid. More like they were a real couple. Because the reality was, he loved her. And he wanted to tell her that. But maybe she wasn't ready. He turned to head to his bedroom and change.

Roxy leaned against the hall entrance, blocking his path. "Hiya."

"Hey." His heart clenched and his head told him to stop being an idiot. "How long have you been there?"

"Not long. I was waiting in your bedroom but when you didn't show up, I figured I better see what you were up to." She was in yoga pants and a crop top. One of his favorite looks. Her gaze swept him from head to toe. She shook her head. "You do amazing things for that uniform."

He laughed. "Thanks. I was so wrapped up in my thoughts I didn't realize you were here."

She walked out to greet him. "You're not the only one who can be quiet, you know." She wrapped her arms around his neck. "I didn't think you'd be gone so long. Everything okay?"

He put the beer down to rest his hands on her hips. "Everything's fine. I took Deputy Blythe's shift since I had so much to do anyway."

She planted a soft kiss on his jaw. "Everything squared away with Jacob then?"

He sighed out of the pure pleasure of her touch. "Done. He claims you met him once at a book signing. Talked to him. You remember that?"

She squinted like she was thinking. "I don't know…wait, I do remember that. It was years ago. He was with Marissa. She didn't even work for me yet. I might have talked to him for five minutes. I don't think he said three words back. Is that the basis for him falling in love with me or whatever?"

"Seems like it." Alex shrugged, using the move to pull her closer. "I can't say I blame the guy. I'm nuts about you."

She grinned. "Good thing I like to drive fast, huh?"

"Yeah, good thing." He bent and kissed her, and the sense of finally being home swept over him. This woman was everything good in his life. Even if she wasn't a shifter. He leaned back. "You're something else, Roxy St. James."

She slid her hands down to rest on his chest. "You don't know the half of it."

"Is that so?"

She nodded. "Yep."

"Then I can't wait to find out. Did you eat lunch? Actually, it's closer to dinner now. You want something?"

She tipped her head. "Are you offering to cook?"

"Yes. If cooking can mean heating up one of the

many casseroles my mother left in my freezer."

"I'm game." Her eyes lit with a curious brightness. "But first, there's something I want to show you."

His body responded to her words and a needy ache settled in his belly. "I have a feeling dinner's going to be late. And I'm okay with that."

"You don't even know what it is yet." She pushed him toward the couch. "Go sit."

He did as he was told. "So I'm leaving the uniform on, then? I'm okay with that too. Just figuring out the details."

"Hush." She stood in front of him, hands on her hips. "This relationship is pretty much perfect. Sure, I know it's early days, but things are good. Comfortable in a way that isn't boring and I…" She took a breath. "I'm falling for you. Hard. I feel things for you I didn't want to feel for any man so soon after my divorce, but you can't tell your heart what to do, can you?"

Warmth filled him. "That's for sure. I feel the same way about you, just so you know."

She smiled, but only for a moment. "The single thing that isn't perfect between us is you're a shifter and I'm not anything. Mostly. But where there's a will, there's a way, right?"

His internal alarm started ringing softly. "You know that doesn't matter to me."

She nodded, her expression slightly sad. "I

know you say that—and I really do believe you, but I think it's the one thing that over time could tear us apart. It just creates such a gap between us. An imbalance that can't be righted."

A chill zipped down his spine. "Are you breaking up with me?"

She laughed as she lifted something sparkly from beneath her shirt. "No. I'm trying to tell you that I talked to Pandora and found a solution."

The chill returned, this time for a very different reason. "Roxy, no—"

Silver flashed in her hands as she said something, then the air shimmered around her and a black panther sat before him.

His mouth came open. He shook his head. "No."

She butted her head against his leg.

He put his hands on the animal's shoulders, pain ripping through him. "Roxy, you don't know what you've done."

A second later, she was human again and staring up at him from where she knelt on the floor. Her face was masked in confusion. "I thought you'd be happy."

He kissed her, then pressed his forehead to hers. He took a breath, trying to find the right words. What was done was done. His beautiful Roxy had sacrificed for him. There was no way she could know what she'd done, but Pandora ought to have known better. Hell, he'd talked to her about this, asked her not to let this happen. Anger built in him, but it wasn't at Roxy. This wasn't her fault. "This spell…it…comes with a great cost. I am so honored that you would do this for me, but…"

She pulled out of his embrace and sat back, staring at him. "It wasn't that expensive. I paid Willa for the silver and I gave her my parents' wedding rings—but that's part of the deal. Her magic requires something personal. And Pandora didn't charge me a thing."

"Willa?" He blinked a few times, trying to understand. "What did she have to do with it?"

Roxy picked up the silver claw hanging off the long chain around her neck. "She made this part of it and Pandora did the main spell. It was a team effort." She dropped the claw. "I just don't get it. I thought you'd be thrilled."

"I am. I would be." He sighed. "My aunt had this same spell cast on her, and I'm so sorry to tell you this, but she died young because of it. The magic takes a terrible toll on the human body. I want forever with you, Roxy. As much time as I can get and –"

"Did I forget to tell you I'm not completely human?"

He went still. "What?"

"Turns out I've got more than human blood running through my veins. Mostly some nymph and a little witch, to be exact. And that other spell you're talking about? Pandora told me about that. She said she'd never perform it on a human, but this spell is different. And it's safe because I'm not entirely human. In fact, that's what makes it work."

His anger faded. "Different how?"

She picked up the claw again. "This amulet holds all the magic and it's tuned to me so that only I can activate it. I can shift whenever I want. I just slip this over my finger and say the word."

"And that's it? There's no magic that will wear you down over the years? You won't lose any of your life force to support it? No bad side effects?"

"Nope. You can talk to Pandora about it if you want."

"I will." He took hold of her shoulders again as what she'd just told him sank in. "Are you saying you can become a panther like me anytime you want to?"

She nodded. "Anytime. I'm never going to be a real shifter. I don't have a half-form and my eyes will never glow, but I can turn into a panther just like you."

"And you did this for me? For us?"

She scooted forward and put her hands on his knees. "Absolutely. I don't want there to be anything we can't share. If we're going to give this relationship a fair shot, we need to be on equal footing. After what I went through the first time, I want everything to be right this time."

"You're the most amazing woman I've ever known. I love you. And I love everything about you. No one's ever done anything like this for me before." He got to his feet and helped her up. "I know you just got out of an awful marriage, but I hope when the time comes you'll be willing to talk about entering into a very different one with me. I can't be without you, Roxy. I can't."

She swallowed. "Are you asking me to marry you?"

"I...hell, yes, I am. Not today or tomorrow or even next year. Just whenever the time is right for you. Please tell me that doesn't scare you away."

She sucked in a breath, her eyes bright with tears. "I've been trying not to tell you I love you for the last week. I thought it was too soon. Thought I couldn't really know this soon. But I do. I can't be without you either and I don't want to be. So yes. When the time is right, I will. And to be honest, I don't think it's going to take that long for the time to be right."

He scooped her into his arms and kissed her, hard. "Then there's only one thing left to do."

She smiled as she wrapped her arms around his neck. "Is this thing going to make dinner late?"

"Yes."

She moved her hands to his shirt and started unfastening the top button. "What else is it going to do?"

He knew his eyes must be glowing with all the emotion coursing through him. "It's going to make you sweaty and tired, but when it's over, you're going to want to do it again."

She laughed as he carried her around the couch and toward the bedroom. He picked his keys off the counter, and with her still in his arms, he headed toward the front door.

She frowned. "Um, shouldn't we be headed toward the bedroom?"

"Nope." He walked outside and went right to his car, where he put her on her feet and unlocked the passenger's side door. "We're going for a run."

She let out a little gasp. "You mean like the way shifters do?"

He walked around to his side of the car. "Exactly like shifters do. What did you think we were going to do?"

She snorted. "Something else."

"You have a dirty mind." He winked at her. "The something else comes after."

Roxy didn't know what was more exhilarating. Running through the forests of Nocturne Falls as a panther with all the speed and agility of the big cat, or doing all that running while at Alex's side, both of them in panther form. It was like the speed of driving the Vette, only so much better.

The run, and the night, wasn't something she'd ever forget even though she knew they would repeat it many, many times over the course of their lives, a thought that brought her indescribable joy. She also couldn't wait to use this experience in her books. The details she'd be able to add now would really bring the world of the shifters alive for her readers.

And, in a curious twist of fate, she felt as though Wolfgang and Marabella had become real to her. She could imagine what they would feel when they went for a run together, and how much more romantic it was than she'd ever realized.

At the end of the run, Alex brought them to a stop beside a waterfall and shifted back into his human form. He was still in his uniform, something that amused her to no end. He could have changed, but his eagerness to do this with her had trumped all else.

Verto. She joined him in human form. "That was unbelievable."

"And something I don't get to do as often as I'd like, but I'm going to make more time for this in the future. So long as you'll come with me."

She linked her arm with his. "Always."

He pointed at the water. "Look."

She turned. Color played over the mist of the

falls where the water caught the moonlight. "That's beautiful."

"It's a moonbow. They're kind of rare, but we get one on the falls almost every full moon." He put his arm around her and they stood that way for a long time, letting their heartbeats slow after the run and enjoying the evening air.

At last he kissed her temple. "Have you changed your stance on soul mates or do you still think they can only exist in books?"

She smiled. "I think I believe in them now. In fiction and in reality."

"Good. Because I know you're mine."

She looked up at him. "You're so sure."

He took a breath. "I am."

"How?"

"I can't imagine being with anyone else. I think about you when I wake up and when I'm going to sleep. You've brought a new kind of happiness into my life. How can you not be my soul mate? How can we not be meant for each other?"

She turned into him, pressing herself against him. "You make a very compelling argument."

He slipped his hands to her waist, then coasted them down her body to cup her backside and pull her closer. His mouth bent in a wicked grin. "I forgot to mention how physically compatible we are."

"Maybe you should remind me."

His grin broadened. "Ready to go back, then?"

"Nope."

His brows lifted. "Right here?"

"Right here."

His eyes gleamed with gold, and a soft rumble spilled out of him. "Is that so?"

She shrugged one shoulder, so deliriously happy that it was an effort not to laugh out loud. This man was her future. She knew that without question. And she was going to enjoy every moment with him. "You did say it came after..."

Want to be up to date on all books & release dates by Kristen Painter? Sign-up for my newsletter on my website, www.kristenpainter.com. No spam, just news (sales, freebies, and releases.)

If you loved the book and want to help the series grow, tell a friend about the book and take time to leave a review!

Other Books by Kristen Painter

PARANORMAL ROMANCE

Nocturne Falls series
The Vampire's Mail Order Bride
The Werewolf Meets His Match
The Gargoyle Gets His Girl
The Professor Woos The Witch
The Witch's Halloween Hero – short story
The Werewolf's Christmas Wish – short story
The Vampire's Fake Fiancée
The Vampire's Valentine Surprise – short story
The Shifter Romances The Writer

Sin City Collectors series
Queen of Hearts
Dead Man's Hand
Double or Nothing

STANDALONE PARANORMAL ROMANCE

Dark Kiss of the Reaper
Heart of Fire
Recipe for Magic
Miss Bramble and the Leviathan

COZY PARANORMAL MYSTERY

Miss Frost Solves A Cold Case – A Nocturne Falls
Mystery

URBAN FANTASY

The House of Comarré series:
Forbidden Blood
Blood Rights
Flesh and Blood
Bad Blood
Out For Blood
Last Blood

Crescent City series:
House of the Rising Sun
City of Eternal Night
Garden of Dreams and Desires

Nothing is completed without an amazing team.

Many thanks to:

Cover design: Janet Holmes
Interior formatting: Author E.M.S
Editor: Joyce Lamb
Copyedits/proofs: Marlene Engel

About the Author

Kristen Painter is a little obsessed with cats, books, chocolate, and shoes. It's a healthy mix. She loves to entertain her readers with interesting twists, entertaining stories and unforgettable characters. She currently writes the best-selling paranormal romance series, Nocturne Falls. The former college English teacher can often be found all over social media where she loves to interact with readers. Visit her web site to learn more.

www.kristenpainter.com

Printed in Poland
by Amazon Fulfillment
Poland Sp. z o.o., Wrocław